THE CRYPTID CLUB

EDWARD J. MCFADDEN III

SEVERED PRESS
HOBART TASMANIA

THE CRYPTID CLUB

1

The SS Coiya cut through the still water, sending a miniature tsunami across Lake Titicaca. Ash stood on the small ferry's bow, hands clasped behind his back as he peered into the early morning gloom. A raspberry sherbet sky filtered through the Andes Mountains in the east as morning came on like a freight train, thin ribbons of cloud trailing off the snowcapped peaks like smoke from a chimney. Calm dark water stretched in every direction, interrupted only by an occasional island, both natural and manmade. The boat's engine growled, the deck vibrated, and the bow lifted as the vessel picked up speed.

Ash didn't know exactly where the boat was taking him, but as the shoreline materialized in the dusk, the faint lights of Achacachi glowed to the south. Where he'd be taken from there, Ash could only speculate.

He'd been met at Inca Manco Cápac International Airport by a driver holding a sign with his name on it. The old Peruvian spoke a dialect of Arawak he couldn't hope to understand, so though the man rambled the entire journey through the brown hills of Huaycho to the edge of Lake Titicaca, Ash hadn't understood a word of it. Then he was dropped at the dock where he met Captain Revvier, who had ushered him onto the twenty-six-foot launch without a word. They'd left immediately, despite there being no other passengers.

Ash walked along the gunnel, a warm breeze pushing over the lake. It was mild for late April in this section of the Andes, though temperatures and weather varied greatly based on location. At an elevation of twelve thousand feet, Lake Titicaca is the largest lake in South America, and it stretches between Bolivia and Peru. Ash figured that was the purpose of the boat trip. At some point the SS Coiya would pass from Peru into Bolivia and there would be no record of him crossing the border. This worried Ash, but he'd agreed to this, along with many other things when he'd accepted the invitation nestled in his jacket pocket.

The wind whistled and brought the scent of smoke and diesel fuel as the vessel knifed through the lake, barely throwing spray, the rumble of the engine echoing off the mountains. Lester Treemont had gone to considerable expense to ensure Ash didn't socialize or make any stops on route to his estate. That was the only conclusion Ash could draw from the available facts, but despite his host's attempt at secrecy, everyone within twenty kilometers knew there was a boat churning across the lake. Ash supposed it didn't matter. If Treemont's place was close surely the locals knew, and many probably played a role in stocking and maintaining the estate. With money on the line, in a place where comforts didn't run deep, if Ash stepped out of line he'd be seen as an outsider who was jeopardizing what little economy they had and would deal with him accordingly.

Light spilled through an open bulkhead door and Ash entered the passenger cabin. A line of lights ran down the center of the ceiling and rows of seats filled the space, tinted windows blocking out the rising sun. He slid into one of the bench seats, nestling up against the bulkhead. His reflection in the tinted glass stared back at him; dark bags hung beneath his brown eyes, his short-cropped black hair in a tangle. Black and gray stubble covered his face, and a thick salt and pepper mustache eased over pale red lips. His stomach gurgled with hunger as his heart galloped, his mouth dry as powder. He breathed deep, but it felt like his lungs weren't filling with air. He was at twelve thousand feet, and the air was much thinner than back home in Stony Creek.

Outside, the lake was coming alive, shards of sunlight streaming through the snow-covered mountain peaks and shining like spotlights on the placid blue water. In the hills beyond the lake, a lone set of headlights pushed through the early morning dusk, following the road that ran along the eastern edge of the lake. He couldn't see what type of vehicle it was, but his gut told him it was his ride. His gut, and the fact that no other headlights pierced the dawn.

Ash drew out the gold embossed invitation and turned it over in his hand.

It was printed on high-end white paper, the kind you didn't see much anymore. Everything had become electronic, and getting snail-mail of the non-bill variety was unusual for Ash. The thick cardstock was folded, and its envelope had been postmarked in Zuric, but he knew that meant nothing. Not unlike a wedding invitation, when Ash had first opened it a reply card and self-addressed stamped envelope fell out. Ash had tracked the French return address to a card store, but it had turned out to be a dead-end PO Box.

The offer the invitation presented was simple enough: it invited Ash to join eight others at Lester Treemont's infamous estate where he conducted his cryptid research, and where it was rumored he housed cryptid specimens. Its exact location was unknown, and rumors had swirled about the facility's purpose for years in the shadowy cryptid community. After Ash received the invitation, he researched Treemont and his menagerie, but he didn't find much, and he'd been unable to locate anyone who had actually been to the estate.

The invite explained that Treemont was dying, and the world's preeminent cryptozoologist planned to give his sizable fortune, assets and research to the cryptozoologist he felt was most qualified to run The Cryptid Club, an exclusive group of cryptid hunters and researchers. Ash wasn't sure he believed the club existed, and he was still skeptical about Treemont's intentions and why he'd been selected to be in the group.

Was he a cryptid hunter? Considering this brought bile up his throat as all the questions the invitation raised came rushing back like the tide. How had Treemont known about him? Ash was new to the cryptid culture, though his story had made all the conspiracy rags as well as several national papers and news sites. Treemont had been watching him, that much was certain, and it worried him. Ash usually didn't race off into the unknown with no planning, no evidence to support his quest, but there was something in the timing of the invite and his current level of desperation that appealed to his sense of helplessness.

He had nothing to lose, plenty of time, and Darcy could fill his shifts at The Foot, so he'd taken the plunge and mailed back a 'yes' response. All travel arrangements had been made for him, free of charge, and thank some god for that, because Ash was on his last dime and wouldn't have been able to afford the $4,000 airfare from Eureka, California to Juliaca, Peru.

He'd become skilled at tempering his expectations, and he wasn't expecting much. If worst came to worst, he could leave, or so he thought.

Through the tinted windows of the passenger cabin, Ash watched a gold Uru reed island slip by. The indigenous people lived on the lake on islands they made from cut totora, a thick, buoyant reed that grew abundantly along the edges of the lake. Four reed houses stood dark, but several Uru walked around the island, their bright red shirts standing out under the early morning sun. Uru islands dotted the center of the lake, and more were lined up in the shallows around regular islands like cars in a parking lot.

Ash slipped the invitation back in his pocket, the gentle sound of water crashing on water as the boat sliced through the still lake easing his nerves. He'd had a few close calls recently and his entire world had been turned up-side-down. He'd gone from respected scientist to loose cannon nutcase in less than two years. He rubbed his temples. Two years. Had it been that long?

Static bleated from a speaker, and Ash jumped, a chill running through him. Isolation and loss had dominated his life since Ophelia had left. That had been what broke him. It hadn't been his colleagues not believing him or the university cutting him loose. None of that had mattered as long as he had Ophelia, but when she'd stopped believing, he started questioning his version of reality.

A swirl of water appeared off the port bow, like a giant whale circled just below the surface, but there were no whales in Lake Titicaca. He inched forward on his seat, straining to see into the dark water. What creatures lay below the surface of the lake? Was that why Treemont had chosen this specific location for his research? Rumors said Treemont was obsessed with the Loch Ness Monster, a cryptid with many faces and many homes. He'd never heard of any sightings up this way, but that wasn't surprising. He glanced at his cellphone as a bolt of disconnection ran through him.

No messages. No service.

He sighed and rolled his shoulders. What the hell was he doing here?

The moan of the engine lessened, the bow dipped, and Ash slid forward on his seat. The shoreline was close, several small houses standing out in the brown rolling hills. Green reeds lined the shoreline, and a thin dock stretched out into the lake. Lights sparkled on the hillside as houses came alive. It reminded Ash of the hills in Napa and Sonoma, which were just south of where he lived. Nothing moved on the road beyond the reeds, and there were no other boats.

The rumble of the SS Coiya's engine died as the vessel rubbed against the dock, a loud squeak reverberating over the stillness. Ash felt self-conscious in the silence, like every sound he made would be heard for a thousand miles.

An old beat-up Toyota pickup sat waiting at the end of the dock, its tailpipe puffing dark smoke. Ash gathered himself and got to his feet. He had to be getting close. He'd been traveling for two days and he was tired and hungry, his feet hurt, and his back ached from the plane ride that required he change planes at four stops. Ash stood in the passenger cabin, waiting for the captain, stillness pressing on him like darkness. Water popped and snapped as it hit the boat, and wind pushed through the open bulkhead door.

The captain didn't come to meet him, so Ash went out on deck, peering around for assistance, but found none. He collected his rucksack, flung it over a shoulder, and headed aft.

The windows of the old pickup were tinted, and Ash couldn't see the driver. The town of Achacachi was several miles south, and Ash saw no other cars. If the Toyota wasn't his ride, he'd need to get comfortable. His brow furrowed and he glanced at his phone.

No messages. No service.

The ferry was drifting away from the dock with the wind because it hadn't been tied off. No sign of the captain. Ash jumped across the two-foot gap between the SS Coiya and the dock, landing with a soft thud on slick wood. He slid in the morning dew and almost fell, but regained his balance by grabbing a support pole that rose above the dock.

The pickup's passenger door opened, and a white hand extended from the dark cab and beckoned him on. Mist snaked down from the higher elevations, the sun baking off the morning moisture. Ash considered not getting in the truck. This could be his last opportunity to turn back and leave this all behind. Find a new life. Maybe even try and get back everything he'd lost. He looked around at the brown hills, the deserted road, the immense lake, and the block of ice in his stomach shifted, his nerves walking a tightrope.

The SS Coiya's engine rumbled to life and the vessel pulled away from the dock.

So that was that.

Ash headed for the Toyota, his footsteps thumping on the rickety pier.

"Good morning to you," came a voice from the darkness of the pickup's cab.

Ash arrived to find the opposite of what he expected. There was no old, wizened local hiding beneath a wool parka and knit cap. A young woman with short cropped, bleached-blonde hair sat behind the wheel, her blue eyes sparkling. She wore jeans, a black skullcap, and a t-shirt that read Climbers Do It Higher. A chain of carabiners hung from the rearview mirror, and two lengths of colorful rope sat on the seat next to her.

"Morning to you," Ash said as he slid into the truck and pulled the door closed. "Surprised to see you."

"Why's that?"

"You're American?"

"Aye."

"You're the first I've seen is all," Ash said.

She laughed. "You just haven't gone to the right places."

"Where are those?"

She leaned forward and pointed up through the windshield at the tall mountain peaks to the east.

Ash said nothing.

"Not a climber, huh?"

"Not a big fan of heights."

"You're in the wrong place, then, my friend." She put the pickup in gear and pulled out onto the road.

"Where are you taking me?" Ash asked. He knew this was a strange question, which was confirmed by the odd sideways glance the driver gave him. "I mean, do you know my final destination?"

"I was told to pick you up and bring you to the fields west of town."

"Who hired you?"

She hiked her shoulders and pointed at the DriveMe logo on her windshield. "I just drive. No idea who arranged the ride. The app doesn't tell me."

"Have you already been paid?"

She wagged her head. "Well."

They didn't speak again as the old Toyota popped and farted its way south, working around Achacachi where the locals were setting up the day's market in the center of town.

As the brown hills fleeted by, Ash cycled through the last few months in his mind, and all the failure and doubts built a mountain of angst. All the fruitless hunts, failed theories, and misguided searches making him question if Ophelia had been right. Maybe he was losing it, or perhaps he already had? Why else would he run off on a crazy quest to South America? What did he hope to find? The more he turned this over the more helpless and foolish he felt.

The pickup came around a bend in the road and an open field stretched into the distance.

A jet-black Sikorsky S-76 sat in the center of hardpacked dirt, its four rotor blades still and drooping. It looked like Darth Vader's helmet shining in the early morning sunlight, and Ash saw the Toyota's reflection in the helicopter's dark glass windows. But it wasn't the copter that made Ash's mouth fall open a crack, it was the group of people standing beside it, waiting to board.

2

Nine people stood next to the sleek black copter looking around like a group of teenagers who didn't know each other. A small pile of baggage sat behind them, and the copter's storage compartment door was open. The invitation was very specific about what you could and couldn't bring to Treemont's place.

The Toyota rumbled to a stop, and the driver put the vehicle in park, the chain of carabiners hanging from the rearview clinking and clanging like a wind chime as the truck settled on its springs.

Ash handed the driver a black paper bill he'd gotten as change at the airport. "Thank you."

"You bet. Maybe we'll see each other down the road," she said, and winked.

"I don't even know your name?" Ash said as he slipped out of the car with his rucksack.

"I know," she said. Then she leaned across the seat, pulled the door closed, and sped off, leaving a trail of dust. Ash watched the rusted pickup cruise around a hill and disappear from view.

He threw his sack over a shoulder and headed for the copter. All nine people were eyeing him like he was a steak and they hadn't eaten in a long time. Worry drained his lungs and sweat rolled down his back. Ash pulled his phone like a gunslinger.

No messages. No service.

As he walked, relief flooded through him when he realized he knew two of the people in the group, Candice Stockton and Sean Macrerie.

"Well if it isn't the man from Bigfoot land," Sean said. The redheaded Scot was muscled and gruff, yet oddly comforting and humorous. "Treemont will let just about anyone up here."

Most of the group averted their eyes at the mention of Treemont's name.

Ash extended his hand. "How are you? Long time no see. When was it?"

"When you came nosing around a few years ago. Remember?" The men shook.

"I do." Ash had broadened his horizons after he failed in Northern California, and he'd taken a trip to the Scottish Highlands to immerse himself in the Loch Ness mystery. The local hunters hadn't welcomed him with open arms. "And how are you, Candice?" The lanky blonde stood behind her on again off again boyfriend.

Candice slipped around Sean, and pecked Ash on the cheek. "Very well, though this is all a bit odd," she said.

Ash nodded, but said nothing.

Sean saw Ash examining the throng and said, "Quite the odd group, wouldn't you say?"

Ash would, but didn't.

"Can we go? I am weary of waiting," said a man wearing a blue turban.

"Goes by the name Snake. Quite the ass," Sean said.

"Snake?"

"Yes. That's it. Snake," Candice said.

A dour man with a waxy complexion and salt and pepper hair stepped forward. He wore jeans, and a blue dress shirt with silver epaulets on the collar. A blue cap that said, "We Drop'm Anywhere" sat crooked on his head. "Mr. Cohen?" the man said.

Ash hadn't heard his last name spoken in so long he didn't answer right away. Candice tugged on his elbow and Sean said, "He been nipping already?"

Ash shook his head. "Yes. Ash Cohen. Call me Ash."

"Good. Very good. We're running late. My apologies, but arms out, please," the pilot said.

The group leered at Ash. The invitation was very specific about its no weapons clause and all guests were subject to search at any point during their stay. Ash lifted his arms and the pilot stepped forward and frisked him. The only weapon he was smuggling, a miniature folding karambit with a plastic handle and razor-sharp fiberglass blade, was sown into the padding of his rucksack base.

When the pilot found nothing on Ash, he said, "If you come this way...." He extended an arm toward the waiting Sikorsky. "We'll get you right up to the ASAS asap." The man smiled as though he'd made a joke.

Nobody laughed.

"ASAS?" said Candice.

"Not sure what the A stands for, but the rest is Special Animal Sanctuary." The pilot shifted on his feet. Flyboys always wanted to fly.

Ash said, "Where is Mr. Treemont?"

The pilot sighed and rolled his eyes. "As you can imagine you're not the only one with questions Mr. Co... Ash. Please get aboard and everything will become clear." He smiled, yellow teeth and the scent of cigarettes revealing a smoking habit. The gesture was anything but reassuring.

Ash added his rucksack to the pile of bags and joined the group as they filed into the copter. Ash saw his haggard reflection in the black tinted glass, and the faces of Candice and Sean behind him. He was happy they were here.

Sean was an expert in everything Loch Ness, along with the creature's closely related relatives, Altie, Champ, Bessie, Tessie and Chessie. Candice was a mystery wrapped in an enigma. Attractive, smart, yet she'd chosen to devote her life and her family fortune to investigating and exploring cryptids of all types. It was her dream to start a museum that would catalog all the reputable research and specimens in cryptozoology.

Ash took a seat, Candice plopped down next to him, and Sean sat directly across from Candice, facing her.

The pilot slid the helicopter's door closed and an uncomfortable silence filled the cabin as nine people did their best not to look at each other, instead using fast glances and reflections. Directly across from him a petite Asian woman stared at the deck, brow knitted, hands clasped before her. Ash thought he'd seen her somewhere, but concluded he hadn't. He would later recall that he had met Emica Sasai, but as she sat before him, he didn't recognize her.

The rest of the strangers looked innocuous enough: a white-haired gentleman with blue eyes, clearly a German, a tall skinny black man, and an Indian female. She wore a sari with a brightly colored floral pattern on it. A younger man with bushy dirty-blonde hair and a mischievous grin sat next to her. If Ash had to guess, he'd say the man was Australian. Snake looked to be a loose cannon, but that was no surprise. These were cryptid hunters, not astrophysicists.

That thought made Ash remember why they were all here. One of them would be rich in a few days and the rest wouldn't. These people weren't his friends or teammates. They were competitors.

A thud echoed from below as the luggage compartment door closed, then the pilot's head bobbed past the window and a door slammed as he got into the cockpit. Two heartbeats passed, and static blared from the copter's onboard speakers. "Please prepare for takeoff. Seatbelts on please." Everyone in the cabin ignored the command except the woman in the sari.

The chopper's turbine whined, its drooping rotors lurching into motion. Ash shifted in his seat and rolled his shoulders. A wave of worry washed over him as he stared out the window at the brown hills dotted with green tola bushes. Something didn't feel right. He looked around at the other eight people in the cabin. Only Snake watched him with hateful eyes. The rest appeared lost in their thoughts, much like Ash.

The cabin went dark and the windows blackened.

"What is this?" Sean said.

"Ya," said the white-haired man.

With the cabin lights out, Ash saw nothing but blackness in the helicopter's windows. Mr. Treemont didn't want his guests to know the estate's exact location. Not surprising. Running lights along the floor came on, providing minimal illumination in the cabin.

The Asian woman looked around, then stabbed a black button on the bulkhead below a speaker. "Pilot? Answer me now. Pilot?"

Static, then, "What can I do for you, Ms. Sasai?" It was hard to hear him with the rotors cycling up.

At the mention of her name, Ms. Sasai looked around at the group, her cheeks turning a light shade of red. "Why can't we see?"

"Boss's orders, Ms. Sasai. If you refer to your invitation, you'll see you agreed to—"

She stabbed the button and cut him off. "Yes. Yes. Whatever." She threw herself back in her seat, turned to look out the window, then snorted.

Curiouser and curiouser. Ash turned to Candice and she gave him a nervous smile.

"The weather is unusually good for this time of year. The visibility must be exceptional," said the white-haired man.

"And you might be?" Sean said.

"Edo Vancharlin. You?" The man didn't extend a hand.

Sean chuckled softly, and said, "Sean."

Edo's steel-gray unblinking eyes locked on Sean's, but he didn't respond.

"Do you know the area well?" Ash asked.

"I've never been here before, but you know, Google." Edo held up his phone, its screen dark.

"Are you able to get a signal?" said Candice.

Edo shook his head no.

Snake, the tall black man, the Indian woman and the young Aussie said nothing as they listened to the conversation.

Ash said, "Perhaps we should all introduce ourselves? I'm Ash. Ash Cohen from Stony Creek, California."

Edo chuckled. "I've been there."

"Really?"

"The Bigfoot capital of Northern California. How could I not visit?"

Ash sighed and said nothing. Bigfoot was his bane, and it didn't help that the cryptid had recently become the butt of many jokes.

"Stony Creek lives off hikers, river runners, and other outdoor activities, but the real bread and butter is the Bigfoot hunters," Edo said.

"I know," Ash said, a little too strongly. "I work at The Foot."

"Splendid," Edo said.

"Yeah, it all started in the 50s when a logger named Jerry Crew came to Stony Creek carrying a plaster cast of a giant footprint he'd found around his logging equipment. Since then, the town has been Sasquatch central," Ash said. He hoped that was the end of it, but it wasn't.

"It's like a Bigfoot amusement park. There's several Bigfoot statues, a museum, several 'foot' related bars and hotels—the biggest one being your place of employment, The Foot, and there's many companies that offer Bigfoot hunts to enthusiasts from all walks of life," Edo lectured.

"It's not that way anymore," Ash said.

Edo frowned and cocked his head to one side.

Ash continued, "Despite Stony Creek's interesting history, several poorly planned and executed Bigfoot hoaxes recently got significant press, causing many tour companies in the area to suffer, and the other businesses in town to suffer along with them.

"People don't like spending money to look like fools, and recently Bigfoot has made many people look foolish. The first blown hoax centered around two men who claimed to have found a Sasquatch corpse, but who had nothing more than a gorilla suit. Another involved a park ranger coming upon two men in the Appalachian Mountains who wore what the ranger called 'large prosthetic footwear that left large animal-like prints.' There had been recent Sasquatch discoveries and sightings in the region, and they all immediately became suspect. Then a Montana man was hit by a car while lurking roadside wearing a Bigfoot suit made of real hair. Bigfoot is a joke."

"You helped with that, didn't you mate?" Sean said.

Anger burned through Ash, but he tamped it down. Sean was an ally. At least until he wasn't. When Ash spoke, his voice was calm and collected. "Now you know about me. Anyone else want to share?"

Nobody said anything, not even Candice.

"OK, then. We're all going to find out soon enough," Ash said.

Sean sighed. "Well, you already know my name."

"And mine," growled Snake.

Candice gave her name, and Ms. Sasai said to call her Emica. That left the majority of the group staring at the three undeclared.

The young Aussie sighed. "I go by Auggie."

The tall black man's voice carried a thick accent. "I suppose you're right. I'm sure Lest... Mr. Treemont will introduce us. I'm Otto Landen. I—"

"Don't tell me!" Sean said. "You're from Jersey."

Otto looked at the floor and Ash couldn't help but snicker with the others.

"So who is she?" asked Emica.

The woman wearing the colorful sari shifted her eyes to the deck and squirmed in her seat, all attention on her. A moment passed and her head jerked up defiantly, and she stared at each member of the group in turn. A silent rebuke. Ash could almost hear the woman yelling "it's none of your damn business" in his head.

"I know who she is," Snake said.

The Indian gave the man a withering glare.

"Her name is Deepali Singh."

"I've heard of you," Candice said. "You're an expert on Burus."

"Among other things," Deepali said.

The copter's rotors pounded, and the party fell silent. The bird lifted from the hardpan, kicking up dust as it climbed.

Candice shouted, "Ash, any idea how far we might be traveling?"

"No idea what direction we're going, but we can't go further than five hundred miles without refueling."

As the helicopter leveled out the pounding of the rotors lessened. Sean said, "So what do you make of this?"

Ash knew what the man was asking, but said, "What do you mean?"

"I mean," he paused to show his frustration. "What do you think Treemont's real purpose is? The guy has a reputation as a fanatic."

"A twisted one," said Emica. "But I never met him, so I'm unsure."

"I heard he was a bit unhinged, also. Killed a servant or something a few years back. There was an inquest an' all that, but he was exonerated," Auggie said.

Edo asked, "Clearly you have ideas in this regard, Mr. Sean."

"Could be a scam. He could be looking for some information he thinks we have."

"Yes. Motives," said Auggie.

"It's also possible his story is true," Otto said.

Everyone looked at the man like that was the most unlikely possibility.

"You think he's going to just give one of us his money?" Sean said.

"No strings?" said Candice. "No, he'll want something."

"Lester and I have had numerous fights on the internet about some of the more dubious claims he's made. Why he's included me here is somewhat of a mystery to me. I think he's up to something," Sean said.

The copter flew on as shadows danced around the cabin. Time ticked by, the eight passengers sizing each other up. Ash felt the fool.

They all knew so much about him and he only had scant memories of Sean and Candice.

After what felt like four hours, but was actually two and a half, the cabin lights came back on, revealing the snowcapped peaks of the Andes Mountains. Blue sky and tattered clouds stretched to the horizon, the steepest peaks fading into the distance in their wake. The copter listed hard to port as it turned, the sounds of pounding rotors and ripping wind filling the cabin.

The valley was no more than a crack in the Andes Mountains. The copter swung east and turned sharply, cutting between two large rolling hills and dipping down into an exotic vale.

"Wow," Candice said.

Green foliage filled the valley, and at its far end a house sat nestled against the mountainside. Sheer cliffs boxed in the gorge, and a lake ran along the southern cliff face.

"How can there be so much vegetation?" asked Ash. "And that looks like a forest of white birch. They're not indigenous to these parts."

"Cochamba isn't... can't be far from here and its climate is moderate. Similar to your Stony Creek, in fact," said Otto.

That was the second time Otto had corrected himself. All of them had secrets. Everyone did. But this group—Ash didn't think this crew would fit the normal demographics associated with their age and economic bracket on the secret chart.

Deepali gasped.

"What is it?" snapped Sean.

The woman pointed out the window.

At the edge of the lake that ran along the southern edge of the valley, a long gray neck with an oblong head stuck from the water, its mouth hanging open, dark baseball-sized eyes gleaming in the sunlight.

3

"It can't be," Sean said. "Nessie? It... it..." The Scot's voice trailed off to a squeak.

A massive gray form floated just below the surface of the lake, the beast's long serpentine neck protruding from the water, its flat, narrow head swaying back and forth, gleaming black eyes watching the copter. Four large turtle-like flippers stroked the lake as the beast tread water, and as the copter approached, the creature lowered its head.

"Some kind of Disney animatronic trick," Edo said.

"It's quite real," Otto said. He looked at the deck and bit his lip.

Otto was suddenly the center of attention, but none of the group pulled their gaze from the creature.

"And you know this how?" Snake said, jaw set, eyes tracking the beast.

"Mr. Treemont and I have corresponded. I've seen video. Pictures. I'm certain the Plesiosaur is legitimate."

Ash thought the man was lying, but he said nothing.

"You know Treemont personally? You've met him?" Emica said.

Otto said nothing.

Ash couldn't contain himself any longer. "Whatever you think you saw in these videos and pictures, how do you know it was here? I don't see how the creature could've evolved in such a remote location. It makes no sense. And it certainly wasn't transported here. It looks like it weighs thirty thousand pounds." He shifted his gaze and found Otto staring at him. Ash recalled how Otto had almost used Lester's first name, then when he nearly revealed the valley was close to the town of Cochamba. Now he was lying about how he knew the Loch Ness creature was real. "Have you met him, or not, Otto?"

"I owe you no explanation," Otto said, chin jutting out.

"You seem chummy with him. On a first name basis?" Auggie said.

Otto looked at the other guests, and his eyes narrowed when he realized everyone was listening to the conversation. "Do you refer to FriendNet 'friends' you've never met by their first name?"

"I don't really care," Sean barked. "How do you know the thing is real?"

"Because Lester," Otto paused, "claims... the creature was brought here as a calf."

"How old is it?" Emica said. "Supposedly."

"Over a hundred years," Otto said.

Edo harrumphed and Ash sighed. This was going to be a long weekend. "Where did the calf come from?" Ash asked.

Otto didn't answer.

The Sikorsky's rotors thundered as it banked hard to starboard, knifing up the center of the valley. The creature's head dropped into the lake, whitewater surging over the surface like a breaking wave. When the lake began to settle the beast was nowhere to be seen.

The gorge was a thin cut in the mountainside, and tall snowcapped mountains and sheer cliff faces boxed the valley in on all sides except one. The eastern end was open, providing an amazing view of the lower Andes Mountains and the Amazon Basin beyond. Sunlight angled into the gorge, the northern slope filled with lush vegetation, and the southern nothing but brown hills marked with green tola bushes. The valley floor, where sediment had built-up over the eons of mountain runoff, was flat and packed with lush vegetation.

Ash was good at estimating distances and size, and he figured the valley was no more than two miles from the northern wall to the southern, with a length of six miles. Stands of trees, both native and non-native, dotted the valley floor and northern slope, and dark brown wood walls zigzagged across the valley like a maze drawn by an infant. Paddocks, but Ash didn't see any of the beasts they contained.

Nestled in the western tip of the valley where the southern and northern cliff faces met, was a house unlike any Ash had ever seen. It was made of blue granite, its heavy quartz content sparkling in the sunlight. It had a red shale roof, and thick timbers boxed in windows, some sealed with closed shudders, others with glass. A small greenhouse stuck from the blue brick on the front of the house, which faced east, and a thin trail of white smoke snaked from a dark stone chimney.

Fields covered the land to the south of the house, and chickens and cows roamed behind wood fences. A yellow brick path wound through a round garden containing a large monument before continuing up the hill to the house.

The Sikorsky leveled out and came in low, buzzing a line of trees that ran along the edge of the yellow brick path. The copter vibrated as it slowed, then stopped, hanging in the air above a patch of blue and red gravel in the middle of a green field. A blue stone path that shimmered in the sunlight led from the landing site to the yellow brick path.

The helicopter touched down with a thump, the craft shook and swayed, and bumps and rattles rang through the cabin. The lights went out, and the nine visitors were plunged into gray darkness, their exterior view blocked again.

"I've had enough of this camel shit," Snake said. He went to pull open the copter's door, but it was locked.

Minutes passed as the copter's rotors slowed, the whine of the turbine dying.

The pilot's voice crackled through the onboard speaker and Candice jumped. "Ladies and gentlemen, we have arrived. Please disembark. If you've changed your mind, stay aboard and I will return you to our point of origin."

The click of the cabin door unlocking echoed through the cabin. The copter's turbine cycled up, the rotors spinning faster as the craft prepared to liftoff.

Ash slid open the cabin door and the scent of flowers and smoke wafted into the cabin. Nobody wanted to be the first to get out, but Ash wasn't stepping back. Not after everything it had taken to get here. He surveyed his companions, searching each face, considering who might stay on the copter. His quick evaluation came up with Deepali only. As he examined the woman, she appeared to read his mind, because she lurched to her feet and jumped to the ground.

Ash followed her, the pounding rotors kicking up dust, the wind swirling like a hurricane as the competitors leapt from the copter. The last out was Otto, and as soon as his feet hit the ground the Sikorsky's turbine whined and the rotors picked up speed. The group stepped back as the helicopter lifted into the sky, where it hovered, rotating its nose so it faced the open end of the valley. Then the copter roared and sprang forward, darting the length of the valley, rising as it went, the pounding of its rotors echoing off the cliff walls.

The group of nine stood in the swirling dust, watching the shining black dot disappear into the mountains, the *womp womp* of its rotors fading.

"Shit. Our bags," Snake said.

Ash sighed. "Why the hell all the rules about what we could bring?"

Candice said, "Yeah, I mean—"

A mighty roar pierced the day, the cry of a beast in great pain reverberating off the mountains.

An uncomfortable silence ensued as a cool wind pushed down from the hills, the tall grass around the landing site shifting and swaying. The scent of cow manure, smoke, and earth carried on the breeze. The path glistened under the midday sun, creating a kaleidoscope of color that danced over the vegetation.

"What now? Head to the house?" Edo said.

Ash looked to Candice, who shrugged, her long hair in a tangle. Sean stared longingly in the direction of the lake, and Auggie glanced around like a little kid who was at Disneyland for the first time. Snake started down the path, and Emica followed. They didn't get far before they were met by a most peculiar servant.

A rectangle-shaped robot glided out of the tall grass like a wraith. It looked like a shoe box standing on end, two long accordion arms protruding from its sides. The machine had a human face painted on it, and two camera lenses focused in and out above an open slit nose and a speaker-type mouth of metal. The bot was a light shade of brown, and as it eased down the path its upper third shifted and turned.

"What the?" said Sean.

"It doesn't have wheels or legs," Edo said.

To Ash it looked like the robot was floating just above the ground like Luke Skywalker's landspeeder.

"Probably using streams of compressed air," said Edo. "See the small stabilizer thrusters along the bottom?"

"You are correct, Mr. Vancharlin," said the robot, its voice metallic and hollow. "I am Rodgers, the caretaker of Atavism Special Animal Sanctuary."

Candice turned to Sean and said, "Atavism, the A."

Sean shrugged as he stared at the robot.

No lights gleamed from the machine. There were no knobs, buttons, or switches.

"Where is Mr. Treemont?" Deepali said.

The robot beeped, and said, "He's been delayed and will join you shortly. I've been instructed to provide you with anything you require."

"My luggage would be nice," Candice said.

Beeps, a chirp, an elongated squeak, but no words. Leaves rustled, wind whistled through the valley, birds chattered, and under it all a hum that sounded like an electric motor.

"What about our clothes?" Auggie said.

"Are you hungry? Would anyone like something to eat? Dinner isn't until six," Rodgers said.

Ash glanced at his watch. 4:19PM. He was hungry and wanted something to eat, but he didn't respond. Neither did anyone else. The faces of his companions looked tired and aggravated. What kind of host didn't show up to greet his guests?

"If there are no further questions, please follow me," Rodgers said.

Ash looked at Sean and Candice and rolled his eyes.

The robot started down the blue stone path, the group falling in behind it. The walkway twisted and turned, and the tall grass gave way to another brick path that led up to the house. The yellow sandstone was worn and chipped, and it passed through a portcullis with a rusted gate that looked like it hadn't been closed in years.

A garden of evergreen bushes and wildflowers stretched out before the party, and at its center was a huge stone statue. The robot paused when the group stopped to gape at it.

The monument had been chiseled from a spire of gray granite that jutted from the valley floor like a rotten tooth, and it was an amazing feat of sculpture. The granite had been rounded off at the top, and a hole the size of a garbage pail lid had been bored through the round section at an angle. All around the hole reflective stones had been mounted in a mosaic pattern that created dancing lights across the garden. Chiseled into the gray spire all along its length, with a finery only achievable over a long period of time and with great skill, were the distorted images of the world's most mysterious creatures.

The beasts climbed over each other like ants, their carven visages trying to reach the monument's pinnacle first. A great Kraken adorned the left side, its serpentine tentacles wrapping around what looked to be a Yeti or Sasquatch and a humanoid-type creature with wings and a large mouth with long fangs. Below was a huge turtle with a cracked shell, two wolf-like creatures, a huge ape head and a giant lizard standing on two legs. On the opposite side, a massive bird stretched its stone wings, and above it a version of Nessie, various smaller creatures, a giant spider, and an oversized cat clawed and climbed, all the beasts entwined in the gray stone. An enormous dragon sat perched atop the monument, wings spread, its stone eyes staring down at the valley floor.

Ash walked around the sculpture as it sparkled in the sun. "It must have taken years to complete," he said.

"Rodgers, do you know who did this?" Emica asked.

"I don't know who the artist was, though I am certain that information is in the sanctuary's library. I do know the founder of the club commissioned the piece, madam," the robot said.

"And who would that be?" Snake growled.

"Why, Bernard Heuvelmans, of course. He lived here for a time."

Ash knew of Heuvelmans. He'd written On the Track of Unknown Animals, the primary text in cryptozoology.

On the eastern side of the sculpture, a block of polished black marble with white veins adorned the front of the monument, and at its top the following was etched therein: Atavism Special Animal Sanctuary.

Below the title was the following verse:

Atavism

Old longings nomadic leap

Chafing at custom's chain

Again from its brumal sleep
Wakens the ferine strain.

Helots of houses no more
Let us be out, be free!
Fragrance through the window and door
Wafts from the woods, the sea!

After the torpor of will
Morbid the inner strife
Welcome the animal thrill
Lending a zest to life.

Banish the volumes revered
Sever from centuries dead
Ceilings the lamp flicker cheered
Barter for stars instead.

Temple, thy dreams with the trees
Nature thy god alone
Worship the sun and the breeze
Altars where non atone.

Voices of Solitude call,
Whisper of sedge and stream
Loosen the fetters that gall
Back to the primal scheme.

Feel the great throbbing terrene
Pulse in thy body beat!
Conscious again of the green
Verdure beneath the feet.

Callous to pain as the rose,
Breathe with instinct's delight
Live the existence that goes
Soulless into the night.

At the base of the black slab, chiseled into the smooth stone was the name John Myers O'Hara, and next to it, 1902.

Out of reach, set atop the fifteen-foot tall black rectangle of stone like prayer rocks on a headstone, were nine small statues, each a different color and made of a different variety of stone. From right to left, there was a red hairy humanoid figure that resembled a Yeti or Sasquatch, a black dragon, wings spread, a gray Loch Ness 'Nessie' Monster, a brown coiled serpent, a spider, a salt and pepper dog that looked like a seal and was clearly a Bunyip, a clear skinny humanoid with wings, a ferocious yellow bear standing on two legs, and a blue creature that looked half machine.

"Shall we continue on?" Rodgers said.

One by one the group pulled themselves from the monument, and walked in a loose line behind Rodgers as the bot glided down the yellow brick path. Sunlight poured through the hole at the top of the sculpture, throwing a giant spotlight on the mountainside to the north. A beast screeched, cows bleated, and insects buzzed as Ash made his way toward the gleaming house of blue stone.

Ash was starting to think he might be out of his league. Cryptid hunters and conspiracy theorists usually weren't the most stable people, and Ash had expected to come to Peru and find a broken-down mansion in the mountains with a damp room filled with dusty books. What he'd found was altogether different. He pulled his phone.

No messages. No signal.

Rodgers saw Ash looking at the phone and said, "Those will do you no good here."

"You don't say," said Ash.

4

The scene was postcard-like, the blue stone house sitting on a hill surrounded by greenery, the steep mountain cliffs in the backdrop. The party entered a stand of trees, the path's edge lined with wild dandelions. The trees had dark bark and broad deep green leaves shaped like a human hand. Ash thought they were a type of oak, but knew that species wasn't native to the area.

As if reading his mind, Emica said, "What type of trees are these?"

"A hybrid variety of Black Oak," the bot said.

"And how did they get here?" Ash said.

"They were created and laid down a long time ago, Professor Cohn. You'll discover—"

"Don't call me that," Ash snapped. Everyone eyed him. "I'm not a professor anymore."

"Very good," Rodgers continued. "Mr. Cohn, you will discover that every resident of the valley brought their own flair to the sanctuary. Because of the wet, temperate climate, many species of flora and fauna can survive here, even at the high elevation."

"How high up are we?" Snake said.

Rodgers beeped, but didn't answer.

It was becoming clear the robot servant had limited knowledge, and that Treemont left vast chunks of information out of the bot's database. So far, Rodgers had been no more than a Frequently Asked Questions page.

A line of tall untrimmed hedges boxed in the yellow brick path, and the party was funneled toward the house's main entrance. Up close it looked even more of a marvel. Though Rodgers hadn't answered Snake's question, Ash estimated the estate was at least ten thousand feet above sea level, so getting supplies of any kind to the valley would be a herculean task. He knew the Andes Mountains had mines that produced blue granite, but he'd never seen it until now. Specs of quartz in the blue rock sparkled in the midday sun, and the red roof and dark wood accents made the non-stone portions of the house look dull and drab by comparison.

Something flitted through the trees to Ash's left and he tracked it, straining his eyes to see through the gloom beneath the dense tree canopy. He slowed his pace and dropped to the rear of the group, covertly searching the dark woods. The underbrush of tola was thick, and roots snaked across the ground and dead leaves swirled like tumbleweeds.

A branch snapped and Ash froze. None of his companions had stopped walking, nor had anyone looked back in his direction. He tuned his hearing, blocking the wind, the call of a bird, and the steady sigh of the mountains. Below it all he heard faint breathing, and a gurgle echoed through the forest, then a growl. Ash's hand went for the knife he usually carried in his back pocket, but it wasn't there. His karambit was gone along with his underwear, and suddenly he felt very alone and vulnerable.

The shadow of a thin form with extended arms cut across the path, and Ash's fight or flight response kicked in. With no weapon, no clue what the beast was, flight was agreed upon by his brain's tribunal in a tenth of a second, and before Ash realized what he was doing he was sprinting down the path after his companions. They weren't far, but when he reached them, he was panting.

Rodgers beeped, and moved in close to Ash. The bot said, in a low metallic voice, "He said you might be the one, Mr. Cohn."

"What?" Ash said.

Rodgers beeped and glided forward, joining the others and ignoring Ash's question.

The greenhouse attached to the front of the house was small and ornate. It served as the house's foyer, and was filled with exotic plants and trees from all around the world. The greenhouse's large wood entrance door stood closed.

Edo opened the door and held it as the party passed inside. Tall tropical trees with broad leaves and a multitude of flowers and ornamental plants filled the greenhouse with a perfume-like scent that tickled Ash's nose. The yellow brick path cut through the dense foliage and led to the house's entrance, where it wove into salt and pepper colored stone steps. The warm humidity inside the controlled environment felt good, and as sweat rolled down his back, Ash pictured the place in winter, snow covering the large windows and blocking out the sun. "Do you clean the snow off the glass in winter?" Ash asked.

"That is rarely needed, but perhaps you might find out."

"Why's that?" Deepali asked. She ran a hand through her long black hair, gold bracelets on her wrists tinkling.

"We get less snow at this location than you might think, Ms. Singh, but early season storms can be fierce," Rodgers said.

The interior walls of the house were covered in poplar boards, a light-brown wood with streaks of black and dark brown. To the right of the front door was a sitting room with a large fireplace, to the left a switchback staircase to the second floor.

Rodgers beeped, and a light came on above, a modern LED that looked newer than the fixtures in Ash's apartment back in Stony Creek. He hadn't seen any solar farms during the descent into the valley, and he wondered where the power was coming from.

When the party of nine was all standing in the entranceway, Rodgers said, "You are free to explore the house and valley, but first if I may show you to your rooms so you can refresh yourselves before dinner." The bot floated up the steps and Snake followed.

"We're just going to trail after this thing?" Auggie asked.

"I'm hungry. Sooner we get on with it the sooner I can eat," Snake said.

Ash's watch read 5:19. His stomach growled. It was going to be a long forty-nine minutes.

Rodgers paused on the first stair landing. Then with an eerie foresight, the servant bot said, "You will find refreshment in your rooms to hold you until dinner, which will be served on the veranda on the side of the house at six. Every room has an intercom so you can call me anytime, day or night, and I will assist you. Now follow me, please." The robot continued up the steps with Snake in tow. Emica sighed, then started to climb, followed by Edo, Deepali, Otto, and Auggie. Candice and Sean held back with Ash.

"You OK?" Sean asked. "What happened to you back there? You looked like you'd seen a ghost."

"Maybe I did."

Sean's head jerked back, his lips thinned, and he squinted. A basic WTF face.

"I don't know what I saw... heard. I didn't see anything. A shadow... maybe."

Candice perked up at this new information. "What did you hear?"

Ash said nothing.

Candice sighed and started up the steps.

"You're going to have to trust someone if you want to make it through this, mate." Sean turned and followed Candice, leaving Ash standing alone at the bottom of the staircase.

"You've got no idea," Ash mumbled as he climbed.

At the top of the stairs a hallway ran to the right and left, six doors on each side. Stainless steel electronic locks shined beneath modern lights, the floor covered with a fine red carpet worn white down its center.

Rodgers showed each guest to their rooms, and when the door closed behind Ash, he fell on the large double bed, exhausted. He'd been going fifty hours, traversing more than four thousand miles and two continents. He stared up at the wood ceiling, a large black and purple knot staring down at him like a bruised eye. He rolled over when a gust of wind pushed through the room, thick white curtains blowing inward from an open balcony door.

Ash sat up, legs hanging off the bed, and stretched. He bounced on the mattress, and found it had no spring. He pressed his palms into the coverlet. Felt like a feather bed. He rose and went to the balcony, pulling aside the drapes and gazing out on the valley. His room faced east, and below, the greenhouse glittered in the sun, the eastern end of the valley open like a window on the world, the Amazon rainforest a lush green carpet on the horizon. Wrought iron spikes twisted to points held iron grating in place atop the bulwark, and Ash stuck his nose through a gap in the wrought iron, peering down at the greenhouse. There was no way he could climb down. He'd probably skewer himself on the spikes before he got over the balustrade.

A glint of metal caught Ash's eye and he turned to find his rucksack sitting on a desk across from the bed. The metal rings on the bag's straps shined, and Ash smiled. How had their host pulled off that trick? They'd waited at least ten minutes for the copter's rotors to cycle down, and Rodgers must have quickly relocated the baggage. Or, Rodgers wasn't the only servant. Perhaps it had been Treemont himself? Little mouse feet clawed at his spine, ice filled his stomach, and his cheeks grew hot when he thought about his host. Ash had come a long way based solely on Treemont's word, and from what he'd seen so far, the guy was a little cracked. Though he had to admit the estate was magnificent, and was surely worth a fortune.

He retrieved his bag and emptied the minimal contents out onto the bed. Some clothes, essential toiletries, his journal, a picture of Ophelia, and a folder with his travel documents. He reached into the sack, felt around the bottom, and was pleased to find the karambit still there.

Ash removed a ring from his finger. It was a silver raised star with a diamond at its center. Ash was the only one who knew the ring's multiple edges were sharp, and not only could it serve as a weapon, it also doubled as a miniature knife. He stripped off the ring and held it between his index finger and thumb, and cut open the bottom of the rucksack. Just a thin slit along the seam. When that was done, he slipped the ring back on, and inserted his index finger in the hole he'd made, fishing around for the knife. When he found it a smile spread over his face.

He pulled the small folding karambit free and slipped his index finger through the finger ring. Ash jerked his wrist, flipping the knife in his hand and releasing the curved razor-sharp fiberglass blade. He shadowboxed with the knife, lashing out with quick strikes, punching and weaving. He tossed his head side to side and rolled his shoulders. Then he folded the knife, slipped it from his finger, and dropped it in his back pocket. He felt much better.

Ash stuffed his clothes back in his bag and poured a glass of wine from a crystal decanter that sat on the desk next to a tray of crackers and cheese. He picked up one of the crackers, examining it, then stopped just short of putting it in his mouth. What if the food was drugged or poisoned? Why would Treemont do such a thing after inviting him to come? It made no sense. To that the rational side of his brain said, but many things hadn't made sense in the last twenty-four hours.

His bathroom had a wash basin full of clear water and a ceramic bowl containing warm towels. He rinsed his face, put on a clean shirt, combed his hair, and examined himself in a floor mirror that sat in a corner. He looked tired, black bags hanging beneath his eyes, thin red blood vessels spidering over his eyes. What the hell had he been thinking coming here? He hadn't. He'd been desperate. Still was, though his expectations had changed considerably. The gentlemanly competition he'd created in his mind was turning dark, and he thought of running. He glanced out the double doors leading to the balcony, and the snowcapped peaks beyond.

Run to where?

He turned the knob on his door and the electronic lock disengaged. The odd juxtaposition of the metal receiver box mounted next to the old, ornately decorated wood doorframe looked strange.

Ash stepped out into the hall and Rodgers eased down the passageway in his direction. "Going to dinner, sir?"

"Ummm. Yeah." He had planned to take a short exploratory walk first, but there was plenty of time for that. Perhaps he could get some answers from the bot.

"This place is amazing," Ash said. "How did it get built way up here? Couldn't have been easy transporting materials."

The robot squeaked and hissed, and it sounded to Ash like Rodgers was laughing. "There is a full description of how the house was built in the library. Almost everything you see, minus the tech and fixtures, was created using mined or milled local resources. There is a mine on site, and plenty of shale, sandstone, marble, and sedimentary rocks to make mortar."

"And the odd trees and plants?"

"Some of the flora in the valley was planted and cultivated by former owners."

"And who might they be?"

Rodgers chirped, but didn't answer.

"Did you hear me?" Ash was getting frustrated.

"Yes, sir, but that question falls outside my ability to respond."

"Of course."

The bot led Ash down the staircase and through the sitting room where Edo and Emica sat drinking and playing chess. On the far end of the room wide double doors stood open, a patio with a roof of grape vines and an amazing view of the valley's northern slope beyond. In the center of the stone portico was a dark wood table with eight place settings. A large roasted bird, bottles of wine, pitchers of water, bowls of vegetables, and a board with a loaf of bread and bar of butter rested on the table. Tall blue candles ran down the table's center, their flickering light casting dancing shadows over the gray stone floor and ornate railing that surrounded the patio.

Snake and Deepali were already drinking and eating. None of the others had arrived.

Ash took a seat next to Snake. When push came to shove, and allies needed to be made, why not be friends with the tough guy? Nobody would care about personalities if bullets started flying.

Between bites, Snake said, "The food's not bad."

"Sorry I didn't wait—my parents taught me better—but I was starving," Deepali said.

"No worries," said Ash.

The chatter of voices floated from within the house and Sean and Candice appeared with Rodgers in tow. "The party can start," said the Scot.

"Anyone seen Auggie and Otto?" Candice said.

Otto had faded into the background after their brief debate on the helicopter about the Loch Ness creature. It was almost as if he'd realized he'd exposed himself and was trying to put the paste back in the tube. "Not recently," Ash said. "Why?"

"Otto. There's just something… off. I don't trust the guy," Candice said.

"I don't trust anyone here, no offense to present company," Sean said. He nodded at Snake and Deepali.

Snake was shoveling it in and didn't look up.

Deepali smiled, and said, "The question you should be asking, is why are there only nine place settings?"

5

Snake stopped eating and looked up, Candice's eyes grew wide, and Sean counted, head bobbing as his eyes shifted down the long table. Ash had noticed their host's missing dinner plate right off. Perhaps he'd underestimated Deepali. "What do you make of that?" Ash said.

Deepali shrugged. "Seems obvious, no?"

Ash said nothing, and Sean snickered.

"He doesn't mean to join us for dinner," Deepali said, her soft brown eyes shifting to the patio entrance as Edo and Emica joined the party, followed by Otto and Auggie.

"G'day, all," said Auggie. He dropped into a seat and started filling his plate.

"Evening," Ash said. "We were just discussing the absence of our host."

"He won't be joining us?" said Edo as he took the seat on the other side of Snake.

Ash smiled. Great minds think alike. "It doesn't look like it," he said, sweeping his arm in a wide arc, indicating the nine spots at the table.

Edo's eyes shifted and scanned, and he raised an eyebrow. "It appears there's a fly in the ointment," he said.

Otto and Emica took the two remaining seats.

A bird cawed from the thick bows of a tall birch tree next to the portico. It was like the beast was trying to speak.

"It's all a bit odd, isn't it?" Candice said. "The entire thing, I mean."

"She's got a point," Sean said. "We came here based on nothing. We don't even have a treasure map and we're surprised when this Treemont character messes with us?"

"Also good points," Ash said.

Rows of liquor bottles filled a table against the blue granite wall of the house, and as Ash went to get a cocktail, he said, "Can I get anyone a drink?"

"That's Rodgers' job," Snake growled. "Where is the levitating garbage pail?"

"Right here, sir. How may I assist you?" Rodgers glided onto the patio, head rotating as the robot's eyes scanned the table. "You're all here. Splendid."

"Where is Mr. Treemont?" Ash said.

Rodgers beeped, whined, and squeaked, but didn't speak.

"He won't be joining us for dinner?" Deepali asked.

"No, Ms. Singh, he will not be joining the party for supper."

"Get me a martini, neat. Chop, chop," Otto said. The other eight guests leered at him like he'd just insulted a little girl's dress, then cast furtive glances at each other. "What? It's only a machine."

"It's a slur, dipshit," Candice said.

Everyone gave their drink orders and Rodgers glided to the collection of bottles and mixed the cocktails, the servos moving the bot's accordion arms buzzing in the stillness. The group filled their plates and ate.

Ash received his whiskey and soda, tipped the glass to his lips, emptied it, and handed the glass back to Rodgers. The robot chirped, and eased off to refill the glass. Ash mounded his plate with turkey and vegetables as he waited, and when Rodgers returned with his second drink, he only took a sip before putting it down. Ash ate in silence as he dispassionately summed up his fellow competitors.

Snake was the most open book of the group, his blue turban and its pin, a crescent moon with a star, marking him as Afghani. Though he wore the Sunni symbol, he clearly wasn't devout based on the food he'd been eating and the amount of vodka he'd consumed. He was big of stature and personality, but small in size. Ash could tell by the vacant stares that spread over his face too often that he wasn't the sharpest sword in the armory, and he was aggressive, which meant he was probably hasty and insecure. He wore black pants with brown leather boots that went to his knees, his shirt a green safari-type thing that looked like it had seen better days. Snake looked up when he felt Ash eyeing him, so Ash looked away.

Sean and Candice were no great mystery, though he knew little about either of them other than their areas of cryptozoology specialization and that they couldn't make up their minds if they were into each other. Candice was beautiful, her spiral curled blonde hair falling around her shoulders, her bright blue eyes heavenly pools. Sean's bushy red hair, freckled face and red cheeks identified him as Scottish, making his specialty of Loch Ness an easy deduction. Candice's philanthropy and research were well known, so Ash didn't think his knowledge of his two acquaintances was of any value when it came to the competition, whatever the hell said competition was.

Deepali had a beauty that crept up on you. At first glance he'd made all the stereotypical judgements, and filed her away in the 'spoiled her entire life' file. His first impression had been wrong, however. Her sari was loose-fitting, but when she moved the fabric tightened, and Ash saw the fine lines of her body. Her ample breasts and toned legs. She pecked at the food on her plate, not really eating. She squinted, mouth bent in a frown. Clearly, she wasn't used to not being in control.

Edo, Emica, and Auggie were blank slates. Edo's short white hair was slicked back, his blue eyes dark and penetrating. Ash felt the knowledge behind those eyes. Competitiveness. His accent marked him as a German, and Ash understood on some primal level that Edo shouldn't be underestimated.

Emica had mastered an aloof and distant persona. Her short black hair, dark narrow eyes, and pale complexion told Ash she didn't get outside much, which was odd for a cryptid hunter, if that's what she was. She was probably a research rat and never left her lab.

Auggie did a much better job concealing his strength and competitiveness beneath a veneer of friendly banter and an easygoing style. He was good looking, even by a man's standards, and Ash was having a hard time getting a read on him.

Otto was a different animal altogether. The thin, black man gave off an aura of ice, dark eyes always shifting and watching, short black hair balding in the middle. He was holding back, everyone had noticed it. Was he Otto Treemont's inside man?

Ash turned to Snake and asked, "So what is it you hunt?" Snake didn't look like he'd appreciate pointless pleasantries.

The man's turban dipped as he looked at the floor and chuckled. "You won't have a guess?"

"Anacondas? Sea serpents?" Ash said. Then he added with a smile, "Giant snakes."

"Ding, ding. We have a winner." The man went back to gnawing on a turkey bone.

"Any particular place?" Ash pushed.

Snake dropped his bone and looked up at Ash. "Are we friends? Do I look like I want to make friends?"

"Just making conversation," Ash said.

"Don't," Snake said.

"I know all about him," Emica said. "He's chased giant anaconda all over the world—Amazon basin, Africa. Anywhere there be jungle."

Snake growled, but said nothing.

"I saw a picture of him standing next to a giant snake. Didn't look real," Emica said.

Snake slammed both his fists on the table, all the plates shook, and Ash caught his wine glass before it tipped over.

"It was most certainly real," Snake said.

"Do you think he might have one here?" Sean asked. "Like Nessie."

"I have no idea what this madman might have, but like your Nessie, I don't see how the species could have developed here, so if there are specimens, they were brought here," Snake said.

"I suppose we could ask Rodgers. Not that the tin can would answer," Candice said. Her plate was empty, and she sipped on a vodka and soda.

Ash said, "I think we can assume none of the cryptids in the valley, if there are any at all, are native to the area."

"A Yeti might be an exception. This environment suits them." Auggie said. "And there are other examples."

Otto leaned back in his chair, eyes shifting from speaker to speaker. When he caught Ash watching him, he winked.

"Rodgers, what creatures live here in the valley?" Sean asked.

Rodgers beeped so long Ash thought Sean's question had broken the servant bot. Finally, it said, "As I have already stated, the house library contains an accounting of the sanctuary. Can I get anyone anything? Are you ready for dessert?"

"I am," Snake barked.

"Me too," Auggie said.

"Me three," said Ash. He was on his third whiskey, and was feeling much better about his situation. Magic, whiskey was. These folks might not be the world's most upstanding, forthright citizens, but his worry drained away as the companions spoke. Ash knew everyone was being guarded with their comments, the information they provided, for fear of giving their competitors an advantage. He didn't take it personally.

Rodgers buzzed from the portico, disappearing through a thin door in the corner of the patio. A gust of wind pushed up the valley, bringing the scent of flowers, cow manure, and something else... The screaming bird was back at it, and the beast's mournful cry echoed over the portico like a warning klaxon. Ash let his hand drop below the table and he felt his back pocket, making sure the karambit was still there.

"And what of you, Ash?" Snake said. He wiped his face with his stained napkin and put his elbows on the table.

Deepali opened her mouth to speak, then shut it. Ash laughed to himself. Old habits die hard, and Ash's mother had scolded him to get his elbows off the table many times.

"You're asking a lot of questions," Otto said. "For a guy with your reputation that doesn't want to be friends."

An uncomfortable silence permeated the veranda, like a fart in a movie theatre.

Then Ash laughed. "My reputation?" He'd been afraid of this.

"You were an associate professor of Zoology at Humboldt State University, where you specialized in comparative physiology and physiological ecology, especially of bats. No?" Otto said. He smiled broadly and appeared to think he'd scored a point.

"You can read. How good for you," Ash said. He felt his face get hot, sweat dripping down his back as anger built in him like a surging wave.

Otto threw up a hand. "You all know the rest, yes?"

Ash looked to Sean and Candice. Sean looked at the ceiling and Candice frowned as she stared at her hands, which were folded in her lap.

"He was—" started Otto.

"I'll tell it," interrupted Ash. If his story had to be told, he was going to tell it. He took a long pull of whiskey and soda, then sighed.

"I was spelunking in Northern California, a great spot just east of Redding in the Cascades. I'd spent many days there observing bats, cataloging their comings and goings. Like a hunter, I had my perfect spots. Places where the bats would funnel through in great numbers. I was at one of my favorite places, just before dusk, the sun just starting to sink on the horizon, when I saw an enormous hulking shape emerge from the foliage outside the cave. The beast was huge, covered in brown, shaggy hair, and stood ten feet tall if it was five, but none of that is what made me fall from my perch atop a large stone just inside the cave mouth." Ash paused for effect, and to collect his thoughts. His nerves were walking over hot coals, and he was suddenly sweating.

The group shifted in their seats, the whir of Rodgers' stabilization jets puffing in the stillness. Deepali coughed and Sean sniffled. The bot chose that moment to glide across the veranda with the dessert tray. Each guest selected a treat and coffee was served.

Ash continued, "What threw me was the creature's red eyes. The way they searched the oncoming dusk. They glowed—that's the only way I can describe how they shined," Ash said.

Snake laughed.

"You think you saw Sasquatch? Bigfoot, if you will," Auggie said. The man sounded skeptical at best.

Ash said nothing. The rest of the story was nobody's business, but Otto wouldn't let it be.

"Then you know what he does? He goes to the—" Otto said.

Ash cut him off, "Enough about me, what about you, Otto?" His story was the only one Ash really cared about.

Otto stared at Ash, looked up and down the table, lifted his fork to his mouth, and stuffed in a piece of chocolate cake.

31

Several minutes passed as everyone ate, and as dessert wound down a sharp beeping sound cut across the terrace. The party went silent, cutlery ceased tinkling on plates, and even the annoying bird stopped screaming. Rodgers hovered at the end of the table, the lenses that were its eyes shining in the shade beneath the ceiling of grape vines. The robot servant said, "Mr. Treemont will receive you now."

Stunned silence as the party considered this, looking around at each other, their faces masks of confusion, excitement and fear. Edo grunted, Sean whistled, and Emica harrumphed. Otto bounced to his feet, and that started a wave as the companions dropped napkins, took final pulls of drinks, and brushed crumbs from shirts.

"This way, please," Rodgers said.

The bot didn't head for the wide double doors Ash had come through, but instead went to the far end of the porch where a narrow door stood open. Rodgers had been going in and out of the doorway throughout dinner, and Ash thought the room beyond was the kitchen.

As he had been several times already on this day, he was wrong.

The party knotted together before the narrow door, a line forming as they filed into a hexagonal room with no other doors and a single white light fixture in the center of the ceiling. The walls were covered in poplar boards like the rest of the house, a single portrait hanging on four of the walls, the other two unadorned. Rogers paused in the center of the room, and the door the guests had entered through slid closed.

"Is one of these pictures Treemont?" Sean asked.

"No, sir. Leaders of the Cryptid Club don't get their portrait in the gallery until their term is over, Mr. Macrerie, sir."

Sean looked at Ash, who hiked his shoulders. Always a piece of the answer, never the complete puzzle.

The light went out and the room was plunged into darkness.

Sharp intakes of breath, and a gasp that Ash thought was Candice.

"Camel farts. What is this? Turn on the—" Snake began.

"Ladies and gentlemen." The human voice was harsh and melodious. "Ladies and gentlemen, may I have your attention please."

A slice of light knifed through the darkness, and a door slid open, revealing an antechamber beyond.

6

"Please take your seats," said the disembodied shrill voice. "There is room for all nine of you. Rodgers? Ask if anyone needs drinks."

The door slid open further, the sliver of light becoming a rectangle.

"Can I get anyone anything?" Rodgers intoned.

"Scotch. Double," Sean said.

The voice had stopped, and a heartbeat of nervous silence filled the room. Then drink orders started pouring from the group. Rodgers listened patiently, and when the assembled were done barking orders at the bot, the door the party had come through opened and the bot floated away without a word.

"Ladies and gentlemen. Please join me," came the voice.

Ash stayed where he was, staring into the rectangle of white light, trying to determine what lay beyond. Snake shuffled forward, leaning over like a broken old man, peering into the brightly lit chamber beyond. Emica huffed, and pushed past him, disappearing into the light. Snake followed, then Auggie. Candice and Sean stood with their backs to Ash, and they both turned, as if asking for permission to continue.

Ash shrugged and said, "We've come this far."

"Get on then," said Sean, waving an arm and ushering Ash forward.

Edo hovered at the door's threshold, his head plunged into the bright light like he was bobbing for apples. Otto stood next to him, ramrod straight. Ash didn't sense any recognition or familiarity in the man now. Whatever he knew or didn't know, this was new to him.

Deepali fell in beside Ash, and from habit she reached out to take his arm, then pressed it tight to her side.

Ash threaded past Sean and Candice, and Deepali matched him stride for stride. As they stepped into the white light, Ash was momentarily blinded, and he squinted.

The lights dimmed, and when his vision cleared, he was looking at a ghost, at least that's what the hologram looked like. Nine black leather chairs sat evenly spaced around a black metal box, and above it a four-foot projection of a man floated like Princess Leia speaking to R2-D2.

The aberration had a thick beard, and his hands were on his hips. He smiled jovially, his blue eyes sparkling through a mane of brown hair that fell about his shoulders, loose strands cutting across his face.

The hologram was paused.

Emica and Snake were already seated, and this time Ash used reverse psychology and sat as far from the irritable man as possible. Deepali sat next to him on one side, Candice the other, with Sean next to her.

When everyone was seated Rodgers glided into the room and served the drinks. Ash had ordered a double Jack Daniels. He took a long pull of the whiskey, its sharp burn tingling his senses and kicking his brain in the ass. A simulation. A fancy message. Treemont wasn't here.

The hologram flickered, then came back stronger and jerked into motion.

"Very good. Good. Please take your seats," the projection said.

A thin beam of light shot upward from the black box, and fog leaked from small jets at the box's edges like a smoke machine. The image was projected on the white steam as it formed a thick cloud above the box.

Nobody spoke, and outside Ash heard the bird calling for attention.

"Good, now that you are all here, let us begin. I am Lester Treemont, for the dullards among you, and I'm here—"

"This is preposterous," Otto yelled. He sprang to his feet, realized he'd overreacted, and sat back down and crossed his arms over his chest.

Treemont's image paused.

Rodgers said, "Please do not interrupt the—"

"I'll interrupt you," Snake shouted. The big man pressed himself to his feet, the arms of the leather chair squeaking under the strain. He balled his fists and went for Rodgers, but Edo leapt in his way.

"Break the bot and we're really screwed," the German said.

Snake panted, anger seeping from him like bad breath.

"Food, water. Let's hear what Treemont has to say. That's why you came, isn't it?" Edo said.

Snake said nothing, but he eased back and sat down.

Edo looked around, and sat.

The hologram restarted. Ash figured there were sound and motion sensors at work, that was the only explanation that made sense. Unless someone was watching? Ash glanced over his shoulder, studied the four walls, but found nothing but brown poplar boards.

"...to tell you why you've been chosen, what lies ahead, and what's at stake," Treemont's image continued.

"This isn't what we were—" Candice started, but stopped when the hologram froze. She sighed and mumbled, "Sorry."

The projection went on.

"First off, I'm sure you're all wondering why you? If I thought you were so important and deserved to have the valley and everything that goes with it, why didn't I introduce myself prior? Yes, you're thinking that's a very curious question indeed, and I'm certain you all considered this prior to deciding to come here, yes?" The projection paused as if it were actually speaking to the group.

"Good, yes," Treemont continued. "In the past, members of the club were allowed to come to the sanctuary to reaffirm their commitment to cryptozoology, but times have changed. It used to be like a trek to Mecca, or an American Indian's test in the wild to become a man. Otto can tell you all about it, if he's there. Are you there, Otto?" The hologram paused and mockingly put a hand to an ear.

Everyone looked at Otto, who seemed to shrink under the hostile stares.

"This true?" Ash asked.

The image of Treemont stayed paused.

Otto looked at the floor, then looked up in defiance. "Yes. It's true. I came here as a boy with my father, but I don't recall much."

"Well, wouldn't you think that information might be relevant?" Sean said. He had his fists on the arms of his chair and his ass was an inch off his seat.

"For who?" Otto said. "It's really none of your business."

"That's how you knew about the creature in the lake, and used Treemont's first name. You've met him?"

The companions sat in stunned silence.

The hologram started. "You all still questioning Otto?"

The projection paused when half the party yelled, "Yes!"

"So? What have you got to say for yourself, mate?" Auggie said.

"Nothing I haven't already said," Otto answered. "Have I met him? Technically yes, but as I said, it was a long time ago. I wouldn't know him today if I passed him in the street."

"And you've had no contact with him since?" Emica asked.

Otto didn't answer.

Candice said, "He said they'd corresponded."

"But that's it," blurted Otto. "That is until I got my invitation."

That seemed to shut everyone down.

"We're not done with this," Ash said. With his suspicions verified, he wondered what he hadn't thought of.

Five seconds of silence slipped by, the bird outside going full tilt. Then Treemont continued. "Yes, yes. Please leave poor Otto alone if he's there. His trip to the sanctuary as a boy won't give him any advantages in the competition, I assure you all.

"So by now you've figured out I made this recording prior to your arrival, and thus didn't know for sure who would come. Think of your invitation like an offer to go to a wedding. The invites to your top guests

35

go out first, then the people you'd like to invite, but can't, and those folks get the slots not taken by the first wave, and so on. So yes, you, whoever is sitting and watching this message, may not have been my first choices, but have faith that I had a pretty good idea. If you can't believe that, get over it." The projection paused two seconds for effect.

"As your invitation informed you, I am dying. Indeed, it is my illness that stops me from being with you, and as you watch this, I may already be dead. No matter. Plans have been made, precautions taken, but I warn you now; don't get too upset or excited. I don't want any of you keeling over from mountain sickness or edema. The valley's elevation is on the upper end of the high-altitude-region scale, and the air in the valley, while not as bad as the peaks, is most likely considerably thinner than what most of you are used to, and it will take time for your bodies to fully acclimatize, so have a care. The effects of high altitude are considerable, and could kill you if you're not careful. The percentage of oxygen saturation in your hemoglobin determines the content of oxygen in your blood. After the human body reaches around seven thousand feet above sea level, the saturation of oxyhemoglobin begins to decrease, but fear not. Your body has both short-term and long-term adaptations to altitude that will allow it to compensate for the lack of oxygen, but you'll need to take it easy for a time. I'm sure you've all noticed your shortness of breath?"

Ash had, and he'd understood why, but hearing it put in such stark terms made him wonder for the millionth time why he'd come to the valley. Then all his problems and desperation came roaring back like a bad ex. His chest heaved, his brain reminding him the air contained much less oxygen than he was used to and somehow he'd need to find the strength to compete.

Treemont rubbed his nose, and static rippled over the projection. "Yes, well, perhaps I should have written all this down." The hologram chuckled. "But I didn't, so bear with me, please.

"It is the longstanding tradition of the club that its new leader be selected by its nine most worthy members via a competition officiated by the club's current leader, and if that's not possible, the guidelines for ascendency would be followed by Rodgers. As membership in the club's current incarnation is nonexistent, you nine have been invited here for a chance to carry on the tradition, and become owner of the valley and the leader of The Cryptid Club. How you choose to handle future membership, and the valley, will be your decision. Know, however, that I kept the sanctuary secret, and didn't cultivate membership because in today's age of technology I feared for the traditions and research that have carried me through my life. Indeed, each of you, most likely unknowingly, has participated in that life and its successes... and failures. Bringing you here puts over a hundred years of work in potential jeopardy."

The image paused, Sean sniffled, and Ash wet his lips with his tongue. He didn't know what to think.

Treemont's image said, "As I'm sure you've all already deduced, I've been watching you for some time, using the wealth of the club and its resources to track your research and progress. You are the nine best cryptozoologists on Earth, or at least the nine most adventurous... or desperate.

"Make no mistake, I know your type, even if I don't know you personally. You yearn for answers traditional science doesn't seek because what they'd find would invalidate everything they believed to be true. It is this drive that brings you here, though I am not naive. Whatever emotional baggage you brought to the sanctuary, I suggest you shed it, and I know you all have matching sets of luggage. I invited you here, after all." A pause, then, "OK. Let's get on with the meat and potatoes, as my pa used to say. Who am I? How was the Cryptid Club formed, and by who and why? What are its goals, and..." The hologram waved a finger at the assembled. "How will I decide who will succeed me? Yes, I said I, because everything to come has been preordained by me."

"Hogwash," snapped Snake, and the projection froze.

"Hogwash?" Ash said.

"How much of this are we supposed to take?" Snake said.

"All of it," Edo said.

Silence, the bird, then, "It began in 1878 when cryptozoologist Franklin Lensington discovered the valley while searching the Andes for Yeti. Though there'd been no credible sightings up this way, Franklin left no stone unturned, and as a man of means with access to his family fortune he hired residents for the labor and constructed the house you now sit in from local resources. The remains of the blue granite quarry are below the house, and a well bored into the mountain provides geothermic energy which we use to provide power and heat. As you saw when you arrived, the valley has a contingent of livestock, as well as vegetable gardens, vines for wine production, and even indoor beehives to make honey, and when the weather is good, pollinate the valley. We're quite self-sufficient, so if you thought maybe you'd stowaway on the supply helicopter, think again. The house is stocked, and supply runs have been suspended until further notice. Those who think they can scale the mountain cliffs; I implore you not to try. An ascent is impossible except by the most experienced climbers, with help, and the most up-to-date gear."

Ash knew that was bullshit. There had to be a footpath that led out of the valley and job one would be to find it. If things went south, he needed an escape plan.

Treemont continued, "Over the last hundred and fifty plus years paddocks were added, modern amenities, and as technology and transportation became more advanced and the valley more accessible, Franklin got the idea to make the valley a sanctuary for his small collection of cryptids. Franklin understood atavism, knew that if the creatures he discovered weren't protected, in defending their lives the beasts would revert to their primal tendencies. As his plans came to fruition, he included others, and Franklin's successor was a member of the club and deeply involved in its creation and the sanctuary's construction. Each leader since has brought something new to the club and the valley."

Treemont took a breath and reached outside the hologram's halo and brought a glass to his lips. The projection tipped back its head, drank, then made a satisfied sound. "So, yes. I'm not going to bore you all with a hundred and fifty years of history, but if you're curious, all active competitors will have access to the house library. The history and background of former leaders is there, all the old wet-fart's stories, but know as you waste your time wading through the pompous accounts of their terms as leaders of the club, it's the creatures here in the valley that truly matter.

"Now, if you're like me, you have many questions. Yes, the black hands that pull the levers of the world know the location of the sanctuary, but not its purpose. In the old days, there weren't satellites watching everyone. No Google taking pictures of ant's asses from space. So, the valley was developed in relative secret, and is safe, as long as things stay that way, which was why I didn't cultivate membership. There's simply too much temptation to blow it all up for fifteen minutes of fame. Everyone I invited will put the creatures first, or so I believe.

"Active competitors," the hologram said. "Yes, you heard that right. Some of you—hopefully not all—may not want to continue. That's fine. Nobody is being held against their will. However, if you fail to participate in the competition—and I mean if you miss one contest, or you refuse to compete, you will be sequestered in your room until the competition is over. Why? The valley holds many secrets, and non-competitors will not be permitted to discover them. What's to keep one competitor from helping another? Nothing, but know I have eyes and ears everywhere, and though Rodgers looks to be nothing more than a floating service tray, the bot has access to resources that could make your stay in the valley… unpleasant. So before you decide to be the squeaky wheel, remember you agreed to come here."

Ash coughed and Deepali offered a silk handkerchief, which he accepted with a nod. He wiped his nose as Treemont continued.

"You're all probably wondering what will happen if you decide not to compete, or to quit, how long might the competition last? Fair enough, fair enough. No one will be permitted to leave the valley until the competition is complete, regardless of how long that may take. The helicopter won't return until there is a new leader of the Cryptid Club."

7

The assembled cryptid hunters and researchers gasped, sighed and growled. The sounds were enough to freeze the hologram, a smile running across Treemont's frozen face from ear to ear.

Then everyone started talking at once, a cacophony of bitching and human braying that made Ash want to yell. So he did. "I can't hear myself think." When the rumble of complaining voices didn't cease, he whistled, and the piercing shriek stopped the chatter. "Why don't we hear the rest of the message before we try and determine what it might mean."

The rest of the group stared at him like he was crazy, and the break in the action was long enough for Treemont's projection to start up again.

"Look. I get it. I was pissed the first time I came here. I thought Mason had lied to me. Cheated me out of the opportunity to control my own life. I felt manipulated. Again, get over it. Each of you were chosen for your strength. There are no cupcakes among you. No wall flowers." Treemont's image took another pull from an unseen glass. "You might be wondering who the hell I am?" He laughed. "Fair. Fair.

"I was an inquisitive lad, probably not unlike all of you. I dug where others didn't, ventured places others feared, and I wasn't afraid to believe what my eyes told me was real. Of course, I didn't have much use for organized school, and my dad was a military man, and we were always moving around. He paid little attention to me and my family's travels took me all around the world. I did pretty much whatever I wanted.

"When I saw a Jersey Devil in the swamps of the Meadowlands, everything changed," the hologram said.

"You've seen one?" Deepali blurted. She put a hand over her mouth, and said, "Sorry."

Ash knew how the woman felt. It was infuriating having to listen to Treemont, but not have the ability to ask questions.

Deepali's question caused a momentary pause, and Ash felt himself getting bored and frustrated. He didn't give a Yeti's ass whether Lester had a good childhood. He wanted to get on with it. He was tired, and wanted to hit the rack, though his twisting gut told him the night was far from over.

The leader of The Cryptid Club foresaw the interruption, and when the projection jerked into motion Treemont was laughing, the hologram's beard jerking up and down. "Yes..." The words slithered from his mouth. "When I was sixteen, I sought out Manson Gregory. You've all heard of him I gather?" A pause, then, "For those who haven't, he was the foremost cryptozoologist at the time. Specialized in Sasquatch and Yeti, Loch Ness, Chupacabra. All the good ones. He was well funded, and when he asked me to be his assistant, I jumped at the chance. Little did I know that meant membership in the club, and that eventually I'd become caretaker of the sanctuary."

When none of the party interrupted or spoke, Treemont went on.

"So, what else? Hmmmm." The hologram stroked its chin. "I've told you the valley is home to a myriad of unique creatures, both big and small. Most came here as younglings, but not all. Is there a list of beasts in residence, you might ask? A zoological operation to take care of them, feed them?

"The answer to those questions is no. We put out food in the winter, but other than a few necessary exceptions for specimens that require..." Treemont paused, took a drink from the invisible glass, "I'm sorry. I get tired so fast. My throat is like sandpaper."

A pause, and it was then Ash knew for certain they were all dealing with a madman. This was all too well thought out.

Treemont continued, "Some of the creatures require assistance due to habitat and food supply constraints, but most of the creatures in the sanctuary fend for themselves, and there are a few species in the valley I haven't seen for several years. In the library you will find accounts of most of the beasts, but don't put too much stock in what you find there, for there are many conflicting opinions and accounts. You will see some of these beasts with your own eyes, even meet one, which brings me to the rules.

"Pay very close attention," Treemont said, then paused.

Ash sighed. It was getting annoying having a recording dictating the conversation, but at this point he saw no option that made sense other than to let Treemont finish. He took a deep breath and let it out slow. He was feeling the effects of the altitude.

In typical showman fashion, Treemont had kept the important information for last to keep his audience's gnat-like attention spans from fading out. "I have contrived for there to be a series of tests. Each involves your knowledge of mysterious animals, your ability to interact with them, and your problem-solving skills. These tests will not always be timed, or clear. Everything you do here at the Atavism Special Animal Sanctuary will be weighed, measured, and ultimately, I will decide who wins. If I am unable to make the decision due to my death, a series of protocols have been put in place to make the decision for me and leave no doubts. The winner will be clear and undisputed and a clear rationale will be provided by Rodgers or his designee should it not be obvious to all."

Designee? Ash wondered what that meant. At this point, anything could be possible, but he didn't speak up.

"You are not allowed to interfere with other competitors without their permission. You may help each other, but there'll be no sabotage. If you are accused of such, you will be removed from the competition." The hologram laughed. "Some of you just said to yourself, 'so you say.'" The projection laughed again. "If you attempt to sabotage the contest," Treemont paused and the hologram crackled, "there will be undesirable consequences. These are, of course, always possible—it's dangerous walking out your front door—but I digress. You will report when asked. You will compete when instructed. Failure to complete a given task, as I've already told you, will lead to your removal from the competition." Treemont paused to let that sink in.

"You will meet Tallboy here in the sanctuary. If you're lucky, and he likes you, you might have the opportunity to interact with the Sasquatch, though he can't speak, at least not in the way you might think. He's tamed, domesticated if you will. This is the product of two generations of breeding and living in the valley, but take care. Not all the specimens of Bigfoot and the like in the valley are as tame.

"Well, that's it from first to last. Questions can be placed in the complaint box." Treemont's image chuckled and it rippled, static cutting through the hologram. "Oh, and I almost forgot. You've already met Rodgers. He can attend to your every need, treat most medical issues you might encounter, and can dispense basic medications should you require any. You may ask him questions, but as you've already no doubt deduced his knowledge base is limited.

"I hope to greet the winner at the completion of the competition, but that might not be possible, so I'd like to thank you all for coming, and for participating in my little contest. It is a most dangerous game, but I'm confident in your abilities. You've all done questionable things, and in the days ahead you'll face your greatest fears. So take care. It would be a shame if you all didn't make it out of Atavism Special Animal Sanctuary alive."

Treemont's hologram smiled, waved, and blinked out.

"What a load of cow crap," Sean said.

"A half-hour of speaking, yet he said nothing," Snake said. "We still don't know shit."

"I'm forced to agree with you," Ash said. Despite Treemont laying out what he called 'the rules' he'd hardly given them any information.

"This guy is mad," Edo said.

"What about that last line. Make it out alive? I didn't much like the sound of that," Candice said.

"Maybe I'm the only one here who didn't go to university, but would someone tell me what the hell the word atavism means?" Auggie said.

Edo said, "It means a tendency to revert to something ancient or ancestral, like an animal returns to its natural tendencies given certain circumstances."

Ash nodded. He guessed that made sense. When in the wild animals act a certain way, in captivity, another. That was why so many species had trouble reacclimating after being with humans.

"I don't know about any of that, but I want to hear from Otto," Deepali said. She looked at Ash, lips curling.

Ash agreed. "You're the only one who's ever been here before. What do you remember? You must've seen something other than the lake monster you can recall."

Otto sat silent, his elbow resting on his knee, chin in his hand as he stared at the black box that had projected the hologram. The mist had dissipated, and a chemical scent pervaded the room. Otto looked up and locked eyes with Ash. "I didn't tell you all for this very reason. There really is nothing to tell. Please believe me," he said. "I didn't even remember the lake monster until I saw it. I was four years old for shit's sake."

There was a hint of desperation in the man's voice, all his confidence having fled with Treemont's image. The message had affected others in the group as well; Candice bit her nails, Sean's eyebrows were scrunched together, and Emica stared at the ceiling, her dark eyes wet with the slightest sheen of tears.

Snake threw up his hands and his turban pitched back on his head. "I'll be the asshole. Anyone else buying Otto's shit? He's a mole."

"That makes no sense," Emica said. "If he's a plant, why expose him?"

Snake's head tilted, and he pressed his lips together, but said nothing.

"Why expose me? Great question," Otto said. "Perhaps I'll remember more when I see it. If I do, I promise to share what I remember with all of you, competition or not."

Ash's opinion of Otto was rising like beer stocks before the Super Bowl. The guy had been so quiet and gruff, Ash had assumed–ass out of you and me–that he was an elite dipshit. Maybe not. Ash hoped his batting average improved, because so far, he'd been wrong more than

43

he'd been right. He tossed Otto an olive branch and changed the subject. "Edo, what do you make of all this?"

The German searched the room, his blue eyes sizing up each competitor. He sounded sad when he replied, "I don't think I'm prepared to give an opinion."

"I need another drink," Auggie said.

"Yes, sir. The same?" Rodgers said.

Everyone turned to look at the robot. Ash had forgotten Rodgers was there. The bot hadn't made a sound throughout Treemont's dissertation.

"Yes please, Rodgers. Right away," Auggie said.

Others chimed in and as the service bot floated off to get the beverages, silence crept over the room, the eight companions searching each other's faces for clues, any hint of what they might be thinking.

Ash was thinking he was screwed, and that he'd made a huge mistake. The bot returned and passed out the drinks. Ash asked, "Rodgers, did you start that hologram?"

Rodgers paused, accordion arm extended, Candice's glass of wine halfway to her. The bot buzzed and squeaked, camera lens eyes scoping in and out, and replied, "Yes, sir. Following Mr. Treemont's instructions."

Snake spoke, teeth grinding, his tone dangerously polite. "Can you replay the message?"

"No, sir."

Snake took two fast steps and pushed the servant robot, who deftly balanced the wine and didn't spill a drop. "Sir Snake, please don't do that."

"I'll—"

Candice put herself between the bot and Snake, and plucked her wine from the robot's claw. "Stop attacking an inanimate object and ask yourself if we can trust the information we've been given," she said.

Ash said, "That's an excellent question. What do we all know of Treemont, other than what he's told us? What we've read on the net."

"Has anyone here, other than Otto," Emica paused and everyone looked at Otto, "has anyone else met him?"

The whir of the service bot's stabilizer jets, the faint whistle of the wind, and the hum of the old blue granite house filled the silence. Ash took a deep breath in through his nose, and let it out slowly through his mouth. It was getting easier to breathe, but it was still an effort.

Sean said, "I've never met him."

Nobody spoke.

"I get that, as competitors you might want to play your cards close, but I think this guy is nuts. Might be time to step out of the contest for a bit," the Scot said.

Candice and Deepali nodded.

"You could be lying," Edo said.

Sean's face scrunched and his blue eyes narrowed. "I suppose that's true. All the same, should we share any information we have?" He pulled his invitation from a back pocket. "You all got one of these? Yes?"

Nods and general agreement.

"We should compare them," Auggie said.

"At some point, yes, but I think you'll find they're all the same, save for a few details specific to us. Have I met him? No," Ash said. "Am I willing to lay out my life's mistakes to seven strangers, so they understand why I'd take a shot in the dark? Maybe. But right now, no. I think the question is, as Candice said, 'Do we think what Treemont has said is true?'"

"His story is preposterous," Edo said.

Deepali's frustration bubbled over. "This is simple. We stay and play, we band together and attempt escape, or it's every man and woman for themselves."

A deep silence spread over the room, the puff and hiss of Rodgers' jets the only sounds.

"Is there anyone else in the valley, Rodgers?" Ash asked. He had a feeling there were staff and Treemont lackeys lurking behind the scenes, though he'd seen no one.

"No, Mr. Cohn. You nine are the only humans in the valley."

"Bullshit, mate," Auggie said.

"I'm forced to agree with my Australian friend. How can we be sure?" Ash said. After that last comment about surviving in the valley he was starting to think that as odd as the situation was, he didn't know the half of it.

"So, what do we do? Search the valley?" Snake said.

"That would prove most fruitless. If someone wanted to hide, like Treemont, it would be easy. There are many tall trees, probably caves," Otto said. "Not to mention secret rooms here in the house."

"We could search for a month and not find every nook and cranny of the valley," Candice said.

"What we can do is search and secure the house," Ash said.

"Agreed. Teams of two," Sean said.

The scramble for companions reminded Ash of a high school dance when the last slow song of the night comes on, or better yet, musical chairs. Sean took Candice's hand, and Emica and Edo looked at each other, nodded, and clasped hands. Auggie smiled at Deepali, who grimaced and took Ash's arm. The woman's hands were like claws and her eyes grew wide when Ash pulled back.

Quickly surveying his remaining options, Ash said, "No. No. Perfect." He pulled Deepali toward him and stroked her arm.

Deepali smiled, her brown eyes darting around. In that moment Ash got a weird vibe from her, the heat between them dissipating, her smile cat-like. Thoughts of needing allies to win screamed in his head and he smiled back as wide as he could.

That left Snake, Otto, and Auggie, and none of the men looked happy.

"Let's start by securing all the doors and windows. If we—"

A guttural, non-human shriek echoed through the stone house.

8

"What was that?" Candice said.

"Sounded like it came from outside," Ash said. What he didn't say was the beast, whatever it was, didn't sound happy. The walls of the hexagonal room pressed in on Ash, and he felt alone and vulnerable. He needed sleep. Time to think things through, but not until he was reasonably assured he wasn't going to be attacked in his bed. Sweat dripped down his back as he downed his whiskey and got to his feet. "Whatever it is, it doesn't sound happy. Let's get all the doors and windows secured. Sean, why don't you and Candice check the upstairs? Edo, Otto, Emica, Deepali and I will handle the main floor, and Auggie and Snake can check the basement. Fair?"

"Is it a good idea to split up?" Emica asked.

Ash had seen plenty of horror movies and understood her concern.

"Why? You don't trust me?" Snake said, and leered.

Ash ignored him. "I understand where you're coming from, but we need to search this place as fast as possible. I think it's worth the risk."

"Is this the start of the competition?" Otto said.

Nobody spoke. The wind gusted outside as the weather picked up. The crying bird had packed it in for the night.

"If there are no other concerns, time is of the essence, so let's get to it," Ash said.

Drinks were finished, and Rodgers collected the glasses as the party separated and started searching.

Deepali stood watching Rodgers, her brown eyes locked on the bot as it went about cleaning the meeting room. "I don't trust that thing," she said.

Ash thought she was lying. "What do you trust?"

She looked him up and down, a slight smile spreading over her face. "Why? You want to be my friend?" Her bracelets clinked when she moved, and as she got closer, Ash felt the heat building between them.

Allies. Allies. And she smelled like Summer and spice. He patted her hand and said, "Let's see if we can get through the night."

Edo and Emica left the octagonal room, heading for the front of the house, so Ash went the opposite way. A hallway ran back to the portico, and a doorway led into the kitchen.

"Say what you want, but this place is amazing," Deepali said. She trailed her hand over the thick butcherblock countertop and examined the old stove like a would-be purchaser. A refrigerator with a rounded door sat in one corner, a sink next to it. Ash had noticed the house had minimal plumbing and he'd seen two bathrooms so far, each with a commode and shower. He made a mental note to examine all the house's systems. Perhaps there was an advantage to be had.

Ash and Deepali crossed the kitchen to a swinging door that led into the dining room. He'd already shifted his mindset as his competitive, desperate mind searched for ways to get an advantage over the other competitors.

The dining room was clear, and they made their way through the library, pausing to eyeball the shelves of books and papers that chronicled the history of The Cryptid Club.

"I've read about this place," Deepali said. She was reading the spines of books, wiping away dust.

"Candice will be sleeping in here," Ash said.

"What do you know of her?"

"Her and Sean are solid people, for hunters," Ash said.

"You say that name with such derision," Deepali said. "Are you ashamed to be a cryptid scientist?"

"It wasn't a choice," Ash said. "You?"

The pair locked the dining room windows as they chatted.

"When you get to know me better, you'll see I'm not overly dramatic, but I can honestly say my life has been mostly devoid of choices."

Ash chuckled. "Know the feeling. Not a cryptid hunter by choice, then?"

"Not at all. I was born in the slums of New Delhi and my family got separated when our house burned down and my parents were killed. Family took in my brother and I, but as that support system failed, I found myself on the streets until I met Ms. Glenda."

"I've been to New Delhi. Not easy streets to live on."

She harrumphed. "Understatement of our short friendship." Deepali smiled as she said friendship, and Ash smiled back. It hurt, even though he liked this woman, there was something about her that kept him on edge, like talking to a cop after he'd been pulled over. "I did OK, but I'm alive today because Ms. Glenda took pity on me. Took me in and taught me. It was on an expedition with her that I saw the monkey man of Old Delhi, what you might call a Sasquatch, Bigfoot, or Yeti. Like you, that experience changed everything for me. But unlike you, my newfound obsession helped pull me from the muck. Glenda was wealthy, and eccentric, and her love for all things cryptid sucked me in."

The pair left the dining room and entered a coat room. There was a sitting room through a large archway to the left leading to double doors that opened out on a garden, and to the right there was a closed door. Ash secured the sitting room doors and Deepali locked the windows as she continued her confession.

"I was nineteen when I first heard of this place, of the club. Glenda and Treemont communicated via letter for years, then email, and she claimed to have met him once while they were both hunting monkey man in India. I never saw any proof, though Glenda had no reason to lie."

Ash nodded. Like him, and most likely most of the other competitors, joining the cryptozoology culture wasn't a choice or a calling. You didn't do it to better the world, or to help humanity. You searched to prove you weren't insane. That what you believed to be true is true, and not a figment of an overactive imagination looking for anything to distract from the fact that Ash's life had been slipping away long before his encounter with Bigfoot in the mountains of Northern California. He figured that was one of the reasons he'd come on this crazy quest. On some level he still needed to prove to himself that his colleagues at the university and his wife had been wrong. He wasn't cracked, and he'd show them.

The scream of a person in great pain came from beyond the closed door.

Ash looked to Deepali, who shrugged.

The door was sturdy wood, and had no lock, and that told Ash it didn't lead to the outside, so he reached out to twist the knob.

"Wait," Deepali said. She darted back into the sitting room and returned with two ornate silver candle sticks with heavy bases. She stripped off the candles and handed one of the makeshift weapons to Ash, who accepted it.

Ash was no longer surprised at Deepali's survival instinct now that he knew a little about her. Anybody who'd lived on the streets of New Delhi wasn't someone he wanted to mess with, but as he watched her, Ash found he was attracted to her. "Like Clue," he said.

"In the drawing room," she joked.

He nodded and threw open the door.

A short passageway led to the backdoor, and a red line ran down the center of the hallway, a track of bloody footprints next to it, the poplar covered walls splattered with blood. Ash and Deepali moved down the passageway, being careful not to step in the blood. The dark red prints were huge, and had five toes, each accompanied by scratches in the stone floor that foretold of long, sharp claws. The door at the end of the hall was cracked open, and the blood trail led out into darkness.

Ash inched through the doorway and Deepali pulled him back. "Where are you going?" Her brown eyes were wide, and worry lines cut across her smooth brown face. "Lock the door and live to fight another day."

Ash glanced back the way they'd come. Was he better off outside with the beasts, or locked inside with the humans? "I've got to see what caused this. Whose blood this is," Ash said.

A scream echoed from the thick forest.

"Someone needs help. Do you want to wait here? I'll be right back," Ash said.

She shook her head violently and fell in behind him.

Moonlight streamed into the valley, and shadows danced under every branch and bush. Ash pushed on through the thick evening gloom, Deepali matching him stride for stride. When he reached the tree line he paused, looking back over his shoulder at the house. The dark outline of the open door he'd exited through stood out on the blue stone, and for an instant Ash thought he saw a silhouette therein, but when he squinted, there was nothing there.

Ash put out his hand to stop Deepali, and listened, blocking out the push of the wind, the rattle of leaves, and the never-ending groan of the mountains. Below it all lay an oppressive silence that filled in the valley between the sheer cliff walls. He inched into the trees. Stray beams of moonlight pierced the thick tree canopy, and spotlights marked the forest floor.

A thin path ran through the underbrush, and Deepali squeaked. Ash's heart galloped in his chest, and he felt like an icepick had been jammed in his ear. Pain raced down his back as every instinctual alarm Ash had sounded off like a five-alarm fire raged beneath his feet. Sweat dripped down his back, and he glanced back at Deepali, her wide eyes white orbs in the darkness. What the hell was he doing? Deepali was right. This was crazy, but curiosity dragged him on.

The huge footprints had faded, but the thick red line still ran across the ground, weaving between trees and bushes. Drips of blood splattered the hardpan and dripped from leaves. Ash strained to see into the depths of the forest, and a dread crept over him he couldn't explain.

Something was watching them.

Deepali stopped walking and pointed at the ground, her gold bracelets jingling.

Another set of footprints crossed the path of the first, a splash of moonlight illuminating a puddle of blood. "These tracks are larger, if you can believe that," Ash said.

A beep sounded off behind Ash and he whirled, crouching as he searched the underbrush. Rodgers pushed through the vegetation, camera eyes glowing in the darkness. "Are you in need of assistance?" the bot asked.

"Shush," Deepali said. "You scared me half to death."

"I'm sorry madam, Sing—"

"Shut it before I shut you down," Deepali said.

Ash plunged deeper into the forest, following the trail of blood. He heard Deepali struggling behind him as he picked up speed, underbrush slapping his face.

Ash formed a picture in his mind that matched the footprints; a large beast with long claws that walked on two legs. Ash's pulse raced, the trail of blood growing from a thin red line to a wide mark that confirmed Ash's earlier suspicions; something, or someone, had been dragged through the forest. The line of blood wove through the trees, the path becoming clearer with each step. Ash pushed through underbrush, climbed over rocks, and traversed walls of trees.

A smell like that of rotting flesh filled the woods as a puff of wind pushed through the valley.

Snake's blood-smeared turban lay crumpled next to a tree, its pin gone. Deepali pleaded with Ash to go back to the house, but he was adamant.

"Go back if you want, but I'm going on," Ash said, and he hoped that would deter the woman, but it didn't. Ash felt something had subtly shifted, his nerves walking a wire, and he needed to know who... what had killed Snake.

A stick snapped. Ash froze, then stepped behind a large oak tree that looked over a hundred years old. Its thick trunk hid Ash and Deepali from view, but the creature they were following was aware of them. The beast's shadow lifted its head, sniffed, and huffed, a loud intake of air that sounded a little like laughter.

Ash paused in the darkness, something on the ground blocking his way, and Deepali bumped into him. They stared down at Snake's twisted, bloodied body, and a snarl reverberated through the forest, an earsplitting cry of agony that wasn't human, but not quite animal. The scent of rot grew, and the tang of blood carried on the air.

Snake's body had been torn in two, his legs at a ninety-degree angle from his waist. His frizzy black hair fell across his face, dark eyes staring blankly up at the star-filled sky. Claw marks streaked across his face, half his right arm was missing, and a large bloody wound covered what was left of his chest.

A large hulking shape wheezed in the shadows, white eyes peering through the underbrush at them. Ash went cold, and every bad scenario he'd envisioned since receiving the invitation came rushing back like a piece of mail with no postage. His knees came unhinged and Ash dropped to the ground. This wasn't happening. This couldn't be happening.

Deepali knelt beside him. "No. No. Don't you checkout on me," she said. "Not yet."

Ash hardly heard her. Sean's words rang in his head; this guy is crazy. Staring down at Snake's body he couldn't help but think his murder was no accident.

Deepali helped Ash to his feet as they watched the Sasquatch. Ash had forgotten Rodgers was with them, and when the bot beeped, he jumped and the creature froze.

Ash pulled his karambit and flicked it open.

"Where did you…" Deepali's voice trailed off when the beast stepped into a cone of moonlight.

The creature was covered in dark brown fur and blood, its face ape-like. Eyes shining in the moonlight, it lifted its huge clawed hand as if to wave, then let it fall to its side. The beast gurgled, its teeth glowing in the moon's spotlight. The Bigfoot inched forward, sniffing the air, watching Ash and Deepali as they stood frozen over Snake's lifeless body.

Rodgers inched forward, eye cameras scoping in and out, servos whining. "Tallboy?" the bot said.

Deepali gripped Ash's arm, her hand vice-like.

The Sasquatch lumbered forward, eyes rolling in its head, blood dripping from the two-inch claws at the end of each of the beast's digits.

"So much for domestication," Ash said.

The sasquatch threw back its head and wailed, teeth glinting in the moonlight.

Ash reeled, and Deepali gripped his arm tighter as Tallboy disappeared into the trees.

9

It happened so fast. Ash blinked and shook his head, his mouth falling open a crack. A chill breeze swept through the valley, and he shivered. Trees creaked and leaves rattled, moonlight cutting through the dense canopy. Shadows danced behind every tree trunk and under every leaf and bough. A haze hung over the valley, and the insects had gone silent.

They couldn't take it all in. Ash and Deepali stood frozen, staring at the bloodied and torn-up corpse of Snake. Rodgers had gone still, his camera eyes locked on the corpse.

Deepali broke her grip on Ash's arm and backed away from the body, eyes growing wide. "He's dead?"

"He doesn't look alive," Ash said.

"Not funny," she said.

An owl hooted loudly three times.

"I'm sorry. You're right. I should check him to be sure." Ash knelt and examined the corpse without touching it. Snake's remaining eye was open, his chest unmoving, lips blue. Deep gashes raked across his chest; his clothes tattered. A garbage can lid-sized pool of dark blood congealed on the hardpan beneath the body, and the right leg was twisted at an odd angle. The left hand was missing, and gristle, muscle, shattered bone and blood leaked from the stump. Ash reached out and felt for a pulse. Nothing. "He's gone for sure."

"Just like that," she said, a bit too flippant for Ash.

Ash got to his feet and scanned the forest, but said nothing. He knew how she felt. The nine... eight of them were already walking the high wire without a net and now one of the beasts had killed a guest.

"He was an ass," Deepali said as she stared up at the stars.

"Seemed tough, though. A fighter," Ash said.

"Yes," Deepali said. "How could he have been caught? Killed so... easily."

"Without a weapon... You saw the size of the thing. It looked ten feet tall. And speaking of getting caught, where's his partner?" Snake had been paired with Auggie.

"Rodgers, do you know where Auggie is?" Ash asked.

Rodgers made no sign, the bot's eyes locked on Snake's crumpled body.

"Anyone out there?" Edo's call came from the forest.

"Over here," Ash yelled. He hid behind a bush and pulled Deepali with him. "There's a good chance Tallboy didn't leave."

Deepali's head twisted around, and her face hardened. "Wish I had a weapon."

"Stay close to me." Ash pulled his karambit, the blade singing as he flipped it on his finger.

Edo and Emica appeared out of the gloom and Ash and Deepali stepped from their hiding spot.

"Are you guys OK? We heard the screaming. What the... oh, shit," Emica said.

"What happened?" Edo asked. He examined the body, his nose crinkling, and his eyes narrowed as they followed the drips of blood that trailed away into the forest the way Tallboy had gone. "Did you see it?"

Deepali and Ash nodded in unison, but said nothing.

"We followed the blood trail from the house. The beast was in the house?" Emica asked.

Ash nodded.

Ash and Edo carried the body through the forest back to the house and laid it out on a patch of turf by the back door. "Rodgers, any clue what we should do with this?"

The bot had floated back with them but hadn't made a sound. It was like the robot's core programing had been erased. Its camera eyes were still lit, but the bot's arms didn't move, and its head didn't turn.

Edo said, "We have to bring the body inside until we can figure out how and where to bury it. If we leave it out here the animals will get to it."

Ash nodded. "Let's go f—"

Auggie inched out into the moonlight through the backdoor, followed by Candice, Sean and Otto. Candice gasped, Auggie looked away, but Sean and Otto strode forward, eyes scanning the body.

"What the hell got a piece of him?" Sean said.

"Tallboy," Rodgers' mechanical voice shrieked.

Everyone turned in the bot's direction.

Rodgers' camera-eyes scoped in and out, but the machine said nothing more.

"That true?" Otto asked.

Ash quickly told everyone what had happened from the moment they'd seen the trail of blood. "Which reminds me, where were you, Auggie? You didn't see anything?"

"We were in the basement where you sent us—it's a maze down there. Snake thought he heard something back the way we'd come, and he took off in the dark. We got separated and it took me a few minutes to find my way out."

"You didn't see the blood trail? Or us?" Deepali asked.

"I saw the blood when I came up. Guess we missed each other," Auggie said.

Ash looked to Candice, and suspicious glances carried from person to person like a virus. Something about the man's posture made Ash think he was lying.

Rodgers beeped, and the bot's head spun, stabilizer jets puffing as it glided forward and retrieved Snake's body.

"Where you going with that?" Ash said.

The robot ignored the question. Snake's corpse sagged in accordion arms as Rodgers whirred off into the darkness.

"Hey," called Edo.

"Should we try and stop it?" Sean said.

"How?" Emica asked.

Sean shrugged.

"I don't know about you all, but I've had enough for one day," Candice said.

"A man is dead. Don't we need to... do something? Say something?" Ash said. He hadn't liked Snake, but there came a time when bullshit became bullshit, and the man was dead. Did he have a wife? Children? People who were waiting for him to come home? Sorrow washed over Ash. Suddenly his game in the mountains had gotten real.

"Tomorrow," Edo said. "Now we need to rest up and get through the night."

Nods and mumbles of agreement as the party shuffled back into the blue granite house via the rear entrance.

"I assume Rodgers will clean this up?" Emica said, referring to the trail of blood that ran down the center of the hallway.

"We'll see," Ash said.

The group didn't speak as they made their way to the staircase and headed up to the bedrooms. It was a slow, weary and dejected procession. When they got to the top of the steps the party separated; Otto, Candice, Deepali, and Sean going right, and Ash, Emica, Auggie and Edo left.

Like the Boston symphony orchestra, electronic door locks beeped and clicked in a musical jingle twenty-four notes long. Ash stood in the darkness of his room, the door clicking closed behind him.

There was a beep and two clicks missing from the symphony.

Had Treemont's house been an old wooden structure with a creaking wood frame and dark shadows around every corner, Ash may have been more concerned, but the blue granite house was solid, its doors thick wood. There were no possible hidden compartments, and why provide the updated door locks? They could be disengaged with a tap of a button, so Ash had to assume they were for his protection.

Ash's stomach ached, but he poured himself a glass of wine anyway. Despite his rationalization of the fancy locks and granite, he still propped the desk chair beneath the door's handle. If Rodgers or Treemont wanted access to his room, there was nothing he could do to stop them, but the chair might buy him some warning time, not that it mattered. He walked out onto the balcony that overlooked the valley, the scent of pine and earth floating on the night air. He pulled the doors closed and dogged down the latch.

He slept fitfully, tossing and turning most of the night, and finally falling into a deep sleep what felt like five minutes before Rodgers tapped on his door and woke him. The bot appeared to be back to its clueless self, and ignored all questions about the prior night as it floated into Ash's room and filled his washbasin with steaming water. He left two towels and a white envelope. "Breakfast is at eight. Don't be late. There'll be instructions."

Ash lifted an eyebrow. The wall clock read 7:38AM. The show must go on. That's why you play the game. Every man for himself, and all that. Looked like the competition was proceeding as if nothing had happened. Ash wasn't sure he was comfortable with that. Did he care about Snake? Not a fly's fart. But what if Tallboy came after him? There had to be guns in the valley, and he needed to find them.

Bird song floated in through the open veranda doors, and everything went still when a shrill cry cut across the morning. He splashed water on his face and got dressed, slipping the folded karambit into his back pocket.

He opened the envelope.

Unlike the fancy gold embossed invitation that had drawn him to Atavism Special Animal Sanctuary, this paper was so thin Ash saw through it. Words comprised of black dots filled the page and Ash smiled. Dot matrix printers hadn't been used for decades. The note read: "I've chosen to make your first challenge clear and defined. I've selected a test of faith. You must trust in that which you know, and can see. Would it surprise you to know that the Loch Ness Monster, Altie, Champ, Bessie, Tessie, or whatever name they've roamed the Earth under are plant eaters? It explains how the Loch Ness Monster and its siblings can live and support themselves at such large sizes with a limited food supply. It eats lake vegetation, but it's not above eating fish, and that's where your test comes in. Report to the lake front after breakfast. Good luck, be safe, and trust what you know." The printout was signed Lester Treemont.

When Ash arrived at breakfast, Sean, Candice, and Edo already had their letters laid out on the table. Breakfast was on the large veranda on the side of the house where they'd had dinner, but this meal felt much different. The mood was subdued, the prior night's events hovering over the group like a dark raincloud. When the remaining competitors were seated, they ate stacks of pancakes, ham and bacon, toast, scrambled eggs, fruit and drank water, coffee and tea. Rodgers appeared, but didn't take drink orders. Apparently, Bloody Marys were taboo on game day. Ash supposed that was best.

"Rodgers, what did you do with Snake's body?" Sean asked.

The bot said, "It has been buried in the graveyard with the other living things that have died in the valley."

"Can we go see where?" Ash asked.

"I will show you if you'd like."

"I'd like," Ash said.

"First we have some business to attend to," the bot said. "Because Mr. Treemont is a fair man, and we're just starting, I will give some additional background about the creature commonly referred to as the Loch Ness Monster for those who have limited knowledge in that area of cryptozoology."

When nobody interrupted, the bot continued, "Kressel, as she was named when she was brought here from the highlands as a calf, and if you're interested in the specifics of her capture a full account is available in the library, Kressel is believed to be the last of her kind. Nessie, and the other comparable creatures seen around the globe may be similar species, or totally different, but despite extensive attempts to document the existence of such beasts, to date no credible evidence exists except Kressel. All the Loch Ness Monster type cryptids are believed to be mutant Plesiosaurs, prehistoric beasts of the sea. The myths about these mutants have grown in furiousness over time, but most tales of aggression are believed to be false."

The bot paused, its camera eyes scanning the seven competitors. "As your letter has stated, the beasts are believed to be primarily plant eaters and your task today is one of Mr. Treemont's favorite things to do. Today you each must feed Kressel a fish by hand. This way." Rodgers whirred across the stone portico and disappeared down the rear steps that led to the garden below.

The eight cryptid hunters sat around the table staring at each other as if trying to figure out whose turn it was to do the dishes.

Emica dropped her napkin and followed Rodgers, and that started a rush.

Ash got to his feet and followed Deepali, but when he saw Candice hanging back with Sean, he paused. "What's up?"

"What's up?" Sean shook his head and looked at Candice. "My mate here wants to know what's up." Sean got to his feet and got in Ash's face. "What's up—is these beasties are fifty meters in length, weigh ten tons and can suck you under with a breath. Do I believe they're violent? Damn right! Plesiosaurs were up there with the apex predators of their day."

"But what about the food argument?" Candice said.

Sean shot her a glance, but said nothing.

Ash helped her out. "Didn't you tell me Nessie ate plants?"

Sean huffed, but nodded. "There's not enough big game in the lochs."

"Or here," Candice said.

"It's your call," Ash said.

"Shit," Sean said. He vaulted to his feet and trailed after the others.

They followed a dirt path that ran through a patch of tall grass and into a forest of conifers and oak. A tall wall rose to the west, and Ash guessed it was the border of a paddock. He covered his nose as he followed Candice and Sean into the forest, the scent of rot, like the sea at low tide, growing stronger as he worked his way through the thin woods that encroached to the lake's western edge. Its southern and easterly shores ended against the steep cliffs.

Ash broke free of the forest, the smell of dead fish, moisture, and sodium filling the air. A narrow dock led from a thin rock-strewn shoreline out into the crystal-clear water. Rodgers stood on a platform at the dock's end with Emica and Edo. Deepali and Otto were making their way out on the thin dock. Sean stopped, gazing up and down the shoreline, then out at the dock.

A thick serpentine neck wriggled from the water, a narrow gator-like head swaying at its tip. White teeth glinted below black softball-sized eyes that were locked on Rodgers, Emica and Edo. Four powerful flippers knifed through the clear water, undulating up and down, driving the slick gray beast through the lake, a knot of whitewater surging before it. Kressel moaned and dove beneath the lake's surface, disappearing in a swirl of water and sparkle of sunlight.

Sean said, "In a Scottish fjord called Loch Ness, so deep there is no redress for proof, Nessie dwells, alone and aloof."

10

The old dock creaked and swayed as Sean, Candice, and Ash made their way out to the platform to join the rest of the party. The sun was hot on Ash's neck, and he instinctively rubbed it and brushed the sweat from his forehead with the back of his hand. He smelled Sean's body odor. Washing up with a basin of warm water wasn't the same thing as taking a shower. Candice's sneakers squeaked behind him, her shallow breaths labored. She was nervous and afraid. That was understandable, Ash felt the same way.

"Very good, we're now all here," Rodgers said as Ash and the others arrived. "We can get started."

A thin dock, almost like a gangplank, jutted from the end of the platform and extended out into the lake twenty feet. A metal bucket sat at the end of the pier. Swirls of water dotted the lake, like whales were endlessly circling, driving their prey into a single mass so they could feed.

"It's real?" Sean blurted. He stood gaping at the swirls of water, a crooked smile cutting across his face.

"Yes, Mr. Macrerie, very real," Rodgers said. "Gather around."

Sean tore his gaze from the water, his freckled face a contorted mess of frustration and anger. He shuffled over to the group like a child who's been told they need to stop playing and come have dinner. Sean passed his tongue over dry lips, his eyes wide as quarters, face tight. "It's just... I'd come to believe I'd never see her... one. Clearly there's more than one?"

"As I stated earlier, that is an unknown. Kressel is the only specimen ever verified. Using records in the sanctuary library, Mr. Treemont calculated her age at over one hundred years."

Lake water rippled, birds sang, and somewhere far off an animal bleated. Ash looked over his shoulder and searched the tree break, expecting to see Tallboy watching them, but there was nothing. A rank scent wafted from the forest and across the lake, the stench of rot and decay, like the sea at low tide.

"Right, so this test is easy. Each of you must give Kressel a fish. You may not toss, flip, drop, or in any way throw the fish. Kressel must take it from your hand. Understood?" Rodgers said.

The party stood silent, each struggling with their own levels of confusion, frustration and anger. Candice looked like she'd just taken a gulp of sour milk, and Sean and Emica's faces were scrunched up in anger. Otto stared vacantly at the lake, as if trying to persuade old memories from the shadows of his past. Deepali's bracelets rang as she fidgeted, her face oddly confident.

"Who wants to go first?" Rodgers said.

Ash felt the familiar feeling deep in his stomach, a cold dread that seeped through him like sewage in clear water. Regret prodded him, stoked the fire that was the rational side of his brain. It had been a mistake to come here. That thought, like a maggot burrowing through dead flesh, preoccupied his thoughts, but he knew one thing, a lesson his father had drilled into him like it was the most important piece of wisdom he could pass on. "Never volunteer," he'd said. He'd learned that lesson the hard way in the military. Be part of the team, don't stand out, because if you lift your head above the rim of the foxhole to take a look, it might get shot off.

"We get to choose?" Edo said, sarcasm dripping from his frustrated tone.

"This time," Rodgers said.

"I'll go," Sean said. "I've been waiting for this moment most of my life, after all." The Scot inched forward across the platform, his eyes straying from the gangplank dock to the lake.

"How will it know it's feeding time?" Emica asked.

A gritty, harsh, mechanical crackling static emanated from Rodgers and echoed over the lake.

"You laugh now?" Ash said.

"Always could, sir. I just haven't heard anything funny lately," Rodgers said. His monotone tinny voice had returned.

Sean hugged Candice, a bit overdramatically in Ash's opinion. Then he nodded to Ash and turned his back on the rest of the party, staring out at the lake.

The water was still, small ripples rolling over the lake. Fish jumped and splashed, snakes wriggled along the surface, and a group of birds flew overhead in a V formation. The birds squawked and hollered as they banked low, picking up the air currents in the valley.

Sean crept out onto the thin pier and it creaked and popped as it bent under his weight. He didn't look back, but his head jerked side to side. A loud crack reverberated over the water and Sean froze, bouncing up and down slightly as the pier moved.

"It's quite safe, I assure you," Rodgers said.

"Shut your oil hole you AC duct," Sean said. He was moving again, and was halfway to the end of the dock where the gray metal pail waited. "Nobody asked you for your input."

Sean reached the end of the dock and braced himself, legs spread apart. He bent, his hand fishing in the pail and retrieving a ten-inch yellow-striped killifish, its scales glinting in the sunlight. He held the fish up, extending his hand out over the water.

A gust of cold wind pushed through the valley, bringing the foul scent of rot and decay. Insects hummed, beasts mewed and clicked, birds chirped and yelled, and beneath it all the steady buzz-like hum of the valley supported it all.

"What now?" Sean yelled. He hadn't moved or looked back, arm out, the fish still extended over the lake.

Rodgers beeped, then began to sing in a series of chimes, bleeps, whistles, and farts that went on for several seconds.

A bird divebombed a fish, something croaked, but Kressel didn't show.

Rodger's repeated his call, getting faster and louder each time.

To the west a fist of whitewater rose from the smooth surface and rolled toward the pier.

Sean shifted on his feet, but stayed where he was.

Bile rose in Ash's throat as the knot of water grew.

Eyes appeared in the whitewater, an open mouth with rows of teeth.

Waves slapped the shoreline, popping and snapping. A growl that was more moo than roar bellowed over the lake as the creature's head rose from the water like a periscope from a submarine. The reptilian head bobbed, its dark eyes searching. Flippers surged through the water as the beast changed direction, pointing its nose toward the dock.

Sean stood still as stone, the breeze pushing around his red hair.

The mound of water grew, then crested, whitewater spilling over the lake's surface as the beast's mouth opened wider. Kressel breached, surging from the water, its mouth swiping the fish from Sean's hand and crashing back into the lake.

Water splashed Sean, but the Scot didn't move. Water washed over the pier, and waves sucked at the shoreline.

The beast circled, heading out toward the center of the lake, its head falling to the waterline as it ate.

Sean screamed and Ash tore his gaze from the monster.

The Scotsman thrust his fist in the air and hooted. "Damn. That was amazing. Someone got a picture of that, right?" he yelled. His fist fell to his side and he turned toward the group, his joy falling from his face. "Of course, nobody did."

With no cell service in the valley, Ash had forgotten about his phone. He pulled it from a back pocket to find its battery dead.

Sean walked down the rickety dock and joined the others on the main platform.

"Guess Treemont is right, ya?" Edo said.

Sean harrumphed. "Who knows. Kressel was raised in captivity. Things probably would have gone much differently had we been out on the Loch."

The party said nothing.

"Who's next?" Rodgers said. "She'll be expecting more."

When nobody volunteered, Rodgers said, "Emica, you're up."

Kressel had made a full circle and was heading back toward the dock, her head lifting from the water in preparation for another food grab.

Emica hurried to the end of the pier and got in position, and the massive beast took the fish as it had before.

Up next was Edo, Deepali, Candice, and then Ash's name was called.

"How many times will the beast come? Is it used to getting a certain number of fish?" He'd watched five people feed the beast, and there'd been no problems, yet his instincts still sounded their warning alarms. Asking a creature the size of Kressel to take food from your hand was nuts, and it didn't really matter whether the creature was an aggressive meat-eater or not. It was an animal, and beasts do strange things when they feel threatened or are hungry.

Ash's worries were for naught. He walked the plank, held out his fish, and it was taken like the others, without incident. His stomach churned as the beast approached, its evil-looking eyes peering out through the whitewater, sharp teeth glistening in the midday sunlight, but he'd felt nothing as the fish was taken from his hand.

Otto went next, and that left Auggie for last.

Having seen his seven companions successfully complete the challenge, the Australian didn't look nervous at all as he strode to the end of the pier and lifted the last fish.

The creature didn't come right away. It circled out to the center of the lake, and Rodgers had to call it again. Kressel responded, and the beast knifed through the lake and surged from the water, taking Auggie's fish. He wore a smile ear to ear as he approached the group.

"Can we do that again?" Auggie asked.

"Perhaps," Rodgers said.

"So who won?" Ash asked.

The crackle of Rodgers laughing.

"Stop that," Deepali said.

Rodgers' mechanical cackling ceased. "Nobody has won, sir. You've all completed the task and may move onto the next challenge, which begins now."

Startled exclamations, gasps and chirps.

"Now?" Emica said.

Rodgers squawked, "Now."

The bot's stabilizer jets puffed, and Rodgers glided down the dock toward shore.

"Wait," Ash said. "What's the test?"

"Rules?" Edo echoed.

Rodgers said nothing. The bot glided off the dock and paused on the thin shoreline, waiting.

"This sucks," Emica said. "Who's up for trying to get the hell out of here?"

Nobody answered.

"No sense staying out here," Candice said as she headed for shore.

Sean and the others followed, the dock swaying and creaking, waves lapping on the shoreline.

The scent of rot and low tide had subsided.

"Sir Chambers, you might find that of interest," Rodgers said.

Ash started. Who the hell was Chambers?

Auggie paused, staring up and down the rock-strewn beach.

Something dark shot through the clear water like a torpedo, leaving twisting swirls of lake water in its wake.

Auggie stepped down off the dock, his eyes never leaving the shape as it scythed through the water.

A head popped above the surface, and to Ash it looked like a dog or a seal.

"Devil," Auggie said as he strode forward in a daze.

"Hey, Auggie," Edo said. "You might want to give that thing some space."

Auggie either didn't hear him, or didn't care, and he continued down the thin beach, the dark figure growing in size as it approached the shoreline.

"Bunyips are your specialty, are they not, Mr. Chambers?" Rodgers said.

Pebbles crunched and popped beneath Auggie's feet as he walked down the beach. He didn't answer Rodgers and didn't look back.

Auggie paused, transfixed by the creature as it slowly rose from the darkness.

Candice and Deepali gasped, and Otto whistled.

The beast broke the surface, its tail flukes driving the creature forward as it snaked through the water. Its angular head was a foot long and had two pointed ears that were thrown back. Two long fangs hung from a long mouth below deep-set eyes, its slick black skin shining in the sunlight. The beast's neck and torso were corded with rippling muscles, and as it breached from the lake, Auggie realized he was in danger. He jumped back, looking toward Ash and the others, as if asking for help.

"Run," Candice said in a low whisper, as if willing Auggie on.

The Bunyip landed in the shallows with a splash, muscles twitching and tightening beneath seal-like skin. The beast growled, throwing back its head like a lion. It pulled itself toward shore, using its two forward flippers like arms, its tail flukes digging into the soft lake bottom, pushing the beast forward.

Auggie took two hesitant steps backward, then stopped.

"Rodgers, what should he do?" Ash said.

The Bunyip splashed its way onto the rock beach, tossing its head and gurgling, its dark eyes finding Auggie.

Rodgers answered, "The Bunyip is a creature of Australian mythology. Auggie called it a Devil because that's the aboriginal translation of Bunyip. It's been alleged that the beasts steal children, and are very aggressive. Thus the various childhood stories. This particular specimen—"

"Auggie, get the hell out of there!" Ash yelled.

The others looked at him, surprised, and in that moment the Bunyip attacked.

The creature coiled and launched from the shallows, jaws distended, forward flippers hitting the ground like legs and supporting the beast.

A surge of whitewater rolled over the beach and Auggie ran, but it was too late.

The Bunyip moved with amazing speed and agility, its tail flukes pounding the rocky beach as its front flippers propelled it forward, its odd gait reminding Ash of a running spider. The beast was on Auggie in seconds, and it launched itself, mouth open, teeth bared.

Auggie screamed as the Bunyip's jaws locked down on his legs, cutting him to the ground. The Aussie pitched and heaved, kicking out with his feet, trying to stay away from the creature.

The Bunyip snipped and pawed, taking small bits from Auggie.

Ash jerked forward, intent on helping, then he pulled up. He only had his small karambit. What could he do?

The Bunyip and Auggie thrashed on the ground for ten seconds before the creature's jaws finally found purchase and locked down on Auggie's arm.

Otto screamed.

Blood poured from Auggie's mouth as he was dragged toward the lake, his hands clawing at the beach, legs kicking. "Help!" he kept yelling.

Ash stood with his feet nailed to the dock, staring out at the chaos, the Bunyip thrashing its head as it tore Auggie apart. A red cloud of blood spread over the lake as the beast dove, and Auggie disappeared underwater, bloody bubbles popping and snapping on the surface.

11

Slowly the forest static came back online, and the creatures of the valley went about their business as though a man hadn't just been killed and eaten by a seal dog the size of a pony with foot-long fangs. Waves snapped and popped on the shoreline, the undertow pulling pebbles over stones. The sound was oddly relaxing, and as Auggie's blood cloud dissipated, pieces of fat and skin drifting away like leaves, the tension that had been pulling Ash apart eased. There was no question any longer that their host, Lester Treemont, was a madman and meant to kill them all.

Except, perhaps, one.

"Anyone want to answer my question now?" Emica said. "There's got to be a way out of the valley. A footpath."

Nobody spoke. Ash had thought the same thing, but they had no idea how far away from civilization they really were. They didn't have weapons, climbing gear, proper provisions. To Ash it seemed impossible and an escape attempt would be folly and a last resort.

Ash sucked his lips. "What are we supposed to do? Do you have any information for us, Rodgers?"

The bot beeped, and said, "Take care. Lunch at the bell."

Ash rubbed his temples with the tips of his fingers, patience draining from him. He said, "Sean, maybe you're right. Maybe it's time to find out what happens when we break something."

"Gladly," Sean said. The Scot jumped from the dock onto shore and headed for Rodgers.

The bot was unmoved, its lens eyes scoping in and out as Sean approached.

Edo stepped between them again.

"Step aside," Sean said.

"No."

Sean turned to Ash, freckled face red, eyes blazing.

Ash shrugged.

Sean turned back to Edo and said, "Move, or I'll move you."

Edo's left foot eased back, and his hands came up. He rolled his shoulders as he stared at Sean.

The Scot sighed as Rodgers disappeared into the forest. "Now it's gone," Sean said.

"Why are you so hell bent on protecting that tin spy?" Candice said.

"Propaganda," Edo said. "We've got to start being smart. Feeding the bot information to flush out Treemont. Clearly he's watching us."

"Thanks, Mr. Obvious. He told us as much," Sean said.

He had, and suddenly Ash felt exposed, and he looked around for cameras, but saw none. He knew that meant nothing. Cameras the size of pinheads could be placed anywhere, and advances in solar cells allowed for an easy and indefinite power supply. He thought of the Truman Show.

"I think we should all stop playing," Candice said.

"I think you should start," Edo said. He stalked off after Rodgers, but nobody followed.

"He is an impatient person," Otto said.

Sean, Ash, Deepali, Emica, and Candice exchanged glances.

"What? He is."

"I'm heading back up to the house to look around, check out the food supply and stuff," Sean said. "Candice, you coming with?"

She looked to Ash, but when he made no sign she said, "Right behind you."

When Sean disappeared into the trees, she pecked Ash on the cheek and said, "Holler if you need us."

Ash actually thought she meant it.

The footpath that led up to the house wasn't the path less traveled, and with his allies Sean and Candice checking out the house, he decided to reconnoiter the surrounding area alone, maybe scope out some of the paddocks and try to see some of the creatures that lived therein. The bookworm in him wanted to search the sanctuary library, but there was time for that after dark.

He worked his way west along the shoreline, searching for another path, but there was nothing but thin animal trails, and without a machete it would be difficult to follow them. Animals tended to stay away from areas trafficked by humans, and in this case that was what he was looking for. Ash laughed at himself. He had no idea what he was looking for, but it was a classic case of he'd know it when he saw it.

Ash reached the sheer rock wall that marked the southwestern edge of the valley. The forest ran along the wall to the west, and to the east the lake stretched into the distance. A vale of shade lay over the southern slope, the northern side of the valley baking under the midday heat. Sweat ran down his back into his underwear, and his knees ached, his stomach reminding him it was almost lunch time.

Trees swayed and shifted, and a gentle chirping sound, like the coo of a dove, carried on the breeze. Ash did an about-face and headed back along the shoreline the way he'd come, pausing at the entrance to a thin animal trail that led north into the darkness beneath the dense forest canopy. Shadows danced, and Ash's hands were clammy and cold. He caught the scent of decomposing flesh wafting from the forest, and sniffed, but the smell was gone.

Ash ducked under a branch and inched into the woods. The trail zigzagged around dense conifers, dead spiked leaves covering the forest floor like a swarm of copper-colored ants. The peeping and squawking got louder as he worked his way deeper into the woods, a painfilled whimper rising over the frantic chirping.

A branch snapped and Ash froze as his head jerked toward the sound.

Tallboy hid behind a bush, watching something Ash couldn't see. The fur on the beast's chest and around its mouth was matted with blood, the ape-like face smeared dark red. Crouched low, Tallboy was the same height as Ash, and the Sasquatch's head slowly turned in his direction. Dark eyes found Ash, and grew wide. Tallboy shook like a wet dog trying to dry itself, then darted off into the underbrush.

Curiosity pulled Ash onward. He needed to see what Tallboy had been looking at. He inched forward, watching every step, slipping under branches and around roots and vines.

The land fell away, a depression two hundred yards across stretching out before Ash. A fence made of timber ran away to the north and south, and through the gaps between boards Ash saw the most amazing thing he'd ever seen. Seeing Bigfoot had changed his life— mostly for the worst—but it had been incredible. That he couldn't deny, even though he knew that obsession is what had directly resulted in his fall.

But this... A dragon... Ash could find no other image to compare the creature to. It was white with black striations, large boney humps running from the top of its gator-like head to the tip of its whip tail. It was twice the size of an elephant, and it appeared that the creature's large opaque wings had been clipped. Yet that wasn't what disturbed Ash the most. A metal collar ran around the beast's neck, and a chain ran to a ring that was mounted to the face of a huge stone.

The creature was asleep, gentle breaths puffing from its half open, tooth-filled mouth.

Rodgers beeped and Ash jumped. "What the hell? How about warning a guy next time?"

"I see you've found Smaug," Rodgers said.

Ash knew the name from somewhere, but couldn't place it. His curiosity beat back his anger. "What is it?"

"We don't know," Rodgers said. "Based on where and how the specimen was obtained, Mr. Treemont believes—"

Three brazen, insistent, loud horn blasts echoed through the valley.

Ash ignored the sounds and watched Rodgers, waiting for an answer to his question.

"Torpor can kill. It would be best if you went," Rodgers said.

"What? Where?"

"To the sound of the horn."

The signal resounded through the valley again and Ash judged the horn blasts had come from the north towards the house. No path ran that way, so he backtracked. When he looked to see if Rodgers was following, he saw the bot was gone.

The lake was flat, the shoreline silent as Ash worked his way back to the main path that ran up to the house. He saw Emica in the distance, and followed her, past the backdoor to the northern side of the house. Ash saw the portico where they ate meals, and as the horn blasted three final times, the path was clear.

Emica saw him trailing after her and waited for him. "Where you been?"

"Around."

She harrumphed.

A brick path ran to the northeast toward the open end of the valley, and shadows danced behind every tree and bush on the northern slope as the afternoon sun angled into the valley like spotlights on a Broadway stage, not a cloud in the sky. The air was brisk and fresh, and as he walked with Emica, Ash felt confident.

The feeling didn't last long.

A paddock wall rose out of the vegetation and Sean, Candice, Deepali, Otto and Edo waited behind a closed gate.

"Where you been, mate? I think we're waiting on you," Sean said.

Ash said nothing.

"Have you seen Rodgers?" Candice asked.

Ash shifted on his feet, and said nothing.

The paddock door had a fancy electronic lock like the ones on their bedroom doors, and its indicator light glowed red.

Hoots, squawks, chirps, and grunts floated from the forest, echoing off the valley walls. The seven surviving competitors waited in silence, eyeing each other. Ash felt Otto watching him. Why did the man pay extra attention to him? He didn't appear to even care about anyone else. Was it he saw Ash as the biggest threat? Could be, but since the man knew little about him Ash didn't know how Otto could make such a determination. He'd been told he had a presence, but when Ash pressed people to explain what they meant by that they usually came up with he was big and loud.

The paddock door lock chirped, and the indicator light flipped to green.

Emica was the first to react, and before Ash knew what she was doing the woman had flung open the gate and passed through.

The competitors clogged the opening, pressing each other aside, pushing and shoving their way through the open gate. It never ceased to amaze Ash how fast people reverted to their primal tendencies. That thought stuck in his mind like a popcorn kernel shell wedged between tooth and gum. Where had he heard something similar? Very recently? He couldn't piece it together, and the inside of the paddock drove all needless thoughts from his mind.

The wood wall of the enclosure ran away to Ash's right and left, curving inward to create a circle with a diameter of roughly five hundred feet. Metal mesh covered the top of the paddock, and at its center was a mound of disorganized stones with a manmade cave on its side. Thick cord-like webbing draped over all the vegetation like slimy white snow, the hardpan torn up.

A rifle leaned against the stone pile's topmost rock, its metal barrel casting a thin shadow across the enclosure. A low clicking sound, like teeth mashing together, floated on the breeze, the sweet smell of meat and the coppery scent of blood filling Ash's nostrils.

Sean started forward and Candice grabbed his arm. "What?" the Scot said, his freckled face haggard. "I don't see anything."

"That's what worries me," Candice said.

Emica darted forward, weaving in and out of the web-encrusted vegetation.

A low hiss emanated from the rock cave, but Emica didn't stop. She launched herself onto the lower most stone and climbed for the gun.

"Screw this," Sean said. He ran after her, veering away toward a section of the pile that looked easier to climb. Edo, Deepali and Candice looked to Ash, and when he started running, they followed.

They'd gone ten feet when a giant spider lumbered from the cave.

The eight-legged monstrosity was black, and white hair-like fuzz covered its body and legs. Six wet eyes of various sizes were barely perceptible against the beast's dark body, and they undulated and rotated until they locked on Ash and the others.

Ash skidded to a halt, and Edo and Candice ran into him and the three companions went down in a tangle.

The massive spider hissed, curved fangs hanging from its cruel mouth. Eight three-jointed legs scuttled across the hardpan as the beast came at Ash.

The creature skidded to a stop without warning, its attention turning to the mound of boulders and rocks.

Sean stood halfway up the side of the pile, tossing stones at the spider. He was connecting with every third throw or so, and the creature was getting irritated.

The spider pushed upward and hissed, spinning around and shuffling toward the rock pile with incredible speed. Before Ash could get to his feet, the spider was spinning web and working its way toward Sean and Emica.

Sean kept tossing stones, but as the beast got closer, his angle got worse. When he no longer had a direct line of fire, he disappeared into the rock pile.

Emica remained focused, eyes locked on the rifle as she pulled herself hand over hand. She was almost to the top.

"No!" Edo said, and he darted forward, running at full speed toward the rock pile.

The spider was almost on top of Emica.

Edo skidded to a stop at the bottom of the pile, the giant arachnid climbing above him. He picked up a stone and threw it at the beast, missed, and tried again. He kept trying and kept missing, the spider ignoring him.

Emica reached the pinnacle, grabbed the rifle and held it up.

Edo yelled, "Emica. Look out!"

Emica spun, pulling open the rifle's bolt and checking the chamber. She slammed it home and brought the rifle stock to her shoulder.

The spider's legs churned, working from rock to rock. Five more seconds and it would be at the top.

Emica fired, the crack of the gunpowder expanding and the zip of the shell bringing a smile to Ash's face. The bullet zipped past the spider and buried itself in the ground, a puff of dust lifting from the hardpan. She flipped the gun, holding it by the barrel like a club. The scene was comical, Emica standing at the summit of the rock pile, her small figure silhouetted against the clear blue sky as she swung the gun.

Edo picked up a baseball-sized stone, planted his feet, and launched the rock. It hit the beast square on the back of its head.

Like a house spider crawling across a ceiling when hit with a slipper, the massive beast dropped on a tether of silk, landing on Edo with a thud that sent a tremor through the valley.

12

A cloud of dust lifted from the ground and Emica screamed, surged forward in her anger, and slipped. Her arms shot out for balance and she dropped the rifle, and it clattered down the rock pile and disappeared into the dirt haze. Clicking and hissing filled the paddock, and as the dust cleared, a giant black spider came into view. Its eight legs churned, pounding the hardpan as it looked for Edo, whose broken and flattened corpse lay beneath the creature. A dark pool spread across the ground, the beast's eight legs splattering blood on the surrounding vegetation.

Ash screamed, a primal call of rage that had been building since he'd walked through the enclosure's gate. He picked up a stone and hurled it at the spider, but missed, and the beast didn't even notice as the stone sailed over its head.

Sean was trying to reach Emica, but what he'd do when he reached her Ash didn't know. Emica had dropped the gun, but unless she had a pocket full of .22 caliber shells it didn't really matter.

Candice, Deepali, and Otto followed Ash's lead, and the four companions threw rocks, trying to get the beast's attention.

The creature had found Edo and was pecking and ripping at the corpse, using its forward legs to shovel chunks of flesh into its maw. Blood dripped from its fangs, its wet eyes focused on its task.

When Sean reached Emica they both disappeared from the summit as they climbed down the back of the pile out of view.

"We need to do something," Ash said.

"No, we don't," Otto said. "He's gone. There's nothing we can do."

Ash fought with himself, and got his bravado under control. What was he going to do? Fight the thing using his hands? Otto was right. None of them could bring Edo back. What they could do, was save themselves. "Let's go."

"You keep an eye on the thing. I'll lead the way," Otto said.

Ash nodded. He backed away from the spider, never taking his eyes off the beast. Deepali took his hand, and headed toward the gate, Otto leading the way, Candice in tow. The four companions shuffled along for a minute, a human chain, the spider tearing and pulling at what was left of Edo.

Sean's head appeared above a large stone as he planned his route to the gate. Emica peered around him. The dining spider wasn't directly in their path, but they needed a diversion, and throwing rocks hadn't worked.

The spider's eight legs strummed the ground, and the beast's torso lifted and swayed as it consumed Edo.

Otto reached the gate and passed through, followed by Deepali, Candice, then Ash. Otto pushed the gate closed and Ash held it open a crack, staring through the slit between the gate and fencepost.

Sean and Emica were nowhere to be seen, and the spider was done eating. The cryptid walked casually around the rock pile, its instincts telling it there was more prey to be had.

Crack!

A stone the size of a football connected with the spider's torso, bouncing onto the hardpan and connecting with a boulder. The arachnid spun, searching for the source of the rock, legs churning.

Sean stood next to the rock mound, waving his arms and yelling.

The beast trundled forward, eight legs spilling over each other in an odd sideways gallop, wet eyes locked on Sean.

"What the hell is he doing?" Candice crouched, peering through the open gate. The tone of her voice made Ash's stomach hurt.

When the spider was twenty yards from Sean he yelled, "Now!" Then he turned and ran, disappearing around the back of the rock pile.

Emica appeared on the opposite side of the pile. As the spider chased Sean she sprinted to the gate and slipped through.

"You OK?" Ash said.

Emica nodded as she caught her breath.

Sean came around the rocks like a tight end going for the end zone, all awkward muscle and pure force. He threw himself forward, legs pumping.

"He's gonna make it," Ash said.

As if Sean had heard him, the Scot skidded to a halt and searched the hardpan.

"What the hell is he doing now?" Candice said.

"The gun," Otto said. He joined Candice, and peered through the cracked-open gate.

The spider emerged from the back of the stone pile, a cloud of dust and dirt trailing after the creature.

Ash searched for the gun, but Sean found it first. It was wedged between two rocks, its barrel sticking up like a signpost, and the Scot bolted toward it, pulling it free without breaking stride.

The spider hissed and called, but they were cries of frustration. The beast had seen Sean, but he was almost to the exit. The spider made a sound that would wake Ash from sleep for years to come. A wail, like an infant in great pain, fizzled out to a hiss as Sean slipped through the open gate and Ash slammed it closed and dropped the latch.

He put his back to the gate and slid to the ground, his head falling into his hands.

"Thanks," Emica said.

"You're welcome. I didn't come here to watch people get murdered," Sean said.

Nobody spoke. That discussion was for another time. The six remaining guests stared at each other, unsure what came next.

The beep and chirps of Rodgers solved that problem.

"Rodgers." Disgust spread over Sean's face like spilt spoiled milk. "Always showing up at the perfect time. Like he knows what we're going to do before we do."

"Perhaps he does," Ash said.

Rodgers stopped and examined the group. "Where is Mr. Vancharlin?"

Nobody spoke.

The bot beeped, sighed, and clicked. "Dinner is at six." Rodgers spun and headed back toward the house.

The sun had disappeared behind the lip of the valley, casting tall shadows over the forest. Emica and Deepali went back to the house with Candice and Sean, tears running down Candice's face creating brown rivers in the coating of dirt that covered her head to toe. Otto hung back with Ash, and when the others were out of earshot, he said, "Do they realize the situation?"

Ash cocked his head. When he'd first met Otto, he'd thought the man an ass, but as time wore on Ash felt like he might be able to work with him. With contestants dropping like flies, it wouldn't hurt to have as many allies as possible. Sean and Candice would stand by him, maybe Deepali, but would any of them choose him first? When push came to shove, and blood started flying?

"I'm not sure I've got a handle on the situation myself, Otto," Ash said.

Otto nodded. "See you at chow?"

Ash nodded.

The weather turned, thick, dark clouds filled the sky, and the temperature dropped ten degrees. The difference between fifty-seven degrees and forty-seven had crushed civilizations and transformed continents, but for the guests of the Atavism Special Animal Sanctuary all it meant was they couldn't eat out on the veranda and instead crammed themselves into the stuffy dining room. Old oil paintings adorned the poplar covered walls, scenes of ships at sea in storms, jungles getting pelted by rainstorms, and night scenes featuring sharp lightning bolts. All the pictures depicted destruction and violence. Ash was the first to arrive and he poured himself a glass of wine with a trembling hand as he took a seat.

The wind howled outside, the window shutters creaking and slapping the blue granite.

Emica arrived, her laser-like eyes scanning the room. "You'd think there'd be some drawings of cryptids and such," she said as she joined Ash at the table.

"In the library," Ash said.

She said, "Let me know what you find in there. After I eat, I'm going to my room, locking my door, and sleeping until Rodgers makes me get out of bed."

The rest of the competitors arrived and took seats. When they were all seated, Rodgers took drink orders, but dinner was a short, subdued affair. Ash was lost in his thoughts, turning over ideas, and trying to make sense of the three deaths. His companions ate in silence, the whistle of the wind leaking through the room's windowpanes creating an eerie melody.

Emica was true to her word and after she'd eaten, she disappeared upstairs without so much as a goodnight. She'd been shaken by Edo's death—so had Ash—but she felt responsible because the man had been trying to help her.

Otto and Deepali said goodnight, and when Ash went to leave, Sean pulled him aside. "Can Candice and I speak with you in private?"

Ash looked around. They were the only ones left, except for Rodgers. The bot sat unobtrusively in a corner, camera-eyes watching.

"Where?"

"Let's take a walk. Get your coat."

Ash went to his room, rinsed his face, grabbed his jacket, and met Sean and Candice in the foyer. Candice looked frightened, but excited, her face a contorted mess of smile and angst. The trio strolled through the greenhouse, pausing to admire the flowers.

"So what's this all about?" Ash said.

The party exited the greenhouse into the chill night. Stars blinked overhead, and night owls hooted, and crickets played their screechy tune.

"Candice has figured the whole thing out," Sean said.

"What do you mean?" Ash said.

"You'll see," Sean said.

A wide smile spread across Candice's face as the companions made their way down the yellow brick path to the monument. "Something stuck in my brain when Sean commented about the stink down by the lake. How it smelled like the sea at low tide. Fragrance through the window and door, wafts from the woods, the sea." Candice smiled, eyes wide, awaiting signs of comprehension. "You don't remember those words?"

Ash shook his head no.

The stone monument decorated with cryptids and the Atavism Sanctuary motto loomed in the darkness. The yellow path bent and twisted, and when the trio came to a stop before the massive granite sculpture, Ash took in a sharp breath. "Oh, shit," he said.

"Yup," Sean said.

"Old longings nomadic leap. Chafing at custom's chain. Again from its brumal sleep. Wakens the ferrine strain," Candice said.

"Tallboy reverting to his primal ways... waken the ferrine strain," Ash said.

"And so the rest becomes clear," Sean said. "Helots of houses no more. Let us be out, be free! Fragrance through the window and door, wafts from the woods, the sea! I know you noticed that nasty smell when we went down to the lake, and then Auggie dies when attacked by a sea creature."

Ash read the third verse, Edo's death rushing back like a fire backdraft. After the torpor of will, morbid the inner strife, welcome the animal thrill, lending a zest to life. "Dear God," he said.

"I don't think he can help," Sean said. "And it gets worse. Notice anything else?"

Moonlight shined through the hole in the monument's rounded top, casting a spotlight to the north of the house, and pinpricks of pale light danced about the garden like fireflies as the mosaic pattern of reflective stones around the hole caught moonlight. The spire of granite cast a long shadow, and in the darkness it was difficult to see the distorted images chiseled into the monument all along its length.

"Here," Sean said. He handed Ash a flashlight.

Ash turned on the light and panned it over the beasts climbing over each other like snakes, their carven visages trying to reach the monument's pinnacle first. The kraken, its serpentine tentacles wrapping around what looked to be a Yeti or Sasquatch, the humanoid creature with wings and a large mouth with long fangs. Ash panned the light down, revealing the huge turtle with a cracked shell, two wolf-like creatures, the huge ape head and a giant lizard standing on two legs.

"Look at this," Candice said. She and Sean still stood in front of the slab of stone with the poem on it.

On the opposite side a massive bird stretched its stone wings, and above a version of Nessie, various smaller creatures, a giant spider, and an oversized cat clawed and climbed, all the beasts entwined in the gray stone. An enormous dragon sat perched atop the topmost portion of the sculpture, wings spread wide, stone eyes staring down at the valley floor.

"There," she said.

There had been nine small figurines atop the rectangle of granite, each a different color and made of a different variety of stone. The red hairy humanoid figure that resembled a Yeti or Sasquatch was gone, as was the coiled serpent and the Bunyip.

That left six: the black dragon, wings spread, the gray Loch Ness 'Nessie' Monster, the clear skinny humanoid with wings, a ferocious yellow bear standing on two legs, the spider, and the blue creature that looked half machine.

"Someone stole three statues when we weren't around. So what?" Ash said. He knew it sounded stupid, but part of him just couldn't believe it.

"Not just any three," Candice said.

The serpent, Snake, the Bunyip was Auggie's area of specialization, but Edo? What did he have to do with Bigfoot? Ash said, "I don't know. Some of it makes sense if you look at it a certain way, but then from another angle it doesn't."

"Either way, this is all crazy. We've got to get out of here," Candice said.

"Or focus on survival. Team up and take this place for ourselves," Sean said.

"Candice, you didn't tell anybody else?" Ash said.

"About what?" It was Otto.

Ash and the others turned as Otto emerged from the shadows, moonlight cutting across his brown face.

"How long have you been lurking?" Sean said. The burley Scot stepped forward and bumped Otto. "You're always sneaking around like Rodgers. Was he here when you were a kid?"

"Yes." Otto looked at Sean, surprise blooming over his face. "Actually, yes, he was here. I just remembered."

"Well good for you." Sean bumped Otto again.

"Knock it off," Ash said. He slipped between the two men. Ash wasn't sure why he was defending Otto, though he knew it was more than the need for allies because his gut persisted in its message that he'd been wrong about the man.

"Look," Sean said, straightening and pulling himself up to his full height. "Three men are dead and shit just got real."

"Screw you, Sean," Otto said, and stormed into the darkness.

"Nice. Real nice, Sean. Why do you always need to be the obnoxious ass?" Candice said.

Sean's cheeks puffed up and his mouth opened to yell, but he said nothing and trailed after Otto, disappearing into the blackness.

Ash and Candice stood in the moonlight, the monument looming up in the shadows behind them.

Candice pulled a flask from her jacket pocket. "Drink?"

13

"Amazing how that beam of light shifts," Ash said. He and Candice had their backs to the monument, facing the house at the west end of the valley. Moonlight shone through the circle of stone at the pinnacle of the sculpture, casting a circle of light on the cliffside to the northwest of the house. Ash took a pull of whiskey and handed the flask back to Candice. He felt the outline of his folded karambit through his back pocket, the feel of the hard crescent edge of the closed blade comforting. Sean had taken the rifle with him when he'd stalked off, and Ash hadn't said anything. Until ammo was found, the gun was nothing more than an awkward club or bluff.

"I think it's meant to show us something," Candice said. "The spotlight, I mean." She took a long sip and wiped her mouth with the back of her hand. Her lipstick was long gone, her face covered in a sheen of dust, but she was still an attractive woman. She had an energy that made Ash want to be near her.

"You mean like in Raiders of the Lost Ark? The map room scene?" Ash said.

"I was thinking The Hobbit, but yeah," she said.

Ash wasn't a literary scholar, but he'd read The Hobbit. He searched his memory.

"Stand by the gray stone when the thrush knocks, and the setting sun with the last light of Durin's Day will shine upon the key-hole," Candice recited.

That knocked it home. "Sun or moon? Time? The date?"

"It could point to a series of things," she said. "A trail of breadcrumbs."

"That cone of light is pretty big."

"I have a feeling we'll find out. In the meantime, drink this." She burped as she handed him the flask.

Ash tipped it back, heat coating his mouth and throat as the liquor spread through him. He licked his lips and looked at the flask.

Candice's hand gripped his leg, and a finger went to her lips.

She was staring south into the garden that surrounded the monument. Patches of wildflowers and brambles filled the clearing, the yellow brick path and its tributaries angling west toward the house.

"Do you see it?" Candice whispered. "It's watching us."

"I don't—"

"Shush," she said as she let go of his arm and snatched the flask from his hand. "See the bend in the path to the west, that large bush overhanging the trail."

Ash's eyes traced the yellow pathway to the curve, saw the bush. Beneath the lowest bough, a figure stood silhouetted against the moonlight. Tall and slender with lanky arms, the creature's glowing eyes stared through the foliage in their direction. It came forward through the underbrush, two pointy ears sticking up from a narrow head.

"Is that?" Ash said, but his words caught in his throat.

"A Jersey Devil? I don't see wings," Candice said.

Ash recalled the dragon-like creature with the clipped wings he'd seen. Had they severed the Jersey Devil's wings to keep it from escaping the valley? What monstrosities had Treemont and his forefathers created in the name of the sanctuary? Ash shifted his position for a better view, and the creature disappeared into the forest.

"Nice work." She took a sip of whiskey and handed Ash the flask. She looked around, her head on a spring. "It is a pleasant place for all its oddities. The valley, I mean."

"Yes," Ash said. He took a thin pull of booze, but didn't give Candice the flask back. "Seems nice a place as any to wait it out."

"Wait for what?" Candice's speech was slurred, but her eyes shined with determination and accusation.

"The end of all this," Ash said. "You know that better than me." He felt lightheaded, the liquor loosening his lips and breaking down carefully built walls designed to keep him away from anyone who might care about him. Take an interest. He might be a cryptid hunter, but he also felt a tremendous guilt for everything that had happened, even though he knew most of it wasn't his fault. But that was the rub. He could've walked away. Blinked. Pretended he hadn't seen a thing. Denial. Some people lived their entire lives in its embrace, yet Ash wasn't able to let himself off the hook that easy. "We're all just waiting around for the end, aren't we?"

Candice's smirk faded, and she reached out for the flask, but Ash didn't give it to her. "I'm not sure I'm following you?" she said.

"None of us is ever going to leave here," Ash said. He couldn't believe he'd vocalized the fear that had been eating at him since the windows of the helicopter went dark. "That's Treemont's plan. What other conclusion can we draw? Shit." Ash took another pull of whiskey and handed off the flask. "Sean's right. We need to get out of here."

"Go where? How?" She drank.

"In a way it feels good knowing we don't have to play games anymore. With everything out in the open. Or, most of it anyway.

Whatever Otto didn't hear he'll learn soon enough, and Emica is no fool."

"She wanted to team up. If the six of us stick together maybe—"

A roar echoed through the valley, silencing the night symphony.

"Whatever we do, the beasts are going to have a say," Ash said. "How the hell did you get into all this anyway? Beautiful well-off woman like you from a good family. Rebellion? Pissing off dad and mom?"

She sipped and handed him the flask. "As you can imagine I had everything as a child."

"Even a pony?"

"Two. I wanted for nothing and my parents adored and smothered me. It wasn't so bad, but when I went off to university, I was like a member of an Amazonian tribe venturing out into civilization for the first time. I was so angry at first. Why hadn't my parents let me experience anything? I lashed out."

"With cryptids?"

She chuckled. "Not at first, but let's just say I got involved with a boy who had a peculiar vision of what science meant. His dad was a conspiracy nut, and by second year I was in the back of his van tear-assing around Britain like Velma in Scooby-Doo."

"You didn't have a... sighting? A moment?"

She shook her head no. "I'd never seen proof of any cryptid with my own eyes until I came here."

"Why do you think Treemont asked you here?" Ash said. It was becoming clear that there was more to Treemont's motivations than the future of the sanctuary. With three competitors dead, all under suspicious circumstances, Ash felt like he had a target on his back.

"I don't know. It's fairly well known that I want to start a cryptid museum, and that I plan to spend a considerable number of pounds to make it happen. Maybe he wants me to take care of the creatures here. Feels I have the best resources available."

Ash harrumphed. "That's better than any reason I've got." He took a long pull and handed her back the whiskey. "Where'd you get the flask?"

"Sean found a bar behind the kitchen," Candice said.

"So are you two..."

Her eyes blazed as her hand shot out. Ash handed her the whiskey. She took a long pull and looked up at the monument, the five remaining figurines staring down at them from their perch atop the slab of granite.

"Didn't mean to poke a wound," Ash said.

"You didn't," she said.

"I kind of did... on purpose." Ash's eyes grew wide when she set her jaw and her lips thinned. "I... So, are you guys together, or not? Sean's a mate, and I wouldn't..." Ash was so bad at this he was amazing himself. There'd been nobody since Ophelia. He had no desire and no opportunity. But Candice. When he was around her, old stirrings churned and possibilities fought through the storm clouds of Ash's sullen attitude.

"You wouldn't what?" Candice said. She drank until the flask was empty and she handed it to Ash. "Make sure that finds the sink, will you?"

Ash laughed. "OK. Sorry. I didn't mean—"

She closed the space between them like a cat, throwing her arms around him and wrapping her leg around his. She caressed the back of his head and kissed him hard, jamming her tongue drunkenly down his throat.

Ash stood like a teenager, nerves pulsing, knees weak, like he was being kissed by his grade school teacher crush.

She pushed him away and smiled. "See you when I see you." She sauntered off down the yellow brick road, the irony not lost on Ash.

He pushed himself to his feet using the monument as support. He'd had wine at dinner, then the whiskey. His stomach gurgled, and his vision was a bit blurry. He hadn't been this drunk in a long time. "Real smart," he said aloud. Cricket song rang through the valley, stars twinkling across a hazy sky.

When the sun had gone down the temperature dropped further. Ash was chilled, and he rubbed his hands together and started up the path to the house, but something made him stop. That feeling of being watched, but not in a threatening way. He sniffed the air.

Something grunted in the dense forest that ran along the northern edge of the house. He hadn't been up there yet, but he knew there were paddocks in that direction. He'd seen them when they swooped into the valley. Going up there in the dark made no sense, but suddenly he wasn't comfortable walking the main path and waltzing through the front door.

He left the path and cut through a field of wildflowers and tall grass. Creatures fled before him, and the bleating of several unseen beasts put Ash's nerves on edge. It sounded as if something was gnashing its teeth, which could mean many things, most of which wouldn't be good for him. Ash went tree to tree, slowly working his way along the northern side of the house. The atrium at the front entrance glowed in the darkness, and pale light leaked from the doors onto the dining portico above.

Ash stopped short.

Tallboy stood looking in a first-floor window, his huge hulking form blocking out the candlelight coming from the study. Ash sucked in a breath and got low. The Sasquatch put the palms of his ape-like hands on the clear glass, leaning forward as he struggled to see.

A scream pierced the silence inside the house, and Tallboy turned from the window and bolted away into the forest, snapping branches and braying birds marking the Bigfoot's trail.

The window slid open and Otto's head peeked out into the darkness.

Ash stepped behind a tree. He didn't know why.

Otto looked around for Tallboy then slammed the window.

Ash chuckled, but went still when a laugh-like gurgle echoed through the forest. Was Tallboy laughing? Imitating him? Ash slipped away, backtracking around to the front of the house and entering via the atrium.

Otto waited on a bench within a tangle of tropical foliage from around the world. Each specimen was labeled with a tag.

"Did you see Tallboy out there?" Otto asked.

"No," Ash lied, but again he didn't know why.

"Why are you lying? I saw you."

Ash sighed.

Otto looked at him quizzically, but said nothing.

Blackness pressed in around them, the flickering light from the candelabras on the walls dancing and swaying. Otto was angry, and again Ash told himself he'd misjudged the man. Ash said, "Tallboy was looking in the window. That was all."

Otto's eyes scrunched up and he shook his head. "And you didn't do anything? Just stood there and let him watch me?"

"I... I'd just arrived, and he wasn't really doing anything. He seemed enthralled and when you screamed, he ran," Ash said, recounting the facts that Otto already knew. "Speaking of which, where is everyone? You screamed pretty loud."

"Emica didn't show her face and I yelled up to Candice and Sean. Candice came through a little while ago. Wasted. You know anything about that?"

Ash said nothing.

Otto pursed his lips, and said, "You heading to the library?"

"The library and my investigation of the house will have to wait," Ash said. "I'm exhausted, and if I don't get some rest, I'll be useless when it counts. I'm sure there's more challenges on tap for the new day, and I don't see them getting any easier."

Otto nodded and the two men went in the main entrance and up the staircase. When they faced each other they shook hands.

"Holler if you need me tonight, OK?" Ash said. "I mean it."

"I will."

Otto went right, and Ash left.

"Ash."

"Yeah?"

"Thanks." The click, beep and tap of Otto entering his room echoed down the hallway.

A cold sweat washed over Ash and drips of perspiration ran down his back into his ass crack. He put an ear to his door, and heard the steady strum of the house, the gentle push of air moving down the hallway. Somewhere two people chatted. A man and a woman. Had to be Candice and Sean. Would they leave without him? Did he care?

Ash punched in his code and the lock chirped, metal slipping on metal as the door closed with a click. He stood in the darkness, letting his eyes adjust, scanning the room. His bag was where he'd left it. A basin of water with a fresh towel stood on his dresser. Nothing appeared out of place.

He stripped off his clothes and washed up, scrubbing his armpits and putting on clean underwear. The room was chilly, and he checked the balcony door before he propped his chair beneath the door handle. With everything secured, he threw back the covers of his bed.

A wool blanket covered the cotton sheets and they smelled fresh and felt clean as Ash tucked himself in, pulling the covers around himself like a cocoon as he buried his head in the feather pillow.

Something hard pushed against his head through the feather-filled pillow. How had he been so lazy, so reckless? He should have searched his room. Standard procedure.

Fearing an explosive of some type with a pressure trigger, he quickly rolled off the bed onto the hardwood floor, his hipbone hitting the wood perfectly, jarring pain knifing through him. Ash whelped and covered his head, but there was no explosion. No poisoned darts shooting from the walls.

He knelt next to his bed, watching for movement, but everything was still.

Ash jerked the pillow away, and there, resting in a fold of the sheet, was the pin from Snake's turban.

14

Ash's second morning in the valley dawned bright and crisp. The storm had moved on and not a single cloud marred the pristine blue sky, the sun angling into the valley through its open end to the east like a wave of light. The view from Ash's balcony was postcard-like, sunshine casting long shadows across the deep green forest that covered the valley's northern face. A cloud of birds burst from the forest to the northwest where the trees met a notch in the mountainside. Ash recalled seeing a paddock wall running diagonally through the forest in that direction, and he'd seen the wall the prior day during his travels.

There was a tapping at the door. "Breakfast, sir."

Rodgers' tiny voice was starting to grate on Ash. He said, "On my way."

Like dinner the prior night, breakfast was a silent affair, the six remaining competitors weighing their options, turning things over in their minds. If they were anything like Ash, they'd all come to the same conclusion he had. Play out the string. What other choice did they have?

The party ate on the veranda as they were serenaded by birdsong and the whistle of the wind. Sean was shoveling eggs into his mouth like he hadn't eaten in days, Candice watching him with a disgusted look. Otto watched the group over the lip of his coffee mug, revealing nothing, as was his norm. Deepali ate in silence, her bracelets ringing each time she moved.

Emica sat frozen, a piece of bacon on the end of her fork poised halfway to her mouth. She cocked her head to one side. "Do you hear that?" she said, and ate the piece of bacon. "Are those footsteps?"

They all heard it, and glances flew around the table as each guest verified what they knew to be true. As far as they knew, everyone in the valley was present at the table. As if sharing one brain, the party rose, dropping napkins and forks, and putting down glasses. The group watched the entrance to the veranda, in that moment as one.

Rodgers glided from the house, his beeping, tapping, and chirping louder than normal. To Ash it sounded like the bot was yelling.

Sean bolted past Rodgers and peered into the house, his head jerking side-to-side as he surveyed the room beyond. He turned back to the group and shrugged.

The pounding of footfalls got louder, and Ash ran to the edge of the veranda, gripped the stone balustrade, and searched the ground below.

A cloud of dust floated at the edge of the forest, but when the wind cleared it away there was nothing there.

Rodgers continued to bray and chirp.

"Oh, will you stop it Rodgers," Sean yelled. "What are you yapping about? Speak English before I…"

Candice put a hand on Sean's shoulder, and he deflated like a balloon.

The stress of the situation was getting to everyone, and Ash felt the icy fingers of worry and fear walk up his spine. He turned back to the group and retook his seat, and the others resumed eating. Ash had lost his appetite.

Rodgers stopped beeping, and floated next to the table, eye lenses scoping in and out as everything the party did and said was recorded and monitored. Ash was starting to think Edo had only been partly right. Yes, destroying the robot wasn't smart, but what about confining it? Cutting it off from communication with Treemont? That seemed like a half measure worth considering.

The companions found conversation difficult. There was no more talking of cryptids, or their adventures. Suspicious eyes and furtive glances told Ash all he needed to know. The competitors had never been friends, and now they were considering whether they were enemies.

When Rodgers piped up and broke the silence, Ash was almost happy for it. "I see you are all almost done eating, so in the interest of time, I will begin." Birds chirped, insects buzzed, and the faint breeze brought the scent of flowers and earth. "Beneath the house you will find a maze, and at its center there lies a prize."

"Funny how the only people I've met who went down there are dead," Emica said. She'd been quiet all morning, but with the challenge afoot, her indignant attitude came shining through.

Rodgers paused, like the hologram of Treemont had, waiting patiently.

Emica sighed, but didn't speak again.

Rodgers continued, "Within the maze you will find creatures that may interest you, but be wary. They are dangerous. So take care."

A crow cawed and in the distance a beast rumbled.

"There are many false paths, and though some may lead to unexpected findings, keep in mind at all times what your main goal is. To find the statue at the center of the maze and bring it to the monument in the garden out front. This must be done by sundown today."

Silence. Even the birds appeared to be listening now.

"The second task of the day has no rules, no time limits or constraints. Today, at any point during your day, you must provide me with satisfactory proof of the existence of a cryptid. Any cryptid of your choice."

Sean laughed and so did Ash. This was ridiculous. How the hell could he prove, definitively, that he'd seen anything? Beast or not? Wasn't that the crux of his entire life's failure?

Rodgers said, "Of course, you're all wondering how you'll prove the feat? You must bring a feather, lock of hair, scales, bones, something that proves the existence of the cryptid you choose."

"What about pictures?" Ash said. He pulled his phone free and tapped the screen. Nothing. He'd tried to charge it overnight. "Still dead."

"Mine as well," Emica said.

"I think you'll all find your phones are nonfunctional. Permanently," Rodgers said.

"Permanently!" Ash couldn't believe what he'd just heard.

"Yes, sir, Mr. Treemont apologizes in advance, but the reason for this precaution is obvious."

Ash pulled back his arm with the intention of hurling his phone off the portico into the forest below, but thought better of it. Instead he grunted, defeat washing over him like wet seaweed, and he dropped the fried phone into his breast pocket.

"This is insane," Otto said.

"You can adjourn to your room and await the outcome of the contest, if you wish," Rodgers said. "But remember, choosing to do so will—"

"Shut it!" Ash was out of patience. "How are you going to stop people from cheating?"

Rodgers beeped and sighed, but didn't speak.

Sean let the empty rifle fall into his hands, and he flipped it, holding the barrel like a club. He swung, a powerful thrust that would've broken the bot in two had the swing not been a warning. The stock of the rifle sailed inches above Rodgers' head, the bot's lenses jerking up as the gun passed.

"Not now," Ash said. "Though I wish you could."

Sean growled, but nodded. The man was incredibly rational for a ball of nervous muscle and angst.

"Failure to participate will result in ejection from the contest," Rodgers said. "Do not forget the rules you agreed to when you accepted the invitation to come here."

"Things have changed. Three people are dead," Deepali said.

"Let us try to keep the number at three," the bot said.

Rodgers paused, before saying, "Good luck to you all."

Six people looked at each other as the bot floated from the terrace, but they could find no words to say.

Otto was the first to rise and leave the group, and that started the rush.

Ash held back, and Candice waited. Sean stopped at the door to the house, looking over his shoulder, frustration painted on his freckled face. "What? We're giving them a head start?" he said.

Candice looked around as if expecting to find someone hiding under the table. "You think it's safe to go down there?" she said.

"No," Sean said. "But is it any safer up here? And we're still in this thing? Aren't we? We're here."

Ash was torn. On one hand Sean was right, until they figured out a way to break the cycle, find Treemont, or escape the valley, why not stay in the game and keep an eye on things, try and direct things in their favor. But the other side of Ash's brain, the one that usually won, kept screaming that the last two people that went into the basement were dead. To say nothing of the fact that the entire task, not unlike the valley itself, was a trap.

"You both know the rules," Ash said. "We have to participate or 'measures will be taken.' We can participate, but how hard do we need to try?"

Sean looked at Candice, then threw up his arms.

She stared blankly at him. Ash knew the look well, it was in most women's arsenal of facial weaponry. It said she thought Sean was a dumbass.

"I get it. The game. The prize," Ash said.

"If we're gonna play, why not play?" Sean said. "We can't all win."

"But we can all lose," Candice said.

Ash and Sean nodded.

"How about this. If it's down to the three of us, and you think the game is still underway, it's every man... person, for themselves," Candice said.

"Agreed," Ash said, "We'll go down there, stick together, and be careful. If we need to pull out or back off, we can."

Candice said, "We might not win, but we'll be alive."

Ash nodded.

Sean frowned, his blue eyes straying to the stone floor, but then he nodded.

The trio made their way through the house to the back of the main staircase where a pocket-door led to wooden steps that trailed down into blackness. Sean flicked on their only flashlight, the beam swaying as the Scot inched down into darkness.

Shards of light bounced off the walls, flecks of quartz in the blue granite reflecting the harsh LED light. Cool air floated up from below, and the scent of sour milk and rotten fruit pumped through the doorway.

Ash held out his arm. "After you, madam."

Candice squeezed through the opening, her jeans riding down on her butt, revealing the top of her pink panties. Ash felt a stirring he hadn't felt in a long time, and he stood gaping like a ten-year-old who'd just seen his first Playboy.

"You coming?" Candice said. She was several steps down, staring up at him, backlit by the glow of the flashlight which faded as Sean delved deeper.

Ash took a deep breath and slipped through the door, sliding it closed behind him.

A steady thrum, like the beat of a giant heart, echoed up the stairwell as they climbed down into darkness. It got colder with each switchback, which came at twenty step intervals. Ash had counted sixty steps when Sean came into view, standing in the cone of the flashlight beam at the bottom of the steps.

"Damn," Ash said, as he and Candice climbed the final section of steps.

"Much deeper than I thought," Sean said. "Auggie didn't say shit."

Awkward silence, dripping water, the faint push of the wind, and that steady thrum...

"You know what I mean," Sean said. "He didn't say anything about us having to travel to the center of the Earth."

"You just had to say that, didn't you?" Candice said.

"What? You didn't like that one?" Sean said.

"Which one? Jules Verne?"

"If at every instant we may perish, so at every instant we may be saved. You can look that up," Sean said.

"Based on my count we're at least fifty feet deep," Candice said.

"Try more like a hundred," Ash said.

Six narrow tunnels ran away from the steps in erratic directions, the roughly hewn walls of blue granite coated in moisture. Sean panned around the flashlight. All the passageways ran straight on, and Ash saw no difference between them.

Candice shivered and hugged herself. "Much colder down here."

"Sure is. Must be like an icebox in the winter months," Sean said.

"What now?" Sean asked.

"I'm thinking of a number from one to six. What's my number?" Candice said.

"Six," Ash blurted.

Sean sighed. "Just pick a tunnel, will you? You Americans, always trying to make a game of everything."

Ash looked at him and raised an eyebrow, but said nothing.

"So what was your number... damn," Sean said. "One. I pick one."

"Six it is," Candice said.

They all laughed, and amidst the chaos that was their current reality it was a welcome sound, and suddenly Ash felt lucky. What if Sean and Candice hadn't come, or weren't invited? What if he'd been truly alone? But he wasn't. They might not be best mates, but Candice and Sean weren't killers, and whatever was going on they weren't part of it any more than he was.

Sean shined the flashlight into what he considered the sixth tunnel, but Ash and Candice felt it was the first. Ash and Candice had numbered the tunnels right to left.

The tunnel was tight, ten feet across, the ceiling random and jagged. The passageway was hand-hewn through sandstone and granite, and they all looked the same, save for the coloring of the granite. The trio soon found themselves lost, but thankfully for Ash and Sean, Candice had eyes like a cat, the memory of a supercomputer, and a better sense of direction than a sea captain. She backtracked to the staircase several times, and that allowed the party to avoid retracing their steps and recalibrate.

The companions fumbled around in the darkness for three hours before they found the center of the maze. At first, they didn't even notice they were there because as the walls fell away there was nothing to see in the darkness. The trio stood in the blackness as Sean methodically scanned the area with the flashlight, finally finding an empty display platform.

The prized statue was gone.

"We're too late," Sean said. "Damn, I told you we shouldn't have waited."

A rock tumbled to the floor with a crack and Ash froze.

Before him a massive form sat atop a boulder in the darkness.

Sean swung the flashlight, putting a cone of light on the creature.

Candice gasped.

A giant bat sat perched atop a stone, wrapped in its black, leathery wings. Dark eyes shined under the harsh flashlight beam and the beast spread its wings, pumping the air and screeching.

"Let's head back," Ash said.

Ash turned back the way he'd come, but froze.

Hooting and screeching filled the tunnel, the pounding of many wings.

Sean swung the flashlight, its wobbly beam slashing through the darkness and finding the tunnel mouth. A cloud of bats roared down the passageway, their squeaking and flapping drowning out the pounding of Ash's heart.

15

"Run!" Sean screamed. He pointed the flashlight toward a tunnel and ran, head down, left arm holding the rifle at his side as it hung from its shoulder strap.

The screeching and crying bats, and the pounding rumble of their wings engulfed Ash like water. He searched for Candice. She was double-timing it after Sean.

The massive vampire bat watched Ash with curious eyes, still as the statues on the monument.

Ash took two slow steps toward the rock the beast sat on, the glow from the flashlight fading.

The creature watched him, but didn't move.

Ash slipped behind the boulder the creature was perched on, shielding himself and disappearing into the shadows.

Still the creature above didn't move. Its eyes had tracked Ash, but the beast's attention turned to the cloud of its smaller brethren filling the tunnel. The swarm of bats moved as one, and they shrieked and cried as the flying rats tore past the massive vampire bat, who looked on with disinterest. When the flock was gone, the bat searched for Ash.

He eased out from his hiding place, light filling the cave. The outline of the massive bat didn't move.

"Wow, that was close, eh mate?" Sean came striding from the tunnel he and Candice had hidden in. "You've got bigger Blarney stones than I thought."

The glow of the flashlight lit the chamber, and for the briefest of instants Ash locked eyes with the bat. The eyes were... Ash rubbed his face with his palms. The eyes looked human.

"It's still here!" Candice screamed.

Ash jumped.

Sean swung the flashlight, its beam finding the giant vampire bat atop the slab of gray sandstone.

The beast squawked and launched from its perch, wings pounding the air.

Sean brought up the rifle, remembered it had no bullets, and let it fall to his side.

The bat sailed overhead, let loose with a glass-shattering screech, and disappeared into the darkness.

Sean did an about face and started back toward the staircase.

"You're leaving?" Candice said.

"Excuse me?" Sean and Ash said at the same time.

"Impressive," she said. "Stop and think for a minute."

"Why?" Sean said. "I know what I need to do. Get the hell out of here."

"Agreed," Ash said. "But I think I know what she's thinking. All those bats, including the big one, seemed pretty determined to go in that direction." Ash pointed down a tunnel that led away from the stairs.

"So…" Sean said.

Candice sighed. "At what age did you start drinking beer? 'Cause I'm thinking you killed a few brain cells. Really."

"There's probably another way out," Ash said. He felt like dad stepping between brother and sister. "We haven't found the mine yet, so I'm with Candice. Let's track those bats."

The flashlight beam wobbled in the blackness as Sean's shoulders lifted and fell as he argued with himself. "Fine," he said. "But you take point for a bit." He handed Ash the flashlight.

The party passed storage rooms with old empty crates and ancient furniture covered in threadbare sheets. The guano path was clear, the only thing missing from the nasty trail of white and black bat shit was the arrow.

"Watch your step," Ash said.

The party walked for what seemed like an hour, but was only fifteen minutes, before they came to a chamber cut from the bedrock.

"There's something here," Ash said.

A skeleton was propped against the wall, a green cap sitting askew atop the white skull, tattered clothes covering bones. A backpack sat next to the remains.

Candice gasped when she arrived.

Sean said, "Did you check the pack?"

Ash darted toward the bag a little too fast as he said, "Was just about to." Ash felt Sean's eyes on him as he went through the backpack. There was tattered and moth-eaten clothes, a weather-beaten copy of On the Track of Unknown Animals, empty food wrappers and a bone dry and cracked water skin. "Nothing of use," Ash said, but as he went to drop the bag, he felt weight in its front pocket.

Sean rubbed his face with the palms of his hands and leaned against the wall, watching Candice, who chewed her nails, her eyes darting around like she'd just done a line of cocaine.

Ash slipped his hand into the bag's pocket, cognizant of the fact that it might get bitten, but when his fingers wrapped around the cold steel of the revolver, he almost hooted with joy. He tossed the old backpack to the floor with a little extra force, dust rising from the ground and drawing Sean and Candice's attention.

Ash slipped the gun into his pocket.

The trio hiked another twenty minutes and the tunnel took a turn, and they were forced to go around a large stone that cut across the passageway like a gate.

Candice called a halt. "Back it up," she said.

Sean shined the light on her, and she pointed at a gap between the tunnel wall and a large slab of stone. He panned the light up. A blue streak of granite ran through the gray and brown sandstone, the jagged edge where the slab of stone had broken off glistening in the flashlight beam, quartz refracting and splintering the LED light into a rainbow of colors that spilled through the darkness like sunrays.

Cold air pumped from the gap like an AC on full blast.

"This vent goes deeper, but it looks like it's blocked by this slab of stone," Ash said.

"Shine the flashlight on where it broke again," Candice said.

Sean complied.

"No," she said. "See those channels that run vertically through the broken area? Those were drilled. Someone broke off that piece of rock to block the tunnel on purpose. No doubt."

"Can we get back there?" Sean said.

Sean poked the flashlight into the gap and inched into the gap, Ash behind him. The space was two feet wide, covered in cobwebs, but there was room to push through.

The space beyond was cavernous. Sean panned around the flashlight. "We've found the old mine," he said.

A rusted cart track trailed away into darkness and mounds of blue and white rubble lined the walls. A stack of blue slabs with white streaks rested in wood rack, and next to it there was a pile of granite bricks. A layer of dust, dirt, and bat shit covered everything, and Sean slipped and almost fell in the nasty white guano.

"I wonder how many men died down here mining the stones for the house," Sean said. He panned around the light. "Looks to me like they took more stone out of here than they used." Granite lacks any internal structures, and is hard and tough. Like most stones it's a natural source of radiation, and even granite countertops can be toxic. Breathing granite dust sure was.

"Probably sold stone to pay the workers. It's amazingly unique," Ash said.

"What? Haul it out a pebble at a time?"

The Scot had a point, so Ash said nothing.

"Sure is cold in here," Candice said as she emerged from the gap in the wall.

Their breaths clouded in the flashlight's beam.

"The mine opens up on the opposite end," Ash said. "Give me the light."

Sean sighed and handed over the flashlight.

The party was halfway across the chamber when the low gurgle of a building growl echoed through the mine.

A tall shadow fell across the blue granite floor, and a hulking white figure disappeared behind a pile of blue rubble.

The growling ceased when Ash pointed the light at the floor.

"What are you doing?" Sean's tone was a restrained scream.

"Trying not to scare it," he said.

Ash pointed the flashlight up at the ceiling, the cone of light blossoming outward and gently spilling across the mine.

The Yeti stood in the shadows. It was covered in long white fur that glowed in the faint light. Ash almost giggled, he was looking at a white Chewbacca. The beast's ape-like face, not unlike Tallboy's, stared through the gloom, deep red eyes shining in the half-light.

The beast raked its claws over a stone and screamed, a thin, powerful wail that made Ash jump.

"It's fantastic," Candice said. "Definitely a Sasquatch of some kind."

The beast barked, and took a long stride forward, its long hair dangling like snakes, sharp fangs glinting in the glow of the flashlight beam.

"How can it..." Sean's voice trailed away.

Despite what they'd seen thus far, Ash knew Yeti had only been seen in certain areas of the world. Known also as Bigfoot, Sasquatch, Kang Admi, and the Abominable Snowman, the tall humanoid-like creatures with white fur were always spotted well above the frostline. Ash had never heard of a sighting in the Andes, though the mountains were certainly high and cold enough.

"Did you hear about the sighting up on Everest last year?" Sean asked in a whisper.

Ash nodded. "Any truth to the stories?"

Sean said nothing.

"I meet a guy in Nepal. Claimed he'd met a guy who was on that expedition," Candice said. "He said the stories are true. A Yeti took down three climbers, left one of them to die with claw marks across his chest and face."

"They never found the other two climbers," Ash said.

The trio fell silent as they stared at the hulking ten-foot-tall apparition stalking the shadows.

"Enough of this shit," Sean said.

"What are you going to do?" Ash asked.

"Sean?" Candice said. It was the WTF tone. When the Scot didn't respond she took it up a notch. "Sean!"

"When in doubt," Sean said, "treat it like a bear." The Scotsman let the rifle fall into his hands. "When I say so, shine the flashlight right on it. Try and hit it in the face."

Ash nodded, but Sean couldn't see him.

"You hear me, Ash?"

"10-4."

Sean brought the rifle to his shoulder and aimed at the creature.

The Yeti sensed something was wrong, because it stopped creeping toward them, its nose lifting and sniffing the air, as if it could smell the gun.

"Now!" Sean yelled. He bolted forward, heading straight at the beast. He yelled, screaming and masking as much noise as possible. "I'll shoot. I swear." Sean thrust the rifle out before him, but it had no effect. Either the Yeti had never seen a gun, or didn't give a turd.

Sean screamed again, but when the creature didn't shift position or run, he skidded to a halt ten feet in front of the beast.

The creature's jaws flexed open, white teeth shining in the harsh light, slime dripping between stunted fangs. Long talon-like claws extended from each digit of its hands, and the beast displayed them to Ash like a bird ruffling its own feathers.

The Yeti sprang, two long, powerful strides, that closed the ten feet between Ash and the creature in the blink of an eye.

Ash drew the revolver and squeezed the trigger. The cylinder spun, the hammer struck home, but the gunpowder in the old bullet didn't expand, and a click, a faint sparrow fart puff, and a small cloud of white smoke were the only signs the weapon had been fired.

The Yeti swiped Ash aside like security clearing a path for a pop star, the creature's knife-like claws raking over his chest. Ash screamed as he went down, the pistol flying from his hand. He lay on his back, panting, and when his hand found his chest, he discovered blood leaking from scratches. It had been a glancing blow, but pain still ran through Ash. He rolled on his side, trying to push himself to his feet, but Sean planted a foot in his back and flattened him back to the ground.

The Scot was swinging the rifle like Babe Ruth, grunting and wheezing as he tried to take the Yeti's head off.

The beast feinted back, avoiding the blows, and lashing out with its claws. The monster threw its head back and roared, anger rippling through its muscular legs and arms.

Ash rolled and pressed himself to his feet like a surfer on a longboard, pain arcing through the scratches on his chest. He pulled free his karambit, flicked it open, and turned to face the chaos.

Sean was losing the fight. His rifle swings were getting slower and less powerful as the Yeti pushed forward, dirty strands of white hair falling over the beast's monkey-like black face. A thin mohawk of gray hair ran down the center of the creature's head, and spidered out to its appendages and snaked down its body.

Ash whistled.

The Yeti hesitated, its head turning slightly.

Ash lashed out with the karambit, slicing off several locks of straggly hair.

The creature growled and pulled back, its dark eyes going wide.

Sean swung the rifle and caught the beast on the back of the legs and the creature fell to its knees, a thin wail of pain escaping its lips.

The Yeti reached out to grab Ash as it fell, and the karambit flashed, Ash striking out. The blade sliced through the creature's left hand, severing two digits and a chunk of the beast's palm along with them.

The creature howled and convulsed on the ground in pain, rolling onto its stomach, grasping the wound with its other hand.

Sean ran, angling away from the creature as he went around it, disappearing into the darkness.

Ash clicked off the flashlight and he and Candice backed into the shadows.

They heard the Yeti rolling on the ground, whimpering, and they saw the faint shadow of its head shifting from Ash to Sean's pounding footfalls. It gurgled and spit, the wet slap of blood hitting the floor unmistakable. The massive beast shuffled in the darkness, heavy breathing and whining mixing with growls and snorts.

"We've got to go," Candice said.

The beast roared, and came at them, its huge shape rising in the blackness, teeth glinting, remaining claws extended.

Candice grabbed Ash's hand and ran after Sean, angling into the darkness away from the Yeti, weaving around piles of blue rubble, old mining carts, and ancient rusted equipment. When she reached the far tunnel, she paused.

Ash pressed his back to the chamber wall, his breaths coming in labored bursts.

"You OK, mate?" Sean stood next to him in the blackness.

"Yeah," Ash said.

"Let's go then," Candice said.

"Not yet," Ash said. "I want that gun."

"About that," Sean said.

"Later."

The trio waited in silence, the Yeti stalking around in the dark mine, grunting and hollering.

Sean motioned for Ash and Candice to follow him, and the three companions slipped from the tunnel and hid behind a tipped over mining cart.

Minutes slid by and when Ash deemed it had been long enough, and they hadn't heard any signs of the beast for over an hour, Ash searched the area with the flashlight without leaving his hiding spot.

The gun lay next to a rubble pile, its dark gray metal blending into the floor.

A little further on, sitting next to a dark puddle of blood, were the Yeti's two severed fingers attached to a chunk of the beast's palm.

Ash collected the weapon, and stood over the severed fingers.

Candice and Sean joined him.

"Seems like we've got our cryptid proof."

"How you figure?" Sean said.

Ash bent, flipping the karambit in his hand, the blade singing through the air. He sliced the fingers from the chunk of palm and picked one up, blood, gristle and bone sticking from its cut end, a foot-long curved talon with red stripes at the other.

Ash handed the severed digit to Candice, then picked up the other for himself. He placed the finger in his jacket pocket, a red stain seeping through the fabric within seconds. With the front of his shirt ripped and blood soaked, it hardly mattered.

"So I get the chunk of flesh?" Sean said as he picked up his proof. The patch of the creature's palm looked like lined black leather, and it was obvious where the two huge fingers had been cut. It would pass.

"Quit bitching," Candice said.

"Let's switch then," said the Scot.

"We'll present all three pieces of evidence together. OK?" Ash said.

That settled it, and the party ran on, the flashlight beam slicing through the mud-like blackness. Ash's heart galloped, his knees and ankles ached, and hunger pain twisted his stomach. A large boulder loomed in the center of the tunnel and the companions sprinted around it and the tunnel gave way to forest. There was no path, and Ash worked his way through the vegetation, Sean and Candice struggling behind him.

16

The house glowed as dusk fell over the valley. The sun had passed beyond the rim of the southern wall of the valley, the blue sky bright in contrast. Shadows danced under every tree bough and behind every bush. The creatures of the day gave way to the beasts of the night, the screech of crickets, the hiss and chirp of birds, and the ever-present thrum filling the valley.

When the trio got to the house they were greeted by Rodgers, who accepted their proof of Yeti without comment. When Ash asked who won the maze competition, the bot floated away without a word.

The party separated, and Ash went back to his room, cleaned up, and tended to the scratches on his chest, which were already pink and puffy. He made a bandage from the torn shirt, and slipped on a clean shirt. His stomach rumbled, and he considered seeking out a snake, but decided to take a fast nap instead. It was going to be a long night.

At 6:30PM he headed back down for dinner. All pretense of their group being social had been wiped away. The veranda table was empty, and Rodgers had set out a buffet of food and drinks. Nobody was there when Ash arrived. He had the gun in his jacket pocket, though he had no confidence the remaining four shells would fire. He'd examined the gun and it looked to be in decent shape, but there were rust stains at the edges of the bullets' primer, but the cartridges appeared to be sealed.

Moonlight angled in through the doors that led out to the portico, thin shadows dancing across the dining room. The scent of roasted meat and onions made Ash's mouth water. There was a stack of plates with silverware rolled in napkins in a basket beside them. He looked around like he was stealing before picking up a plate.

Rodgers floated into the room. "Sir, is there anything I can get you that's not available here?"

"Where is everyone? No dinner party tonight?"

"Some of the contestants have chosen not to socialize. There is no rule saying they must," Rodgers said.

Ash harrumphed and filled his plate.

When he was done eating and drinking a bottle of Muscat of Alexandria, he declined dessert and asked Rodgers to show him to the library. The bot led him through the sitting room, and into a portion of the house Ash hadn't explored. Through the windows to his left, Ash saw the atrium entrance, and beyond the dark star-filled sky at the end of the valley. From his POV Ash felt like he could leap through the window and jump off the Earth.

Rodgers stopped before a large set of double doors that stood closed. Flickering light leaked under the doors, and the rumble of conversation echoed from within. A wood sign with red lettering over a white background read: So we may remember those who came before, and preserve their contributions and understand our purpose.

"Deep," Ash said.

Rodgers' head spun, the camera lenses that were its eyes telescoping in and out. "There are some rules."

Ash sighed.

"You may not remove anything from the library for any reason. You may not modify or otherwise deface anything in the library. To uncover a riddle or make something 'visible' are not valid excuses to damage library documents or artifacts." Rodgers paused. Just like a lawyer would have.

"If you have a question, seek me out. I am the curator of the library. You may not take, or otherwise restrict access to any materials. All members can see whatever they want. Basic manners as to the progression of materials is expected."

Ash looked at the hallway ceiling. There was a spiderweb in an upper corner and a black spider an inch-wide stared down at him from the edge of its web. How all these rules would be enforced, he didn't know, but Ash no longer doubted that Treemont was always watching.

"Do you understand the rules as they have been described to you?" Rodgers said.

"Yeah," Ash said. "How do I know other competitors aren't holding out on me? Hiding pertinent documents and information?"

"We operate on the honor system here, Mr. Cohn. You know that well." The bot paused, its head rotating toward the closed doors. "And Mr. Treemont would know." The bot tapped a code into the keypad, the lock buzzed and disengaged, and Rodgers pushed open the doors.

Emica and Otto sat around a small table, stacks of books covering its entire surface, except for a spot cleared for a tray, atop which sat a decanter of brown liquor and two empty glasses. The room wasn't what Ash had envisioned. There were no grand bookshelves, no ornate display cases showing preserved artifacts. It was attic-like, and one that hadn't been cleaned or organized in years. A coating of dust covered everything, and wood crates and carboard boxes lined the walls, along with stacks of books.

"What a mess," Ash said.

"You've got no idea," Otto said.

"You mind if I steal a glass?"

Otto chuckled. "Suddenly I don't want whiskey anymore."

Ash sat and filled a glass with three fingers of liquor.

Otto studied an old yellowed copy of Atavism Special Animal Sanctuary's odd pledge poem. The one printed on the monument. "So you know about the poem?" Ash said.

Otto nodded.

Ash glanced at Emica, who hadn't looked up from the file of old maps she was going through.

Otto nodded again. "Thanks for telling us."

So that was it then, everyone knew. "Do you know who won the maze challenge?"

Otto shrugged. "Not me." He lifted the paper with the poem on it. "What do you make of this? Seems obvious."

"Obvious," Ash said. He went cold. "Did you see the statue? The maze prize?"

Otto said nothing.

Emica lifted her head. "I saw it. It's where... the others were," she said.

Ash didn't know what she meant at first, and apparently Otto knew less. He said, "What do you mean? The other ones?"

"The statues. The ones atop the slab with that poem on it," she said, pointing at the sheet of paper in Otto's white-gloved hand.

"You're saying the remaining five statues are gone? Replaced with... what?" Ash said.

"You need to see it yourself," Emica said.

Ash didn't need to. He felt the trap closing around him. He knew now that he was in a fight for his life.

Emica rose from her seat, poured herself a glass of whiskey, and refilled Ash's glass. There was no question who was in charge as she prepared to take command of the room the way Ash had seen her do before. Emica took a long pull of booze, draining her glass. She said, "We've searched the house the best we can, but in the end that means nothing. The valley is vast."

"Are you going somewhere with this?" Otto said.

"Where I'm going," she said, and sighed, "there are but two conclusions that can be drawn. Treemont, a designee, or someone who has assumed his identity is hiding in the valley, and has plotted to kill all of us."

"Except maybe one," Ash said.

"We already know this," Otto said. "We need to figure out how to save ourselves. Isn't that the most important thing now?"

"I have yet to address the second conclusion I referred to. A second, much more likely option," Emica said, her voice cracking, "is that the infamous Mr. Treemont is in the valley, orchestrating this entire affair for injuries unknown and aggrieved. In other words, there's a distinct possibility that Mr. Treemont is one of the original nine competitors."

Ash almost spit out his whiskey, and holding it in burned his nose as the liquor backed up in his mouth and throat. He coughed, his mind racing, heat spreading over his face.

"Can't be," Otto said. "Why would Treemont go through all the trouble? If he wanted all of us dead, why not crash the helicopter? And if he already knows who he wants to give the sanctuary to, why all the bullshit?"

Emica turned a keen eye on him, and said, "Denial isn't just a river in Africa. The facts are the facts. We're all screwed, regardless of which of my scenarios is correct. Nine people came to this valley, and either one of them is a homicidal maniac, or there's another person or more.... hiding in the shadows."

The thrum of the house, the gentle push of the air, and the faint echoes of the night chorus of insects filled the library, the tension so thick Ash's chest tightened. He said, "Well, Snake, Auggie and Edo are beyond suspicion."

"Why?" Emica said.

Ash laughed. "You've got eyes."

"I do." She used them to stare through Ash.

"Are we missing something?" Otto asked. The bluster had left his voice, and dark bags puffed out beneath his eyes.

"I'm sure you are," Emica said. "Missing something. But you do have a point. I saw Snake's body, and he sure appeared dead."

"Ash, you took his pulse, didn't you?" Otto said. "And cutting your own hand off to fake your death is pretty hardcore."

Ash nodded, but as his mind spun, doubt seeped through him. There were ways to fake death, at least for a short time. Various poisons, venoms, and the like. He felt Emica staring at him as he worked things through. "Auggie got ripped apart right in front of us, and Edo got flattened. So, unless Treemont is Steven Spielberg, I think we can rule them out."

Emica said, "Yes, on the surface it would appear Edo and Auggie can be eliminated, but where is Snake's body?"

"Rodgers said he buried him..." Ash's voice trailed away, and he took a long pull of whiskey. The familiar burn, the heat blossoming in his chest.

"Assuming the three presumed dead to be eliminated, that leaves Rodgers, the three of us, Deepali, Candice and Sean, and possibly…" Emica's voice trailed away, then her eyes searched out Ash and Otto. "Have I missed anything?"

"Auggie's remains were dragged into the lake, and Edo's corpse… or whatever is left of it… should still be in the spider paddock. So, yeah. I think you've covered it," Ash said.

"I can't believe we were stupid enough to come here in the first place," Otto said.

"Something like this goes beyond simple suspicion and caution," Emica said. Her eyes shifted from Otto to the tabletop.

Ash said, "I agree with everything you've said, but I can't help thinking none of it matters."

"Really?" Emica said, the indignity of her tone displaying her arrogance. "You don't want to know if you're breaking bread with a psychopath? And who that might be?"

"Thoughts on that?" Otto said.

Ash met Emica's eye, then Otto's. He didn't know either of these people, and even if he did, he knew that meant very little when it came to an unhinged mind. Some of the most lethal murderers in history managed to keep their secrets from those closest to them. Ash said, "We're all equal suspects, myself included."

"It would be easy, wouldn't it? Pretend to be one of us," Otto said.

"Is Rodgers a real threat?" Ash asked. "Could Treemont be remotely controlling him?"

"I thought of that. I don't think Rodgers could've taken out Snake, but he certainly could've helped orchestrate Auggie's death. He picked Auggie last," Otto said.

"And the bot led us into the spider paddock," Emica said.

"Busy little helper bee," Otto said.

"Any ideas on the next verse?" Emica said.

Otto shook his head no.

"Does it matter anymore?" Ash asked.

"Mr. Doesn't Matter." Otto's chin dropped to his chest and he stared at Ash over the rims of his reading spectacles. "Why wouldn't it matter?"

"Our statues are gone," Ash said. What that meant, he wasn't certain, and the more he turned the riddle over in his mind the less logic he found. What he did know was when the first three statues were removed the contestants associated with them were killed.

"Banish the volumes revered. Sever from centuries dead. Ceilings the lamp flicker cheered. Barter for stars instead," read Otto.

"Ignore the library, ie the past," Emica said. "Banish volumes revered... centuries dead."

"Maybe," Otto said. "I rather think the stars part is important."

With that the conversation died, and the three companions read through old books, scanned maps of the valley, or areas where cryptids had been captured or seen. There were journals from past club members, papers, magazines, printouts, pictures, fossils, but as Ash sat reading, a hollowness crept through him. If in a court of law, so far, he'd be able to claim very little proof, and it would take days to search the library. Days he didn't have. He was about to call it a night when Rogers arrived.

"Rodgers, I'm looking for—"

"It is time for bed. Tomorrow will be a long day," the bot said.

The three competitors stared at the bot opened mouthed, but when Emica got up and left, and Otto followed, Ash figured pushing the issue would serve little purpose.

Ash swayed on his feet as he made his way up the stairs, the whiskey going to his head. As he listened to the chorus of door locks beeping and clicking, a positive thought buzzed into his head.

Nobody died today.

Ash's stomach turned when he thought of the coming day.

17

Ash cleaned and dressed the scratches on his chest the best he could and went down to breakfast early. He wanted to see everyone's face, look them in the eye. Pain lanced through him as he went down the stairs, his chest itching, the new bandages made of cut towel pulling and squeezing. Rodgers had warned of bad weather coming through, so he wore his heavy coat, his long underwear, and he'd brought his gloves and a fleece hat.

The atrium foyer was dark, black clouds pushing in through the open end of the valley like an invading army and obscuring the sky. The house was cold, and no fire roared in the stone fireplace in the sitting room, and when he got to the dining room, Ash found it empty. A basket with bread and pastries sat on the sideboard along with decanters of coffee and water.

"Rodgers?" Ash called. His voice fell dead against the poplar wall coverings. "What, no juice?" His voice echoed in the empty room.

Rodgers didn't come.

Ash tossed his head side-to-side and cracked his neck, his wounds reminding him he needed to take it easy. He filled a mug with coffee, grabbed what looked like a donut with no hole, and headed for the terrace. A blast of cold air assaulted him when he opened the door, so he quickly closed it and eased back inside.

Faint light leaked through the windows. The sky was ashen, and it looked like snow was on the way. Ash bit down on his donut-thing and found it surprisingly tasty. A cross between a Danish pastry and chocolate donut. He stuffed the rest of it in his mouth and washed it down with coffee.

"Morning."

Ash jumped, and turned to find Otto.

"Sleep well?"

"Eh. You?" Ash said.

"Eh." Otto poured coffee, filled a plate with bread and butter, and sat at the table.

Ash paced. "Have you seen Rodgers this morning?"

Otto shook his head no.

"Strange, that, no?"

Otto nodded yes.

Ash sighed and grabbed another pastry. The two men ate in silence, and the other four competitors didn't come. He wasn't worried. Everyone needs food and Ash was pretty sure he'd been the first one to take a pastry off the carefully stacked pile.

"So, I've had an idea I'd like to run past you," Otto said.

Ash looked over his shoulders, around the room, then he shrugged.

"Come on. I thought maybe we were past that shit?" Otto said.

Ash sighed. "What's your thought?"

"We offer to let the others search our rooms, so we can search theirs."

Ash felt that momentary zap of guilt run through him. He liked the idea, but any fool could see that Otto could've cleaned his room in anticipation of the search prior to making the suggestion. Still. It was just him and Otto. Sean, Candice, Deepali and Emica weren't around.

"Let me spin it to them," Ash said.

Otto's brow knitted, then he frowned as he nodded his consent.

Sean might buy the idea from Ash, but there was no way he'd trust Otto.

Emica waltzed into the room, eyes scanning the food and locking in on the coffee. She headed straight for it without so much as a grunt.

"Morning," Otto said, a little extra loudly.

She waved a hand in his direction, got her cup of joe and sat, cradling her mug and watching Otto and Ash.

When Emica got up to leave, Otto kicked Ash under the table.

"Emica… wait up a second," Ash said.

She stopped and stared him down like she was trying to burn him to dust with her eyes.

"Do you want to go back to the library and take another look?" Ash said.

Her eyes darted to Otto.

"Excusa," Sean said as he wiggled past Emica with Candice in tow.

"Morning," Candice said. She attacked the coffee while Sean divebombed the pastries.

"Listen, Ash, about last night. We had a little whiskey. That doesn't mean we're partners, or sharing information, or sending each other birthday cards," Emica said.

"Yeah, sure," Ash said. "But we need to do what I suggested. We have to."

Emica stared at him with a blank face.

Sean stopped shoveling food into his mouth and asked, "What did you suggest?"

"That we search each other's rooms. Make sure someone doesn't have an… advantage," Ash said. There it was. The pressure in his chest eased like a deflating hemorrhoid cushion.

Stunned silence. Five sets of eyes each looking for answers, but saying nothing.

Outside, a crow cawed.

"What the hell are you talking about?" Emica said.

"What? You can search my room, and I'll search yours," Ash said. He hated gaslighting the woman, but desperate times called for desperate measures. "Are you in or not?"

Deepali entered the room and Rodgers floated in behind her. She said, "In on what?"

.Ash sighed. "Room searches."

Deepali's eyes grew wide.

"For once I'm glad to see you Rodgers," Sean said.

Rodgers beeped and chirped, then said, "I cannot determine if that is a compliment or an insult, sir."

"That's called wit, dipshit," Sean said.

Otto ate, eyes focused on his plate.

"I've got nothing to hide," Candice said.

If Ash could've kissed her, he would've.

"What about you, Sean?" Ash said.

"What about them?" Sean gestured toward Otto, who still ate like there was nobody else in the room.

Deepali stood frozen, holding the coffee urn, watching. She said, "I'm in."

All eyes turned to Otto.

"I see you have your gun, Sean," Otto said.

Sean nodded. "For all the good it'll do."

Otto nodded. "Still no bullets?"

Sweat dripped down Ash's back. Why was he dragging this out? Trying to sell it more? They were good.

"No bullets," Sean said, and rolled his eyes.

"Ash, I've heard you have a gun?" Otto said.

Anger welled in Ash and he wanted to draw down and put a bullet in the man's head. He locked eyes with Otto, the man trying to tell him something without speaking. Then it hit him. Otto was covering for him. He knew Emica was the only one that didn't know about the gun, and by putting it out there he'd be OK if it was found in his room. Or, if he had it on him, he could put the speculation to rest.

Ash pulled the old revolver and placed it on the table. "I found it yesterday in the tunnels when I was with Sean and Candice. It's only got four bullets left, and I doubt they'll fire."

"That's true," Sean said.

"Anyone want to examine it?" Ash said.

Otto dropped his napkin onto the table and rose, a smile spreading over his face.

Ash thought the man was having fun, playing to the crowd, enjoying an inside joke.

Otto lifted the gun, snapped it open, and knocked the four bullets into his palm. He closed the gun with a flick of his wrist and put it back on the table. Then he examined each bullet, taking his time turning each one over in his palm.

"Can we get on with this, sir?" Rodgers said. "I have—"

"Shut it!" Ash yelled.

Otto put the bullets back in the gun and handed it to Ash. "I wouldn't fire it close to your face."

Ash nodded. "So? You in?" Ash looked around. "Everyone is up for a room search. Are you?"

"Fine," Otto nodded. "I've got nothing to hide."

The six competitors headed upstairs, where as a group they searched each room, even those of the deceased. They'd found nothing of note in Auggie, Snake, Deepali, or Candice's rooms, but as Ash punched in his code to open his room to inspection the icy chill of fear spread through him and his knees grew weak.

Ash had forgotten about Snake's pin. It was hidden in his rucksack, which was sure to be searched. His lungs emptied and he sucked for air. He felt lightheaded, the edges of his vision going blurry. Time. He needed time. He typed the last digit of his code incorrectly and the lock beeped, but the light stayed solid red.

He took a deep breath, and said, "Sorry about that." He cracked his knuckles. If he could get Candice, or Sean... or even Otto, to search his bag, maybe they'd keep what they found therein a secret?

Outside a creature roared its displeasure with the icy rain that pelted the closed shutters and stone roof.

Did it matter? Ash looked over his shoulder at the four faces. Rodgers floated in the background, lens eyes telescoping in and out.

Ash tapped in the correct code and pushed into his room. He had to make a split-second decision. Otto was his partner in crime—at least in the current caper—so he leaned in close as the man entered the room and whispered as low as he could, "Hurry. Search my bag."

Otto's nod was barely perceptible, but it was all for nothing.

Sean went right for the rucksack, and within seconds he was holding the gold pin that had adorned Snake's turban. The coiled serpent wrapped around the pin, its green emerald gem eyes staring at Ash along with the other competitors.

"What's this shit, mate?" Sean said.

Ash tried to play it off. "I'd forgotten all about that. I found it under my pillow," Ash said.

Emica spoke up. "Under your pillow?"

"Yeah. What? I was the one that suggested we search the rooms," Ash said, his glance straying to Otto. "Why would I do that if I was hiding evidence here?"

To that nobody had anything to say.

The silence stretched out. Finally, Sean said, "And you chose not to tell us. Again. Just like you tried to hide the gun when you found it. The evidence is backing up against you, mate."

"Don't be an ass," Otto said.

Ash felt an inrush of gratitude, but it faded. Why was Otto defending him?

"If Ash is Treemont he's done a half-ass job of it. The gun is useless," Otto said.

"Maybe he has bullets hidden?" Deepali said.

"Why let you know I've got the gun at all? Surely, I could've hidden it better. Gotten it when you and Sean weren't around." All true, but he felt his anger growing.

"A red herring?" Emica said.

"We done here, Agatha?" Ash said.

"For now," Sean said.

The party moved on and searched Emica's room. They found nothing.

"Can we proceed with our day's task?" Rodgers asked when the search was complete.

The bot had said nothing during the presentation of evidence in Ash's defense, and he wondered if it had been the robot that put the pin in his room. Or one of the other competitors? The 'Treemont is one of us' theory was messing with his head.

Nobody spoke.

"The next challenge is simple," Rodgers said. "You must make a choice. Follow me, please."

The party followed the mechanical butler like a chain gang, and Ash found himself admiring the back of Deepali's head. The house creaked and moaned as wind swept up the valley like a funnel, pounding the house.

Rodgers exited into early morning snow, the tiny ice pellets having been replaced with snowflakes as fine as dust. The wind whipped, tiny white cyclones spinning across the thin strip of turf between the back of the house and the tree line. A small green canvas pavilion had been erected on the grass, and it snapped and twisted in the gale, but the area beneath it was dry. A table sat at one end of the tent, but there were no chairs. The bot floated toward the pavilion without pausing, gusts of wind pushing it around like a boat on a storm swept sea.

Sean laughed. "Like a garbage can getting blown down the street, eh?"

Emica lowered her shoulder and pressed into the cloud of snow, head down, arms tight at her sides.

Sean chased after her. Candice and Deepali followed.

"This is—"

"A trap?" Otto said.

"I was going to say nuts," Ash said.

Rodgers and the others had reached the pavilion and were staring back through the snow in their direction. Sean put his hands on his hips and Candice waved them on.

"Guess Rodgers is waiting on us," Ash said.

"We can head back in. Grab a bottle and lock ourselves in your room," Otto said.

Rodgers' tinny voice, elevated by his speaker mouth, boomed through the snowstorm. "You have one minute to join us or retreat to your room and be eliminated from the competition."

"As fun as that sounds, Otto," Ash said, "what could possibly happen?" He tried to smile and failed.

Otto sighed. "Let's go."

Ash and Otto ran to the tent, and when they arrived, they were greeted with a series of taunts, complaints, and jokes that left Ash feeling almost normal.

Until the monstrosity inched from the forest.

"Meet Mira, everyone," Rodgers said.

The creature was half machine, half flesh. Six steel, multi-jointed legs supported a torso of metal, circuits, wires, blood vessels and flesh. The beast shuffled forward in a spider-like sideways gait, legs churning. The transition from metal to flesh was a bastardization that reminded Ash of tangled fishing line. Blood vessels and muscle encased in wires and intertwined with circuits and metal supports gave way to a short torso. Four arms hung loose, three long talons protruding from the ends of each. A pumpkin-like white head with four dark, glassy, softball-sized eyes sat above a sawblade slit of a mouth.

"Oh, shit." Ash drew the revolver.

"You will not need that," Rodgers said.

"Says you," Otto said. "You keep it out, Ash."

The spider-thing came to a stop across from the table just outside the protective covering of the pavilion. Its bulging eyes searched the party, but gave no sign.

"Mira, are you ready?" Rodgers asked.

The supports in the beast's chest creaked as it wagged its head up and down.

Snow gusted under the tent, and Ash hugged himself. The weather was getting bad.

Rodgers said, "Otto Landon, Ash Cohn, Emica Sasi, Deepali Singh, Sean Macrerie, and Candice Stockton are present. Who will go first, Mira?"

"Me," Emica said. She stepped forward, transfixed, staring at the creature with longing.

"Bio-mecha is her thing," Sean said.

"Really," Ash said. Pain shot down his spine.

Mira boomed, "Mr. Landon will go first. Please step back... Emica."

"Fascinating," Emica said as she retreated.

"Mr. Landon, step forward, please," Mira said. The voice was more human-like than Rodgers', but it still had a noticeable metallic twang.

Otto inched forward, eyes never leaving the monstrosity that stood before him. He glanced at Ash, but there was nothing Ash could do to help him. He'd been chosen to go first. Hopefully he'd get extra credit for that like you did in grade school.

When Otto stood on the opposite side of the table, he paused, shifting on his feet.

Two of the creature's serpentine arms snaked from behind its torso and produced a statue of a Jersey Devil with wide wings. The one that had sat atop the monument with the others. Mira placed it on the table, and with another arm produced a knife.

Emica gasped.

The twelve-inch clipped blade was made of black carbon steel, with a full tang and a notched back. The handle was dark wood with gold and brass mosaic pins. Mira placed the knife on the table next to the statue, and in its booming mechanical voice, the creature said, "Choose one."

18

The choice was a simple one. At least that's what Ash told himself as he watched Otto wrestle with the decision. Mystery behind door number two, or a guaranteed way to defend yourself.

A gust of wind tore through the pavilion, snow pelting Ash's face. Something glinted in the forest beyond and Ash thought he saw Tallboy hiding behind a tree, but when a cyclone of snow tore from the woods and cleared, the Sasquatch was gone.

Otto stared down at the knife and statue of the thin, lanky figure with wide wings. Ash knew very little about Otto, but his MO as described by Sean was he was an American generalist, specializing in Bigfoot and Chupacabra, Jersey Devil, anything cryptid or exotic found in the U.S. Treemont was from Jersey, and the Jersey Devil had started his obsession.

Otto reached out, took the statue and stepped back, never taking his eyes off the creature towering before him. When he bumped into Ash, he slipped behind him.

Mira said, "Who will be next?"

Emica strode forward.

The spider-thing's metal legs shifted and stomped, the creature's four black eyes doubling in size as they bulged, slime dripping from two curved fangs. "You will go last, Emica Sasai." The tone of the creature's voice was so harsh Emica flinched and hurried back to the group.

The creature left the knife and produced the statue of the black dragon-like creature with its wingspread. "Candice, what do you choose?"

Sean and Candice exchanged glances.

So that's how it was. Ash had always known when the bullets started flying Sean and Candice would stick together. They might not be marriage material, but Ash didn't think they'd have a problem coexisting if they could somehow win as a team.

Ash looked over at Otto, who hiked his shoulders.

Candice stepped forward, took the statue, and faded back, all in one smooth motion that lasted three seconds.

The arms on the creature's torso rotated, producing a statue of the Loch Ness Monster. "Sean?" said the bio-cryptid.

Now they'd come to it. Would Sean take the knife, so the team had one of each? Should he take the knife for the same reason? Thing was,

Otto wasn't his partner and if he took the knife, he'd end up protecting the man.

Sean didn't move as fast as Candice, but he was confident and quick. He took the knife.

The creature's six legs bent, and the beast lowered its head to the ground, rocking forward until the slime dripping from its open maw smacked the table like big raindrops. The thing rotated its arms and replaced the knife with another, exactly the same as the one Sean had taken. A mecha claw covered in skin and wires snatched the statue of the Loch Ness Monster and produced the figurine of Bigfoot, and Ash had no doubts it was the one from the monument.

"Mr. Cohn?" To Ash it sounded like the monster's shrill mechanical voice was full of derision.

Ash inched forward, trying not to look timid, but also trying to buy a last few moments to think. The statues could be nothing more than a trick, or they could be of great importance. The knife required hand-to-hand combat to be truly useful, and based on some of the creatures he'd seen so far, Ash didn't think the knife would be of much use. Roll the dice or play it safe?

Ash lifted the statue of Bigfoot and turned it over in his hand. It was finely sculpted, and the dark marble was cold to the touch. He stepped back and joined the group.

The spider figurine was placed on the table, and Deepali took it.

That left Emica. The woman's face was beet red, and Ash was enjoying watching her seethe. She so much wanted to examine the cryptid she'd forgotten where she was, that she was being manipulated, and not very subtly.

To Ash's surprise, Emica didn't step forward. She stood rigid, shaking with rage, and when Mira called her name, Ash definitely detected the ring of sarcasm.

The spider-bot pulled back, moving away from the table until twenty feet separated it from the group. Its mechanical arms rotated and pulled free the statue of a biotech-creature that looked to be more of a monstrosity than the spider-thing. The beast extended its long arm and placed the statue on the table. "Ms. Sasai?"

Emica shifted on her feet, cheeks puffing out, face turning a deeper shade of red. Ash thought the woman might turn and bolt, but instead she strode forward and took the statue.

The creature moved further back.

Ash chuckled and Emica looked over her shoulder and shot him a look that could've wilted fresh lettuce. Mira was messing with the woman, making it hard for her to see the creature.

Emica harrumphed and turned, but as she did so she reached out with her free hand and snagged the knife from the table.

The bio-bot shrieked like the woman had stolen its child, legs going straight, the beast's body lifting above the pavilion's roof. The creature charged forward, head down, mouth open.

Snow gusted beneath the tent, and Ash drew the revolver. He held it at his side like a gunfighter preparing to draw, and fired, squeezing the trigger four times in fast succession.

Four taps as the hammer fell, four puffs of smoke, but none of the shells fired.

Emica rolled on the ground, vaulted to her feet, spun and faced the creature, knife out before her.

The spider-bot pulled up short, stabbing at Emica with the sharp tips of its legs. The creature pushed beneath the tent, pulling up its stakes as it jerked and heaved. The green canvas flapped in the wind, then tore away, exposing the group to the snow squalls.

The creature pulled itself up to its full height, and suddenly Emica looked very small and frail. The urge to help her, that primal feeling that makes a stranger help another, rose in Ash. He rolled his shoulders as the beast danced and swayed, coiling to strike.

Emica rocked on her feet, and her blade looked like a kid's pocketknife next to the sharp tips of the beast's metal, servo-driven legs.

Ash dropped the gun in a pocket and flipped the statue in his hand like a football. He gripped it with both hands and pulled it tight to his chest, lining up his throw. He brought his arm back, flexed and twisted his hips, feet firmly planted.

The creature bellowed and Emica thrust her knife forward, but the beast was quicker. It knocked aside the blade with one leg, another leg stabbing at her.

Ash torqued his hips, twisting and building strength as he brought his arm forward. He released the statue at the highest point of his throwing motion, capturing maximum velocity and power. The statue spun off his fingertips and spiraled through the air, striking the creature in one of its four bulbous eyes.

The beast screeched and bucked, pulling itself upward and back.

Emica crab-walked backward until she ran into Sean, who lifted her to her feet.

The mecha-spider surged forward with a hiss, mouth open, fangs exposed.

"Mira. Halt. Now." It was Rodgers. The bot had faded into the background when it had ceded control of the proceedings to Mira, but the mechanical butler was controlling everything.

The spider-bot pulled up and froze.

Rodgers turned to Emica. "Give Mira the knife back."

Emica looked around searching for help, but found none. That's what happens when you don't even say good morning. She backed up like a cornered animal, holding the statue in one hand and the knife in the other. "I'm not going anywhere near that thing."

"You will give Mira the knife or you will be—"

"It tried to kill me!" Emica screamed.

Rodgers beeped, chirped and hummed. The bot said, "You must comply, or you will be excused from the competition."

"Fine!" Emica took two steps and threw the knife. It landed five feet in front of the bot.

A crackling that sounded dangerously like a sigh escaped Rodgers' speaker mouth. "Mira, take the knife."

The beast inched forward. To Ash it looked afraid. It scooped up the knife and scuttled away into the snow, then disappeared into the forest.

With the pavilion gone, the group stood in the swirling snow, freezing.

"What will that thing do if we encounter it in the wild?" Otto asked.

Rodgers didn't have a chance to respond because a steady trumpet blast echoed through the valley.

Ash sighed. The day wasn't even half over, and it had already gone to shit.

Tiny shards of ice bit at the company as they made their way around the side of the house and down to the monument, which was where Rodgers said the horn blasts had originated. A thin coating of snow covered the ground and the yellow stone path, icicles hanging from tree branches and shrubs. The wildflowers were struggling in the cold, but they were weeds, and the blossoms that got destroyed would sprout ten new buds.

Rodgers buzzed through the thinning snow, swaying like a drunkard as the wind pushed the bot around.

When the party arrived at the monument, what Emica had asserted the prior night was confirmed. The eight figurines were gone, replaced with one slightly larger statue. Ash eyed the statue of Bigfoot in his hand.

The new solitary statue was an amalgamation of the nine, like the cryptids that climbed and crawled over each other to reach the top of the monument. The figure was two feet tall and made of blue granite. It was an amazing work of sculpture, the finery of the beasts as they intertwined, an incredible display of patience and time.

The six surviving guests and Rodgers stood in a half circle in front of the monument, the wind roaring, pinpricks of dancing snow twisting and writhing, biting Ash's face. He'd put on his hat and gloves, but he was still cold. It rarely snowed in Stony Creek. That was one of the reasons he liked living in Northern California.

"Now we've come to a most important challenge. One that will test your physical and mental stamina and abilities." Rodgers paused, snow and ice building-up around where his telescope eyes connected to the bot's face.

Wind gusted, no birds or insects sang.

"As you have no doubt already surmised there are nine statues representing the nine competitors. This task involves collecting as many of the nine as you can. Those wise enough to select the statue instead of the knife, already have one point. Mr. Snake, Mr. Chambers, Mr. Vancharlin, Mr. Macrerie and Ms. Sasai's statues will be hidden within the valley. Find th—"

Emica blurted, "Wait. What about my statue?"

"Because you failed to comply with the rules set out for the last task, you have been assessed a penalty."

"By who? This is bullshit. I'm not—"

"You will give me your statue immediately." Rodgers wailed over the howling wind and gusting snow. "Or you will be removed from the competition. You agreed to abide by the rules set forth by Mr. Treemont, did you not?"

Emica stared at Rodgers in disbelief, snow pelting her face. She tossed the statue at Rodgers, but unlike Mira, the bot deftly caught it.

"You will collect as many statues as you can. A horn blast will mark the end of the contest, and the task will be completed. Food and drink will be continually available in the kitchen and in the dining room at regular times. Per Mr. Treemont's instructions, the basement of the house is henceforth out of bounds. Good luck. I hope to see you all at the completion of the task."

"That's it?" Otto yelled. "No other rules?"

Rodgers spun and floated down the path, disappearing in the white haze of snow.

There was no mad dash this time, no scrambling to get the upper hand. The six cryptid hunters stood in the freezing cold, snow pelting them as they watched Treemont's robotic emissary leave them to fend for themselves.

"So that's it then. Every man for himself?" Otto said.

Emica, Candice, and Deepali turned their lethal stares in his direction and Otto flinched. "Sorry. Sorry. Person for themselves?"

Emica said, "Ash, any sign of a way out of the valley when you were in the tunnels?"

"That's what I was thinking. Treemont doesn't want us down there," Sean said.

"Seems too simple, and no," Ash said. "The main tunnel dumps into the valley, but there's got to be a footpath out of here. Has to be."

"Unless it's been blocked or otherwise destroyed," Otto said.

Ash hadn't thought of that.

A faint buzz, like a giant bee approaching, stuck in Ash's ear like a worm. The wind howled, and he focused, eliminating sounds. There was something there, and it was getting louder.

"Do we think this competition is legit in any way at this point?" Emica said.

"I have serious doubts," Deepali said. Her bracelets jingled as she rubbed her hands together.

"That's an excellent question," Ash said. One he'd been asking himself over and over as he thought about what he was willing to do to win, and how he might justify it to himself. Ash was no killer, but he was desperate. If he could bring Ophelia to the valley, show her the creatures that lived here, that would fix everything. Proof. Living, breathing, proof.

Ash laughed at himself. Those types of thoughts were what had gotten him into this mess in the first place.

"Are we going to stand out here and freeze?" Otto asked.

None of the six wanted to be the first to leave, to forsake a possible alliance that could save their life. So they stood in the snow, shivering from lack of movement.

"We could do both, right?" Candice said.

Nobody spoke, but they all stared at her.

The buzzing sound was getting louder.

"We could search for the statues and a path out of the valley, agree not to go after each other, and if a way out is found, tell the group," Candice said.

Sean looked at Otto, then said, "How do you plan to ensure compliance?"

"Can you ever assure compliance?" Ash said.

The buzzing reached a crescendo and a drone appeared out of the thinning snow, flying low and circling the group. It was dropping something. Shiny brass items that stood out against the white when they hit the snow-covered ground.

The drone was dropping bullets.

19

In the swirling snow it was difficult to see, but Ash watched the drone spin and twist in the gusting wind as another bullet fell from its undercarriage. Four rotors spun and buzzed, a camera-head turning atop a sleek fuselage, two cord-like arms hanging motionless. The flying robot circled Deepali and Emica, who stood close to the monument. More bullets fell, and Ash was slow to react.

Sean and Candice bolted toward the first bullet to hit the ground, but they were the furthest away from it.

Otto stood still as stone, snow wrapping him in its embrace, mouth hanging open as he stared up at the craft as it dipped and dived as it was blown around.

The drone's engine whined as it cycled up, and the black craft flew in a wide circle and headed back up the valley toward the house, disappearing into the fog of snow.

By Ash's count, six brass shells had been dropped. One for each of them. He jerked into motion, veering sharply and heading for the bullet closest to him. He slipped in the snow, arms going out for balance, but he managed to stay on his feet as he scooped up a bullet.

Deepali and Emica claimed a bullet each, and Sean changed direction and barreled down the path toward a shell that lay ten feet away from Otto, who was still gazing at the drone like he'd never seen one before.

"Otto!" Ash yelled, and the instant the words were out of his mouth he wished he could have them back.

Otto wagged his head, brushed snow from his face, and looked at Ash.

Sean was halfway to a bullet that lay by Otto, and Candice had collected one shell and was headed for her second.

Ash lunged forward, throwing himself into an awkward run, slipping and sliding in the snow. Otto was still staring at him as Ash's mind spun. If he pointed to the bullet Otto would get it, and he would definitively and irreparably harm his relationship with Sean and Candice. Do nothing, and Sean gets a bullet, which would effectively give him two because of Candice's. Ash ran harder, skidding to a stop feet from Candice as she beat him to the bullet.

Ash spun, shouted, and pointed. "Otto! Otto! Look! The bullet."

Otto hesitated, confused, then he began searching the ground around him, arms out like he might fall.

Sean skidded to a stop and picked up the bullet, straightened, and turned to look at Ash.

Ash ignored him and scrambled, searching the ground. When the others realized what he was doing, they joined in. Ash was pretty sure only six bullets had been dropped, and they'd all been collected, but he was buying time, trying to think of a story to tell Sean. He didn't know why he'd called out.

"Hey, Ash," Sean shouted through the wind. "What the hell was that, mate?"

So much for stalling. Ash didn't respond as he continued his search.

"So that's it then, huh? You're with... him?" Sean said.

Snow pelted the man's red face, but the disappointment and pain he saw in the Scotsman's blue eyes hurt more than Ash would ever admit. "I'm not with anyone," Ash said. That sounded ridiculous. "I'm with myself," he added. Much better.

"You think I'd shoot you?" Sean said.

The snow had eased, the dark clouds breaking overhead.

"I don't know, Sean. Things have gotten out of control," Ash said.

"Says the guy who had the first victim's pin hidden in his room, then hid the fact that he'd found a gun. Now I'm the one who can't be trusted? You Americans are so full of pigshit."

The guy had a point. Ash sighed and decided to put it all on the table. He snuck a glance at the bullet in his hand. A .22 caliber rifle shell. Useless for a revolver that took .45 caliber cartridges. Ash stopped searching and faced Sean.

Deepali, Emica, Candice and Otto stood watching, heads jerking from speaker to speaker like they were watching a basketball team pass around the rock. "So, you're telling me, that if it came down to Candice or me, you'd choose me?"

"You think this guy is going to help you when times get tough? Where the hell you been?" Sean said.

At this, Otto stirred and stepped forward.

Ash put up a hand. "I know he acted like an ass when we first arrived, and that he withheld information, but I can't say I trust him any less than any of you."

"What about me?" Deepali said. She brushed snow from her hair and her bracelets tinkled, despite her gloves.

Emica crossed her arms, looked up into the swirling snow, but said nothing.

"Here, Sean," Candice said. She made a show of giving Sean the two bullets she'd retrieved.

He couldn't be sure, but based on the fast glance he got through the pelting pinpricks of snow, Ash thought the two shells were the same as his; long and narrow with a silver point. Now Sean had three of the six bullets, he, Emica, and Deepali the other three. Anger rose in Ash, burning the pit of his stomach like when someone passed him on the highway. He said, "Emica and Deepali, let me see your bullets, please."

Both women held out their shells. Basic .22 caliber.

The snow stopped, but the wind still pushed around the thin coating on the ground. The six people stood there, suspicious glances moving among them like poison.

Sean strode purposefully toward Ash, who spread his legs and braced for an attack. The Scot let the rifle fall from his shoulder into his hands, and he pulled back the slide and dropped a shell into the firing chamber. The crack of the bolt slamming home echoed off the cliffs and resounded over the valley. Sean stopped a foot from Ash, who was doing his best not to shake like a little boy going on his first roller-coaster.

"Good luck, mate. Stay away from me..." Sean looked back at Candice who stood behind him. "Us, mate. Stay away from us." Sean slung the rifle over his shoulder and stalked off in the direction of the house.

Candice shot Ash a look that was mostly disappointment, but part anger. She eyed the rest of the group as she followed Sean without a word.

When the pair were out of earshot, Otto said, "Thanks."

"For what?" Ash said. "I made things worse."

"Maybe," Otto said, his gaze searching the ground. He lifted his head, the black bags beneath his eyes making his brown skin look darker.

Deepali came forward and gently took Ash's arm the way she had when they'd first arrived. That seemed like eons ago. "What now?" she asked.

Emica, feeling the odd man out, took a step back as she eyed the three competitors.

Ash said nothing, and he deftly untwined his arm and Deepali's.

The woman's dark eyes appeared to well with tears for an instant, then they turned hard and cold.

This was the moment. Most of the lines had been drawn and Ash needed to pick allies with care. He was attracted to Deepali, but what did that mean? She wasn't a good fighter, and he'd end up having to protect her. What would he get of value? Emica was tougher, but there was no way he could trust her, but she could be of help in a pinch. Keep your friends close and your enemies closer, and all that.

That left Otto, who everyone assumed he was paired off with thanks to his own stupidity. Ash said, "What do you think, Otto? I've got no substantive ideas of where to start looking."

Otto's gaze shifted to Emica, then Deepali.

Emica huffed. "You better hope you don't need me." The woman turned and stalked down the path, heading back in the direction where the helicopter had landed, toward the open end of the valley in the east.

Deepali shifted on her feet, her honey-colored cheeks going red.

Otto looked everywhere but at Deepali, his eyes rolling around like marbles.

A beast howled in the distance, a mournful cry that sounded like a wolf with a cold.

Deepali took Ash's arm again, her grip vise-like. She whispered in his ear. "I know you don't owe me anything, and I'm not rich, but I do know some things that you don't."

Ash rolled his eyes and started to pull away, but she tugged him in close. He smelled her perfume, felt the heat building between them, despite their heavy jackets.

"Trust me now, and we can win this," she said.

Ash had always been a fool when it came to women. He could be hard as nails with men, but all a woman had to do was cry and most of his defenses were rendered useless. But this was a special circumstance. This was life or death, and he couldn't put his own life in danger for anyone. Not without getting something equally as important in return. He harrumphed, knowing it didn't really matter how he felt. There was no way he could stop the woman from following, but he said nothing.

Otto threw up his hands. "Three's a crowd," he said.

"Then hit the road," Ash said. He'd destroyed his relationship with Sean without thought, and now he was alienating Otto for no good reason.

Otto's head jerked back, and his eyes went wide.

Ash went into damage control mode. "Look, I'm sorry, OK? I didn't mean that." He sighed and made a show of throwing up his hands. "I'm an ass. Talking out my ass without thinking."

The anger fled from Otto's face, and his eyes shifted to Deepali.

"She's with us," Ash said. "That OK?"

Deepali, realizing the make-or-break situation, went to Otto. "I know you don't trust me. None of us can trust anyone, but I promise to help in any way I can. Please. This isn't about the contest anymore. If we win through, or I do, you can have my share. I never want to see this place again." She took Otto's hand and the man's face softened like he'd just eaten a thick piece of cake stacked with icing.

Otto nodded.

Deepali smirked.

Ash got that feeling again, like Deepali was lying.

The three companions stood in the cold, the monument looming behind them. Wind tore through the valley, but it was letting up. The mountains sang and whistled, their snowcapped peaks obscured under clouds of white.

Otto said, "I think we should start at the paddocks. Specifically, ones relating to the missing statues."

"I thought of that. Seems too obvious, no?" Deepali said.

Otto looked at her like she had no right to speak.

"Me also," Ash said. "But without any clues maybe it's that simple. I don't know which paddocks are which, anyway, do you?"

Otto shook his head no.

Deepali crossed her arms and looked defiantly at Otto, who hiked his shoulders. She said, "May I speak, your grace?"

Ash chuckled.

Otto looked at his feet.

Deepali waited, reveling in Otto's discomfort.

The wind blew, trees bent and creaked, Ash's breathing echoing in his ears. His stomach churned and ached.

"OK, what?" Otto said. "I'm sorry, OK?"

Deepali pursed her lips in triumph and said, "I know where each paddock is."

Ash and Otto exchanged glances, but said nothing.

A sneer ran across Deepali's face as she commanded her audience.

"How?" Ash blurted in his frustration.

"I've got this." She produced a yellow folded piece of paper from her tunic pocket.

"And that would be?" Otto said.

"A map," she said.

"So, you stole that from the library?" Otto said.

Deepali's face tightened, her credibility and worth again being drawn into question. She recovered quickly. "I borrowed it. And now WE... We, have it," she said.

"I'm gonna tell Rodgers," Otto said, imitating a child's taunting call.

"Let's get under cover and take a look," Ash said. "Aren't you worried Treemont will know?"

Deepali answered with a wry smile.

***

As the three co-conspirators walked toward the forest, Rodgers inched out from his hiding place, his eye-lenses telescoping in and out.

***

Ash found a tall conifer with wide, spreading boughs, and the trio slipped beneath the ice-laden branches out of the wind and churning snow.

Deepali unfolded the paper and handed it to Ash.

The hand drawn map reminded Ash of the atlas of Middle Earth at the beginning of The Lord of the Rings. The Andes were clustered triangles with curved tops, and they surrounded the interior of the valley, which was most of the sheet. The house, monument, and lake were marked, and multiple paddocks had outlines with dark lines that spidered through broccoli-like trees.

"We're looking for the serpent, the seal-dog, Sean's Loch Ness Monster, a giant bear and Emica's bio-monstrosity? That right? Does that account for all the figurines?"

Ash did a fast count. He'd retrieved the Bigfoot statue, Deepali had the spider, Emica gave hers back to Rodgers, Otto had the Jersey Devil, and Candice the black dragon. That made nine in total.

"Seems clear the Loch Ness statue and the Bunyip would be by the water. Make sense?" Deepali offered.

Otto and Ash nodded. "If anything, it seems too easy. Too logical. And I've got a good guess where Emica's statue is," Ash said.

"With Mira, wherever the hell her hole is," Deepali said.

"The paddocks on the northern slope would be the best snake and bear habitat." Otto pointed at the map. "See these two paddocks. They appear to have structures of some kind."

"Bears like caves, right?" Deepali said.

"They do at that," Otto said. "I think she's onto something." Otto smiled at Deepali and she smiled back.

Had Ash made a love connection? He felt some of his tension drain as he allowed himself to think of normal things, like life and love, for a minute. Things he himself hadn't paid any attention to for far too long.

"We're looking for a path out of the valley. The largest caves would be notched in the cliff face, I'd think," Otto said.

"Plus, we could also search the forest as we make our way north to the valley wall," Ash said. "And based on what happened to Auggie, I don't want to see that Bunyip thing again."

"Tangling with a giant bear or a forty-foot snake might be just as bad," Otto said.

"I can run faster than I can swim," Ash said.

"We should grab some food and supplies, just in case we get... waylaid," Otto said.

Deepali nodded so vigorously Ash thought the woman might hurt her neck.

Ash's stomach gurgled at the possibility of a drink and food, his nerves stretched tighter than piano strings. Pain arced through his groin. He had to take a pee.

As the small party walked the slick yellow path to the house, Ash scanned the hillsides for sniper roosts. If Sean picked the right spot, he could knock off the three of them anytime he wanted if he was a decent shot. Thankfully, Ash didn't think the man was a killer.

Ash frowned. Was he?

20

The air was brisk and fresh, the sun a white orb in the dissipating storm, blue sky with a mask of tattered cotton candy clouds stretching across the eastern end of the valley. Ash led, and he pulled the straps of his rucksack tight as the party plunged into the forest. He'd brought food and water, a bottle of whiskey, some towels, a flashlight, and six dull steak knives and three forks. His hand dropped to his pants pocket, and he traced his folded karambit through the fabric. His nerves bounced and stretched, and every few seconds a chill cut through him like an electrical shock, but knowing the knife was there, feeling its presence, eased his tension. Nobody had questioned him about the knife yet, but he knew the next time it appeared he'd have to explain another lie, another example of Ash holding out.

Ash followed a thin path shown on the map that meandered northeast through a tangle of silver fir and juniper. The trio was heading to paddock C, the one with a small coiled snake drawn in its center. It was the smallest of the paddocks, and would be easy to search. The vote had been unanimous.

Deepali followed Ash, bracelets jingling, her perfume tickling Ash's nose.

Otto watched their backs. He held the sharpest knife at his side, but it was comical. The two-inch serrated blade would barely break the skin, but it was better than nothing. Ash and Deepali held onto their own bullets. They hadn't addressed the issue as a group because there was no reason to. If they had a gun that could take the bullets, maybe they'd combine the ammo, but they didn't.

Deepali said, "Ash, I'm thinking the statues will be displayed prominently."

"Do you always talk like that?" Otto said.

Deepali eyed him with derision.

"Prominently?" Otto mocked. He pranced like a pony and stuck out his jaw.

Ash laughed and she turned her smoldering gaze on him. Ash stopped laughing.

"Do you morons know what I mean or not?" Deepali said.

"Easy. Sorry... never say easy to a woman unless you want to get punched. Sorry," Otto said.

Ash lifted an eyebrow. Sorry? Ash hadn't thought the man knew the word.

"You're saying the statues are small, and if Treemont wanted to hide them where we'd never find them, that would be easy enough to do," Otto said.

"And? You guys think that means he'd serve them up on a silver platter?" Ash said.

"No, but if they're hidden well, there'll have to be clues," Otto said.

The brisk breeze pushed around the dusting of snow, and there were small footprints in some of the thin drifts around boulders and trees.

A scream pierced the day, floated down the valley on the wind, hung in the air, then faded.

"That was human," Otto said.

"It was Emica. I'd bet good money on it," Ash said.

"Any idea what direction it came from?" Deepali asked.

Ash looked back down the path the way they'd come, toward the house and the lake beyond, then ahead at the mountainside. There was still no sign of the paddock, but Ash said nothing.

The small party picked their way through the forest, traversing wide conifers, and thin oaks with hand-like deep green leaves. Spiderwebs hung under tree boughs, and small rodent and bird tracks marked the remaining patches of hardpan still covered in a thin coating of snow.

"Look here," Ash said. He knelt before a set of footprints that trailed northwest.

The prints were two feet long with five toes ending in sharp claw-like points.

"The beast was moving fast," Ash said. He'd seen Bigfoot tracks before.

"I agree," Otto said. "See how the footpad is so narrow? Because it was barely touching the ground."

Ash nodded. "Running from us?"

"Let's find out," Otto said.

Ash looked at Deepali, who shrugged. "The paddock and the cliff face are in that direction anyway. Right?"

Deepali nodded.

The trio lost the trail after five minutes, but continued northwest. Though the weather was clearing, a stiff breeze still pushed through the valley, rattling leaves and pushing around snow. The terrain and underbrush were thick. It was slow going, and the party hiked for an hour before the wall of paddock C appeared in the dense forest. The ground was covered in brown pine needles, and the fence was a sun worn wood of similar color. The way the ground blended into the fence made the paddock wall almost invisible.

A low gurgle rumbled through the woods and echoed off the wall.

Ash dropped his pack and put his back to the fence.

"Shit," Otto said. He held a knife out before him, but his hand shook so violently Ash thought the man was going to drop it.

"Sush," whispered Deepali. She grabbed Otto's arm and pulled him against the wall next to Ash.

Shadows danced in the forest as the afternoon sun fought through the cloud cover. The wind whistled, and the insects went still.

Grumbling. Panting. Snarling. Like the biggest dog ever to walk the Earth was frustrated and angry.

A tall shadow fell across the fence to the south.

"Move," Ash spat. He sprang forward, hurling himself into the forest, slammed into a tree, and fell on his ass.

Cracking branches. Pounding feet. Gurgling and grunts.

Otto yanked Ash to his feet. "You OK?"

Ash rubbed his forehead, a kaleidoscope of rainbows dancing in the air.

A roar boomed through the forest, followed by a cold inrush of air.

"Otto?" Ash rubbed his eyes. "Otto?" Ash's vision began to clear, blurry images moving between dark sticks of black.

"Be quiet."

Blood ran into Ash's eyes, his head pounding in rhythm with the scratches on his chest. In that moment, he wanted to drop to the ground and go to sleep. Otto urged him forward, tree trunks and dense underbrush coming together like a puzzle as his vision cleared.

Another roar pierced the day, a big animal that was very angry.

The party took cover beneath the thick boughs of an evergreen, its small pointy leaves poking and scratching at the trio as they slid under the tree's branches.

The shadow on the wall shrank as it got closer, the grunts and gurgling getting louder.

Time stretched, like nature itself was waiting to see what would happen next, and when Ash saw the creature, his chest hurt and his knees went weak.

Tallboy was a teddy bear compared to the beast that came into view along the wall. The creature was smaller than Tallboy, but looked more muscular and furious. The Bigfoot's brown fur was matted and dirty, and it slouched as if carrying a heavy weight. Its eyes burned like cinders from within deep sockets, the beast's ape-like face twitching. Two long fangs hung from a mouth full of teeth, and the dime-sized nostrils of the creature's flat nose pulsed open and closed.

Little imaginary mice crawled up Ash's spine onto his shoulders and he tossed his head, cracking his neck, trying to shake the angst.

The Sasquatch bent, dropped to a knee, then leaned forward as if kissing the ground. The beast sniffed and sighed, its claw-tipped fingers raking the ground where the party had stood. It sniffed again and threw back its head and howled, a long, angry cry that carried up the hillside and echoed through the valley like a gunshot.

The beast moved in a blur, lurching forward in an awkward gait, nose sucking in air like a vacuum, eyes locked on the pine needle covered ground. Branches snapped and cracked as the Sasquatch surged into the forest, smashing into the conifer tree the party hid under.

The flexible, sap laden, evergreen branches accepted the beast like a trampoline, flexing and stretching, building force. They bent, but didn't break, and the beast was pushed back a step as the branches resisted.

Otto screamed and lunged forward, plunging the steak knife into the Bigfoot's leg, then peeling off and disappearing through the tree boughs without breaking stride.

The Sasquatch howled in pain, a cry that sounded oddly human.

Deepali ran after Otto.

Ash pulled his blade.

The beast gurgled and coughed, arms outstretched, branches snapping, trees bending and swaying.

Ash ran, this time with his eyes up like a running back picking his way through a defense. He jumped over fallen branches, dodged underbrush and bushes, and cut around tree trunks.

Ahead, Otto veered north, and when he reached the wall, he made a right, Deepali on his heels.

When Ash got to the paddock, he turned and put his back to the wall, knife out before him, heart galloping. He searched the forest, but didn't see the Bigfoot. He'd seen the Yeti, Tallboy, yet the creature he'd just seen was very similar to the one that had changed his life. In many ways, had destroyed it. But it was real. He wasn't crazy. It was real.

The forest stayed still, and no grunts, gurgles or howls echoed from within. It appeared the beast had given up the chase. Otto had stabbed the creature. Ash could hardly believe it. The man had stepped up. Ash knew it was probably the fear and adrenaline taking over, but those were just details.

He stayed still with his back to the fence for several minutes, making sure the beast wasn't waiting for him to move so it could attack.

Ash found Deepali and Otto waiting for him by the paddock's gate.

The large wooden entrance stood open. An intricate wrought iron portcullis surrounded the gate, black metal twisting and spiraling upward, each bar ending in a small metal star.

"The beast gone?" Deepali said.

"Not sure, but it didn't follow. Not yet, anyway," Ash said. "The gate wasn't locked?"

"This is exactly how we found it," Otto said. He gazed into the paddock through the open gate.

Had the Bigfoot escaped? Had it been protecting the paddock? What lay within? Ash said nothing as he strode forward and joined Otto and Deepali.

Paddock C definitely didn't house Sasquatch.

Multicolored gravel, mostly sandstone rubble and small chunks of granite, filled the enclosure, and the bleak Mars-like terrain rolled and mounded into dunes. Bushes with dark green oval leaves dotted the landscape, but there were no trees. The hardpacked path that ran from the gate led to a hole with a diameter of ten feet.

Ash eased forward, moving carefully through the gate into the paddock. Otto and Deepali trailed after.

The scent of rot and decay assailed Ash. The coppery smell of blood. Of death. Just inside the gate there was a stained wood platform. Flecks of bone, streaks of black dried blood, and globs of hardened fat covered the decking.

"Feed station," Otto said.

"I thought Rodgers said the animals didn't get tended?" Ash said.

"He said most don't," Deepali said.

"How big would a snake need to be to need so much food?" Otto asked.

"Maybe forty feet," Ash said as he pointed.

A huge snakeskin trailed over and between mounds of gravel, the dried opaque shell speckled black and gray. Drips of fresh blood trailed away from the platform and disappeared around a mound of blue pebbles.

Otto whistled. "Damn."

"Explains the hole," Deepali said.

A faint hissing carried on the wind.

The trio exchanged glances.

"Doesn't sound close," Otto said.

The trio followed the thin trail of blood through paddock C. The terrain reminded Ash of the fish tank he used to keep his turtle in as a kid. Dull, hard, and unattractive. With no trees or underbrush, Ash and company were able to walk the circumference of the paddock in fifteen minutes, and when they didn't find the statue, the team took cover under a bush with prickers the size of stilettos.

"The statue must be by the hole," Deepali said. "You can forget that."

Ash's blood was pumping, his heart racing like an engine with a pinned gas pedal. "What about you, Otto?"

Otto made a face like he'd just downed a skunked beer. Then being ever practical, he said, "If we both go, and retrieve the statue, who gets it? We can't break it in half, can we?"

"I'd think not," Ash said. Trying to be a team while playing an individual sport was making things extra difficult. "Do you want to go after it? I'll step aside if you do."

Otto looked embarrassed, his brown cheeks going deep red. "No, you take it. I'll take the next one."

"Or I will," Deepali said.

Hissing still rolled through the paddock, but Ash kept under cover behind rocks, bushes, and behind dunes of pebbles as he worked his way to the center of the enclosure. There were deep ruts in the sand going every which way, but Ash saw no other signs of the giant snake.

A large dune of blue and brown stones gave way to Ash's right, revealing the southernmost edge of the hole. It was massive, much bigger than he'd originally thought, and was easily thirty feet around.

Emica's crumpled body lay next to the hole, a small puddle of blood leaking into the ground around her. Her dark eyes were open, and they stared up at the tattered clouds. Ash bent and took her pulse. Nothing. She was already cold. Two quarter-sized fang holes in her chest leaked blood, and Ash followed the drag marks in the gravel with his eyes. The snake had brought her to its hole for later, but why hadn't it brought its prize all the way home?

Ash closed his eyes and sorrow washed over him. He hadn't known Emica, and what he had known he hadn't particularly liked. She'd been a moody, overconfident, unfriendly bitch. Did she deserve to be murdered by a giant snake? He didn't think so.

He searched the woman, and slipped her bullet into his pocket. Then Ash tried to move on, but guilt stopped him. He couldn't just leave the woman's corpse to be devoured. He quickly gathered football-sized stones and covered Emica's mutilated corpse. It took him several minutes of hard labor, and when he was done, he dropped his pack and took a long drink of water.

The hissing was getting louder.

Ash put away his water bottle and worked his way around the edge of the hole. Piles of gravel and rocks blocked his view, and pricker vines and brown, stumpy bushes that stuck from the pebble-covered ground like boils caused him to retreat from the hole's edge several times.

The small monument sparkled, and Ash went to it. The thin column was sculpted from blue granite with a dense concentration of quartz, and the brass nameplate affixed to it read Titanoboa. The flat top of the pedestal, clearly designed to hold a statue, was empty.

The figurine Ash assumed had been there, most likely a coiled snake, was gone.

21

Ash searched around the hole, thinking maybe Emica had hidden the statue as she struggled for life, or dropped it, or used it as a weapon the way he had, but it was nowhere to be found. Either the snake had eaten it, or Sean and Candice had beaten Emica to the paddock, which seemed unlikely.

The day was waning, and he'd accomplished nothing. In fact, one could argue he was worse off than when the day began. His stomach grumbled, his mouth dry. Ash headed back to the others, the wind pushing around dust and dirt. It was oddly quiet, the chatter of birds and the buzz of insects distant. Ash had gotten used to the comforting confines of the forest, the crunch and rattle as small animals scurried over dried leaves. Paddock C was barren and harsh, and Ash wanted to leave.

When he got back to Deepali and Otto, Ash told them what he'd found, but they wanted to see for themselves, so the trio backtracked to Emica's stone-covered corpse.

"You couldn't find the statue, huh?" Deepali said, her keen dark eyes scanning the area.

"If there ever was one," Ash said.

Otto said nothing, his eyes sweeping over the scene, brow furrowing.

"The pillar is on the eastern side toward the entrance," Ash said. He felt waves of suspicion rolling off his partners. It made him angry, but he understood. He could've hidden the statue anywhere in the paddock to be picked up later. Also, he'd found the woman's body, therefore it wasn't a stretch to surmise that he killed Emica and took the statue.

Deepali said, "Did you take her bullet?"

Sweat rolled down Ash's back and he cracked his knuckles. He was no poker player, and as his stomach grumbled and pain ran down his spine, he knew he needed to tell the truth. Ash reached into his pocket and brought out two brass shells.

"You are lucky I don't think you're a killer, because someone is sure as hell trying to make you look like one," Otto said.

Ash opened his mouth to rebuff the man, then closed it. Otto was right. Of the nine, he had the most evidence stacked against him and the argument could easily be made that Ash was Treemont.

The hissing reached a fever pitch. Stones tumbled and landslides of pebbles and shifting rocks cascaded into the hole.

"I think it's time to make like a tree," Ash said.

Otto turned to go, but Deepali stared blankly at Ash.

"And leave," Ash said.

No reaction from Deepali.

Ash gently took her arm and the pair followed Otto, who was moving away from the hole and circling around a large mound of gravel topped with a thicket of pricker bushes.

"Trees have leaves. It's an old joke," Ash said. He picked up the pace and let go of Deepali's arm.

She jogged beside him, the crunch of gravel and sharp hissing rising over the blustery wind and her panting. "Not a very good one," she forced out between breaths.

Otto bolted around the mound of gravel, cutting between Ash and Deepali, and disappeared around the hill the way they'd come, heading back toward the hole.

Ash and Deepali skidded to a stop.

An angular head with two obsidian eyes and a red tongue lashing out through two-foot fangs rose above the hill of stones. The massive snake slithered into view, its body undulating and expanding as it moved, pushing aside gravel like the bow of a boat threw whitewater.

Ash turned and ran, following Otto's footprints as close as he could. He didn't look back. If Deepali didn't know she needed to run, so be it.

He shook his head and looked over his shoulder. Deepali ran behind him, and a smirk spread over her face when she saw him looking at her.

The snake saw them, and its head lifted, swaying back and forth, glassy eyes locking on the trio. Ash estimated the creature to be sixty-feet long, at least, and as the Titanoboa surged through the pebbles and stones, he realized running wasn't an option. The creature was fast, and moving in its familiar habitat.

He made a hard right, darting between two large bushes.

Deepali screamed. Rocks popped and cracked as gravel shifted.

Ash skidded to a stop and looked back. Deepali had fallen, and was sprawled on the brown gravel covered ground. In the second it took Ash to decide to help Deepali, the argument he'd had with himself more times than he could remember ran through his head like a ten second recap of a very long story. She wasn't his responsibility. He didn't know her. She was a competitor, and could be a killer. He brushed all the rationalizations aside and when he reached Deepali she was struggling to get to her feet.

She flinched when Ash took her arm, but when she realized it was him, she smiled and said, "Thank you."

The duo ran on, cutting around thickets and piles of gravel like moguls on a ski mountain, the snake's tracks everywhere. Rocks snapped and cracked as the beast pursued them. Ash saw Otto, pumping hard toward the open gate. He was going to make it. If he could be ready to slam the gate closed as soon as Ash and Deepali made it out they might make it also.

A red tongue lashed out, just missing Otto.

The snake's flat head surged through a pile of rocks and pebbles, pushing a landslide toward Otto, who skidded to a stop twenty feet short of the gate.

The creature's massive girth came down with a thud, a cloud of dust and shards of stone rising from the ground. The beast slithered and swayed, throwing stones as it wiggled forward, black glassy eyes locked on Otto.

The Titanoboa paused, its angular head shifting toward the open gate. Its head swung back to Otto in disbelief, then abandoned the chase and slithered out the gate and disappeared into the forest beyond.

"Not good," Deepali said as she came to a stop next to Ash.

"At this point, who gives a turd," Ash said.

"Can it get out of the valley?" Otto asked.

Goddamn people and their caring and ethics. "I don't know," Ash said. He wondered if Otto was more concerned about the creature's welfare, or the havoc it might create as it destroyed the valley and moved on?

Deepali said, "Did that just happen?"

"I do believe it did. You OK?" Ash said.

Deepali nodded.

Ash shifted on his feet, not sure what to do next.

"Should we check the snake den? See what it's got down there?" Deepali said.

Otto and Ash looked at each other, then laughed.

"Are we in a horror movie?" Otto said.

"You are joking, aren't you?" Ash asked.

"No, I wasn't."

The laughter died like the two men had heard the bubble and suck of an empty beer tap.

"You want to climb down the snake hole?" Otto said. The man normally sounded arrogant, but his tone was laced with sympathy.

"I just thought with the thing gone we could—"

"Gone? It could come back at any minute. In fact, that's the first thing it's going to do as soon as it catches more prey, if it behaves anything like a regular snake."

"And there could be more than one," Ash said.

That comment struck home, and the three companions exchanged wary glances.

If there was a moment to break the fellowship, it was now, but Ash said nothing.

Deepali looked around nervously, her bracelets tinkling as she put her hands on her hips.

Otto said, "We can't stay here. The statue is gone, so I'm gone. You guys coming?" He didn't wait to hear an answer and started walking.

There was strength in numbers, and until that changed, Ash saw no downside to sticking together. Plus, he liked that Otto was taking charge. That gave him some time to think.

Ash and Deepali followed and the party eased stealthily through the open gate. The snake's path through the forest was easy to see, the beast's massive girth having flattened the undergrowth. The sun had disappeared over the lip of the valley, and tall shadows fell across the woods. A fresh breeze had replaced the chill wind, and the scent of cedar and flowers hung in the air.

The companions halted under an odd shaped conifer that looked like a disguised cell tower because it was missing every other branch. Ash broke out the food and water, and the trio ate what they had as night came on like a freight train with no station in sight.

Ash pulled free the bottle of whiskey, twisted off the cap, and sniffed the contents. He sighed and took a pull, then offered the bottle to Otto, who accepted it with a smile. "What are your plans now? Tonight?" Ash said. His gaze shifted from Otto to Deepali and back to Otto.

"I'm useless if I'm overtired, but at the same time I don't see how I'll be able to sleep," Otto said. He took a tentative sip and passed the bottle to Deepali, who sniffed it, wrinkled her nose, and handed the bottle back to Ash.

Ash held the whiskey out to Otto, who shook his head no. Ash capped the bottle and put it away. He felt better with the alcohol flowing through his veins like gasoline, rousing his senses and heating his body.

"We could all go to one room. Keep watch," Deepali said.

"While Sean and Candice collect statues?" Ash said.

"You still care about that?" Otto said. "We're fighting for our lives here."

"I know that, but I—"

"Then start acting like it," he shouted.

Ash ate the last bit of his tongue and cheese sandwich. How could he explain he was doing both? But was he, really? Otto had a point. By all accounts he should be scaling mountains to get out of the valley, yet he knew that was impossible. Treemont—whoever the hell he was—planned things well, and he'd closed his trap efficiently and completely. The more Ash spun the situation around in his mind the more he realized that even if there was a footpath or tunnel out of the valley, which there most certainly was, it would be secured or blocked. So what did that really leave to do? Survive. It was perfect. The valley, Rodgers, everything was designed to force Ash and the others to play Treemont's crazy little game. The rules, statues and the rest of it were bullshit.

"I want out of this godforsaken valley," Deepali said, but something in her tone made Ash think she was just saying what she thought he and Otto wanted to hear.

"Do you have some piece of information I'm unaware of that will guide us safely from this valley?" Otto said, his tone dripping with condescension.

Deepali's gaze shifted to the forest, shadows swaying and writhing in the failing light. She shifted on her feet, bracelets clinking. She turned her dark eyes on Ash, her fierceness tempered by vulnerability and beauty. Deepali didn't even look at Otto. All her frustration and anger was focused on Ash. He was the one she wanted. He was the person she needed to guide her, help her, support her, be her partner, but Ash couldn't—wouldn't do that. This had been his worry. Otto had been right; they should've never let the woman join their little fellowship. Ash cracked his neck and rolled his shoulders as he fought with himself like Gollum. He was being an ass. The woman was afraid, that didn't mean she couldn't kick his ass. She was asking for a little humanity, and that didn't make her weak. It made her human. So why didn't Ash trust her?

Ash wasn't so far gone that his mother's mantra of 'practice kindness' didn't still hold sway in his psyche. He'd been slandered, abandoned, ridiculed, mocked, fired, and thrown in the trash, and he'd become a cynical, unforgiving, attack first, ask questions later person, but he still felt an ache in his chest when he saw someone in pain or disabled. His cheeks still burned when he saw injustice, bullying, or the downtrodden being abused. He was who he was, and though he often to tried to shake the morals of his past life, they stuck to him like superglue.

He took Deepali's arm and turned to Otto. "I think we can make it to the bear paddock at the base of the northern cliff face before dark. There should be caves and we've got some light left. I'm sticking with the plan and going on," Ash said. Though the sun had long passed over the lip of the southern valley wall, dusk hung in the air like smoke. When night came, Ash planned to slip away and go back down into the house's basement and explore the caves. Try and see if there was a way out of the valley. But there was a yeti down there. A pissed-off, eight-fingered yeti, and who knew what else?

"I've got a flashlight," Otto said. "But no food, and only a little water."

"Me also," Deepali said. Her bracelets clinked and clanged as she pulled a flashlight from her bag, and held it up as though displaying evidence.

"Great. We've got three flashlights," Ash said. "We can burn Bigfoot with our light beams."

Nobody laughed as the group plunged back into the forest, angling away from the snake paddock. Ash heard hissing once while the trio debated their next course of action, but there was nothing to be heard now except the whistling wind, the crack and snap of trees and the rattle of leaves.

22

Night was coming on, tall shadows crawling across the valley like boney fingers, when Ash and the others arrived at what Deepali's map labeled Paddock F, which had a rendering of the bear-like beast at its center. The forest of evergreens and spruce thinned as the trio approached the mountainside, two large wooden gates standing closed like the entrance to Jurassic Park. The fencing was twenty feet tall, and angled inward at the top, which would prevent even the most skilled and equipped climber from getting over the wall from within. To ensure full security, the upper part of the wall had nails and spikes protruding from its side, sharp dagger-like pimples waiting to rip and tear anything that tried to climb into the paddock from the outside.

"This was a bad idea," Otto said.

"In a series of them," Ash said.

Deepali sighed long and hard. "How the hell did you two even find your way to the Andes?" She stormed past them and strode up to the gates.

A crossbar lay between two grooves securing the doors, but there was no lock. She jerked on the handle, pulled up the latch, and slid the long bar out of the locking grooves. The gates swayed and creaked, the right one falling open a crack.

Otto took a step back and looked at Ash, who shook his head.

Deepali kicked open the gates and got low, scanning the paddock. She waved them on and disappeared through the open gates.

"Why do I feel like we're at Disney going ride to ride?" Otto said.

"Last ride for the day," Ash said. "Suck it up."

"No speed passes?" Deepali said.

Ash had no idea what the woman was talking about.

Otto sighed and trudged after Deepali.

Ash's nerves did summersaults. Otto's observation brought home again that they were being manipulated. They were all playing right into the madman's hands. By structuring things the way he had, Treemont ensured that members of the group would be in certain locations, within certain time periods. Treemont had been two steps ahead of them the entire way, so there was no reason to believe anything had changed. He... or she, was watching, waiting... for what? One to rise? All of them to die? But what would the purpose of the whole stupid affair be then?

Madness rarely has a purpose.

Ash searched his mind for people who might hold a grudge against him, injustices in and out of his control, but he could think of no reason why a stranger might want to kill him.

The inside of the paddock was the same as outside, like a Dr. Seuss machine had run through the forest cutting down trees and spitting the wood fence out its backend. There were no trees close to the wall, but the thin forest extended across the habitat to the rock face, where the mountainside turned sharply upward. A large cave mouth stood out on the side of the cliff face like a cockroach atop an ice cream sundae.

Insects buzzed and clicked, birds argued and sang, and a gentle breeze rattled leaves and pushed around dusty snow from the shadows that hadn't melted off. Nothing moved in the paddock, everything still and quiet.

"Let's get up there and out as fast as we can," Ash said.

"Do we all need to go?" Otto said. "It might make sense to leave a guard at the entrance. We could create a signal incase ther—"

A gunshot echoed off the stone walls of the valley, lingering for several seconds before dying away.

The three companions stood still, feet frozen to the hardpan, all of them looking over their shoulders toward the house, the direction the sound had come from.

"That can't be good," Deepali said.

Ash shrugged. "We should close the gate, and Otto's got a point. Someone keeping watch at the entrance could be helpful."

"We going to have the same stupid argument each time we have to make a decision?" Deepali said.

Ash and Otto stared at her wide-eyed.

She sighed loud and hard. "Who gets the statue if it's found? Certainly not the person who stays at the gate." She pulled down her knit cap, put her hands on her hips, and stared down Otto, who flinched like a beaten puppy.

"Let's worry about that when we've got it. I'm going," Ash said.

"Me also," Deepali said.

Otto said nothing, and when Ash didn't start walking, he stormed forward and pushed past his companions, angling up the hillside in the direction of the cave.

Ash and Deepali followed. No one spoke as they threaded through the sparse conifers and huge juniper bushes with tiny purple flowers. The scent was oddly therapeutic, and Ash sucked in fresh air, trying to calm his grumbling nerves.

A branch cracked and Ash and Otto paused, Deepali taking Ash's arm.

Something big was pushing through the forest, the creature's harsh, erratic breathing like a large engine about to stall. Trees swayed and bent, branches snapped and popped. The trio stayed still within the shadows of a large evergreen, waiting for the beast to pass.

Ash's heart galloped, pain shooting through his chest to the tips of his fingers. If the thing smelled them the way the Sasquatch had, they were all dead. He pulled his karambit from a pocket and opened it with a flick of the wrist. The fiberglass blade glinted dully in the failing light, but Ash felt better with the weapon in his hand.

The creature moved away, the sounds of its retreat faded, and Ash let out the breath he hadn't realized he'd been holding.

"That was close," Otto said.

"Any idea what direction it was going in?" Ash asked.

Nobody answered.

Ash could take a guess where the beast was going as night approached, but he didn't want to think about it.

Rocks slid and cracked, and miniature landslides of gravel and sand pushed the small party backward as they tried to scale the hillside. Small birds wheeled overhead, watching and occasionally yelling at the companions as they trekked. Ash thought of the crebain from the Fellowship of the Ring, how the dark cloud of birds could be seen miles away. Was Treemont watching the birds with the knowledge they were marking Ash's location? That couldn't have been planned, but like finding a dead body in the desert, it was never a bad idea to follow the birds if you were looking for something dead… or alive.

Ash threaded through rocks and boulders on an animal path worn into the hardpan. Devil grass and weeds lined the path, the forest falling away as the hillside got steeper. Natural stone steps led up to a plateau that stretched before the cave mouth and overlooked the valley. The view was amazing. Ash saw the house and the lake beyond, the monument, its spotlight waiting for moonlight. Ash strained to see, but he thought he saw a figure walking around the side of the house, but it was too far to be certain.

Bones, blood stains, and dried fat and gristle coated the stone before the cave entrance. It looked like the entry to a troll den. Ash pulled his flashlight and flicked it on, panning the light around the inside of the cave. Rocks and boulders lined the walls, and when Ash shined his light upward, the beam disappeared into darkness. A thin trail of black dots, dried blood by the looks of it, led into the cave.

Deepali and Otto pulled their lights, and Ash said, "Hold off for now. One should be enough. We don't want to alert the world, and I don't want to get stuck in there with no light if my batteries die."

Deepali nodded and dropped the light back into her bag.

Ash flipped the karambit on his finger, the blade singing through the air as he inched forward into the cave. He wrinkled his nose as he was assaulted by the scent of rot and decay. Paw prints, bone shards, and dried fat covered the floor, but no sound came from within. He paused and looked back. "Someone should stay at the entrance and keep watch. In case the thing shows. I know—"

"I'll stay," Otto said, no hesitation.

Deepali and Ash went on, moving slowly around boulders and piles of rubble.

"I'm surprised you're so open to exploration," Ash whispered, but his voice still rang in the tunnel like he'd screamed.

"Why's that? Because I'm a woman?" she said.

Ash chuckled. "For real? You know damn well it has nothing to do with you being a woman, and everything to do with you not wanting to play Treemont's game."

"This isn't about Treemont or his game," she said.

"What the hell is it about then?" Ash said.

"You just don't get it, do you? For some of us cryptids didn't destroy our lives. They're not the reason we're miserable, or see ourselves as failures. We do that all on our own."

Ash didn't understand, but he was smart enough to keep his mouth shut.

"I'm here for the beasts. That's the only reason I came in the first place. The chance to see some of the creatures I've dreamed about most of my life. Take care of them. Study the world's most unique creatures up close."

Ash said nothing, his flashlight beam bouncing off the stone walls as he trudged forward.

"Edo said he'd seen a Yeren. You know what that is?" Deepali said.

"Beast from the orient someplace," Ash said. "I didn't know that was his thing."

The shadow of Deepali's head nodded. "It's not... wasn't, really. But he said the thing resembled a giant bear, and there's been numerous accounts around the world of similar creatures. To actually see one, be able to verify something that the cryptid community has been trying to find for more than a hundred years. Don't you care about that? Or is it all still about you proving you're not crazy?"

Deepali's lecture made Ash think of Edo, and sorrow seeped through him. The image of the massive spider dropping on top of the man, flattening the life out of him. That sound, the pop, snap, and crunch of Edo's body being broken would haunt his sleep forever, as would

Auggie's screams and Emica's eyes. Leaving out Snake made Ash run through all the possible scenarios again.

The pair reached a fork in the cave and they stopped to drink water. The passage on the left appeared to plunge downward into blackness, but the cool air that pumped through the opening smelled fresh and earthy. The cave on the right was rank and smelled of rotting meat and festering wounds.

Ash and Deepali went left.

The plop and tap of water dripping, and the hiss and squeak of bats filled the cave. Ash angled the flashlight up, light spilling over the ceiling. Thousands of bats hung on and around stalactites of various lengths and thicknesses. The flock of bats undulated and swayed as one, wings flexing under the light.

Ash pointed the flashlight at the ground and the bats settled down, packed like bees on a rough ceiling.

"The tunnel is getting narrow," Deepali said. "We couldn't see the ceiling when we first entered."

Ash realized that. He also realized the walls were slowly closing in on the duo as they pressed forward, the tunnel plunging downward into colder air. The floor was slick, and water ran down the cave walls. Bugs and worms slithered and shifted in the darkness, the tapping of their feet like a swarm of cockroaches.

"Is that a light?" Deepali said.

Ash halted and flicked off the flashlight. Blackness filled the cave, a dark nothingness so complete Ash couldn't see his hand five inches from his face.

In the distance, a spec of green light leaked down the tunnel, but it was so far away Ash didn't know if he was actually seeing a light, or if it was his mind wanting to see something that wasn't there.

"Come on," Deepali said. The pounding of her footfalls as she hurried through the cave echoed off the walls, her bracelets tinkling.

A warning bell sounded in the back of Ash's mind, that primal alarm that told you something wasn't right, no matter how clear the path was.

"Careful," Ash yelled. His call bounced around the cave and fell dead.

Deepali's flashlight clicked on. She was about fifty yards down the tunnel. She put the beam on Ash, and said, "There's definitely something there. Come on."

"Slow up," Ash said. "There might be traps, holes, who knows what."

Deepali skidded to a stop.

When Ash arrived at her side, she snapped off her light. "See it?"

The green light had grown to a small rough circle, but it was still far off.

Behind them, a faint grumble resounded through the cave.

Ash stopped and listened hard, eliminating the dripping water, the breeze, and the incessant screech and tap of bugs, but the grumble was gone.

They doubled their pace, and the team of two covered the remaining two hundred yards quickly.

Green light emanated from a jade statue. The likeness of the giant bear with ferocious teeth and long claws outstretched sat atop a stone, light shining up through the statue and illuminating the chamber with pale green light.

The room was roughly spherical, and if Ash didn't know better, he would've guessed the chamber had been formed by a lava bubble, but that was impossible. Yet what did that really mean? Impossible. He'd learned in the last forty-eight hours that nothing was impossible.

The grumble was back, and footfalls drummed through the cave.

"Let's get that thing and get out of here," Ash said.

"Wait one second," Deepali said. "You warned me, now let me warn you. Be careful." She turned on her flashlight and scanned the floor, but there were no traps or impediments. The statue sat atop a roughly hewn pillar of cave stone, a light glowing from within and pushing through the jade figurine.

"How do you figure that light is powered?" Deepali said as she examined the walls and ceiling.

"Battery or fuel cell of some kind. Treemont did know when we'd be here, after all. He could have sent Rodgers up here," Ash said. He hadn't thought about the bot in hours. The little tin can could be two steps behind, watching them.

A fierce roar echoed through the chamber, a loud booming cry of anger that made Ash and Deepali spin and shine their flashlights down the tunnel.

A massive bear-like creature lumbered into view, walking on two short legs, all rippling muscles and dark fur, two long, thick fangs hanging from a mouth filled with knife-like teeth. The beast filled the tunnel as it attacked.

Ash looked at the glowing statue, then back at the creature as it charged. He sighed. "Great. Just great."

23

Ash searched the chamber for another way out, but found none. The giant bear barreled down the tunnel, galloping on four legs, head low, jaws distended. Ash darted toward the statue, daggers of green light cutting through the gloom, his flashlight beam dancing, shadows writhing. Fear oozed into him like a cancer, but he was already in motion, and there was no other way out anyway.

Deepali screamed and pressed her back to the wall next to the tunnel mouth. That was smart. The beast would come roaring into the chamber, run right past her, then she could slip away down the tunnel while Ash tangled with the beast. He reached the statue, the roar of the creature echoing through the tunnel. It was close, but Ash didn't look back. He scanned the glowing jade statue of the bear, looking for traps. His mind flashed back to his adolescence. He'd seen Raiders of the Lost Ark sixteen times in the theatre, and as he stood before the jade figurine, he saw the gold monkey head and the giant rock chasing Indy through the tunnel.

The bear burst into the chamber, raking the walls with its claws, roaring and growling as it rose on two legs, arms out like a boxer.

In his peripheral vision, Ash saw Deepali slip behind the beast and disappear into the dark tunnel beyond. She didn't look back. At least Ash didn't need to worry about the woman now. Had that been the plan all along? To leave Ash alone, trapped inside the mountain with a creature he couldn't hope to beat in a fight? He yanked the statue from its stone pedestal, dropped it in a pocket, and turned to face the creature.

The giant bear swung at Ash with its massive paw, two-inch curved claws at the end of each digit. Ash feinted back like Neo in the Matrix, the scratches on his chest pulling on their scabs, the beast's claws passing inches from his face.

Ash spun on the tips of his toes like a ballerina, pirouetting and slamming the side of the creature's head with his flashlight as he pulled his karambit and flicked it open.

The beast reeled, bringing up its paws to protect its head, but Ash was faster.

He spun again, the karambit singing, the blade slicing across the beast's forearms.

The cryptid howled as pain brought the creature to its knees. It clutched its wounds, whimpered, but then appeared to get its second wind. The mutant bear turned its black glassy eyes on Ash as it pushed itself to its feet, blood dripping from its wounds.

Ash turned off the flashlight and the cave fell into partial darkness, the faint light that had illuminated the jade statue still sending a cloud of pale green light through the darkness that spilled across the chamber.

Flight or fight.

Ash turned the flashlight on and off several times in fast succession, strobing light into the creature's eyes as it came at him. Ash ran straight at the creature, the two on a collision course that would break Ash in half.

The bear swung its immense paw, and Ash dodged, veering sharply and slipping beneath the beast's outstretched arm. As he passed the bear, Ash lashed out with the karambit, slashing the back of the creature's leg.

The beast bucked and heaved, reaching out for Ash as it fell to a knee.

Ash cut into the tunnel and turned it on. He was forty-two. Not out of shape, but certainly not fit. He was twelve thousand feet up, where the air was as thin as a sparrow's fart, and Ash's lungs burned after twenty strides, pain cutting across his chest, his scratches pulling and shifting. He slowed, sucking for air, but he didn't stop. Grunts, growls, and roars chased Ash up the tunnel, but he heard no footfalls.

He spun the karambit on his finger as he jogged, looking over his shoulder every few seconds. Darkness pressed in on him, his head pounding in rhythm with his heart like when he had a fever. Discomfort inched through every joint like maggots, his throat dry and sore, stomach aching with stabs of pain.

He reached the fork in the tunnel and found Deepali waiting.

"Are you alright?" she said.

Ash didn't stop jogging, though he'd slowed to a turtle's pace. "Let's... go..."

Ash's flashlight dimmed, and blinked out. He slowed and waited for Deepali to light her candle. When light blossomed through the tunnel again, Ash pulled back his arm, intent on hurling the dead light into the stone wall and watching it break, but something held him back, some survival instinct learned long ago and deeply buried. He had nothing, so even an unusable flashlight might serve an unforeseen purpose.

The duo ran on through the cave, the ceiling giving way to deep blackness above. The commotion had stirred the bats, and the flying rats darted and flew around the cave, several divebombing Ash and Deepali as they ran. The beasts didn't like direct light, and Deepali worked her light like a gun, putting the flashlight's beam on any creature that came near.

"You need help?" Otto called through the cave.

The cave walls fell away and the massive cavern that opened onto the mountainside stretched out before them. Ash didn't stop, and he jogged past Otto and punched him on the shoulder.

"What the hell was that for?" Otto said.

Deepali yelled, "What were you doing out here? Napping? You were supposed to warn us if the beast showed. How did it get by you? Did you hide?"

Otto stared at the woman, his mouth falling open.

Ash put his hand on Otto's shoulder, and he flinched. "You OK? What happened? Why didn't you warn us?" As the questions rolled from Ash's tongue, a horrible thought burrowed into him like a tapeworm. Otto is Treemont, and he didn't expect to see Ash and Deepali again.

Otto blinked, but said nothing.

"You awake? Hello!" Deepali said.

"I didn't see anything," Otto said. "I was here the entire time. I heard some commotion down the tunnel, but I stayed here. You were attacked?"

"Give me that flashlight," Ash said, and Deepali handed over the light.

Ash searched the floor, scanning the ground in the tunnel, then moving out onto the precipice that reached out over the valley. The ground was stained with blood, dried fat and gristle, and shards of bones. There were paw prints everywhere, and it was impossible to distinguish new from old. A more experienced tracker might have been able to discern something, but he couldn't.

"You don't believe me?" Otto said.

"I don't believe anything anymore," Ash said. "Let's go before that thing sneaks up on us."

"There must be another way in," Otto said. "Did you see side passages? Any sign where it may have come in from?"

The fork in the tunnel filled Ash's mind's eye, but he said nothing.

The trio climbed back down to the valley floor the way they'd come, darkness settling over the forest, the day chorus giving way to the night symphony. A faint orange-white glow leaked over the western rim of the valley as the sun sank below the rim of the world. Another night had come to the Atavism Special Animal Sanctuary, and the party was down to five, as far as Ash knew. Sean and Candice could already be dead.

When the small party arrived at the tall set of double wood doors, one stood slightly ajar, shifting with each push of the wind. The latch was open, and the board that fell into the locking grooves and secured the doors had been removed.

"No beast did that," Otto said.

"Nope," Ash said as he flicked his wrist, spun the karambit on his index finger, and used the momentum to snap the blade closed. He slipped it into a pocket without Deepali noticing.

Otto was a different matter. His eyes locked on the pocket where Ash had dropped the knife, then they shifted to his other pocket which contained the statue. Otto said, "You find the statue?"

"Yup," Ash said.

Deepali stared at Ash, waiting for him to spill the entire story.

Had Deepali seen him take the statue? She certainly hadn't seen him put it in his pocket. She'd been hightailing it down the tunnel saving her own ass. Ash said nothing.

"And?" Otto said. "Where is it?"

Ash did his best to fain sorrow, and he looked back forlornly at the animal path, then up at the dark opening that marked the cave mouth.

"You don't have it?" Deepali shrieked. "Bull turd. That's the biggest pile of American shit I've ever heard."

She stalked through the open gate, then realized she was alone, and turned around and came back. She stood behind Otto, arms crossed, foot tapping.

Otto looked back at her, then at Ash as he lifted his eyebrows.

There'd been a shift in allegiance, but Ash didn't care.

Otto, either knowing he had no right to the statue anyway so what was the point fighting, or sensing he'd lose a fight with Ash if he pressed the issue, decided to do nothing.

"So that's it then?" Deepali said. "What do you have in your pockets?"

"A box without hinges, key or lid, but golden treasure inside is hid," Ash said.

Otto chuckled. The wind pushed around his hair, and dirt marred his face.

"Look I don't understand your redneck language, OK?" Deepali said.

Otto and Ash laughed.

"Redneck?" Ash said.

"I don't think that word means what you think it means," Otto said.

"I believe the insult you're looking for is geek," Ash said.

Deepali shook her head and planted her hands on her hips.

"Gollum? The Hobbit? Didn't your ma or pa ever read you The Hobbit?" Otto said.

"Sure. Short people with furry feet, a magic ring, a dragon. So the hell what?"

Ash sighed. "Forget it."

The trio left the paddock and Ash found a large dead branch and used it to secure the gates. The dead tree limb wouldn't last under sustained pounding, but it might slow the creature down. While searching for the large branch, Ash and Otto found three sticks they made into staffs by stripping away small sucker branches.

Blackness pressed in as the companions worked their way through the forest, sticking to the path, Deepali's flashlight beam cutting through the murkiness. Otto hadn't brought out his light, but he did offer up the last of his water.

Ash had the feeling he was being watched. He'd felt that way continuously since arriving in the valley, but it was stronger now than ever. Something stalked them from the shadows.

"Let's take a break for a second?" Ash said.

"If you need it," Otto said as he took the final pull of his water.

Deepali jerked to a halt, bracelets clanging.

"Jesus," Ash snapped. "You're like a constant alarm."

Both men stared at Deepali.

When Deepali ignored them, Ash said, "Deepali, kill your light for a second."

She sighed louder, but complied.

Ash dropped into a crouch, scanning the forest behind them the way they'd come.

"What the hell—" Otto said.

"Be quiet. Just act normal, like we're taking a break," Ash said.

"We are taking a break," Deepali said.

Anger surged in Ash, but he beat it back, taking a deep breath and rolling his shoulders.

Moonlight cut through the tree canopy and shadows danced under every branch, behind every stone, and next to every bush. The forest shifted and swayed, the gentle breeze pushing around dead leaves, brown pine needles, and the occasional small tornado of snow.

Ash went tree to tree with his eyes, going slow, focusing. There was something there, he could feel its presence, but he couldn't see it.

This went on for several minutes before Deepali clicked her light back on and started for the house. "You boys have fun. I think I'm done for the night."

Ash said nothing, Deepali's flashlight beam bouncing around in the darkness.

"We're gonna let her walk up there alone? In the dark?" Otto said.

Ash shook his head as he started after her.

The trio didn't speak as they threaded their way to the yellow path that led to the front of the house. They entered the atrium, the fresh scent of water and earth assailing them. Moonlight slanted through the glass windows, and the slick green leaves of tropical plants shined as if wet. The table at the center of the atrium stood empty.

The house beyond was quiet. The trio moved through the atrium into the house, and Ash closed the door behind him. He said, "Anyone getting food?"

Deepali didn't answer. She climbed the steps without a word, leaving Ash and Otto standing alone in the foyer.

"What the hell do you think that thing out there really was?" Otto said.

Ash was surprised at the sudden question. "You heard the description. Could it be Edo's Yeren?"

Otto raised an eyebrow. "You knew about that?"

"Deepali told me."

"Could be a Yeren, an Ozark Howler, many different things. As I think of all the cryptids listed in the sanctuary library, creatures resembling giant bears are the most common. Makes sense, right? I mean, to someone who's never seen a grizzly bear, in the right light the big ones look scary. Odd fur coloring is easy to explain."

Ash rubbed his forehead. "It's all just so crazy, you know? I thought I'd seen all the crazy there was. Apparently, I didn't know shit."

Otto laughed. "You know you need something to eat. Let's go."

There was cold ham on a platter with bread, potato salad with vinegar, and bread that had long gone cold. There were bottles of wine on the sidebar, with pitchers of water, but Rodgers was nowhere to be found, and when Ash called, the bot didn't come.

"Sean's right about that tin can," Ash said. "I could really use a martini."

The two men ate in silence, and when they were done, they went up to their rooms. The house creaked and moaned in the silence, and Ash thought he heard classical music playing far off. Maybe in one of the rooms.

The duo got to the top of the steps, and paused.

Then Ash did something on impulse, something he didn't exactly understand. He pulled the statue of the giant bear from a pocket and showed it to Otto. "A piece of this is yours," he said.

Ash expected a wry comment, a cynical account of how that would work, but instead Otto nodded, headed down the hall, and disappeared into his room.

Ash stood before his door, glancing up and down the hallway. He was going back down into the maze, but it was important to keep up appearances. He tapped in his code and entered his room, letting the door click closed behind him. He'd give his companions time to go to sleep, then he'd find a way out of the valley.

24

Ash searched his room, but nothing appeared out of place. The water in his basin was cool, but there was a clean towel and decanter of wine on the washstand. He poured a glass of vino, and went out onto the terrace, the faint glow of the atrium below, moonlight knifing across the forest. Clouds fleeted past, the chill breeze pushing out the remainder of the storm. Bright, clear patches of star-filled sky stood out in the clouds. When Ash saw a true clear sky, he was always amazed at how much light pollution there was. Even Stony Creek, where the Northern Californian climate produced clear skies, didn't compare to stargazing at twelve thousand feet.

Something howled, and Ash went to the railing and leaned over it, the sharp edge biting into his stomach. Nothing moved along the house. Everything was dark shadows and stillness. He tossed back his wine and went to get another, but froze. Sean stood watching him from his balcony.

Ash waved.

Sean disappeared back into his room without a sign.

He went inside, blew out the candles, flicked off the single light, and sat on the edge of the bed in the darkness facing the door. The house creaked and moaned, but the place was made of stone. Conversation and footfalls traveled, and he'd hear anyone who came down the hall, even Rodgers.

Rodgers. Where had that bot got to? It had disappeared at the perfect time. Emica's death, suspicion and mistrust among the players. Perhaps he should have let Sean take its head off. But would it matter? Treemont could have three spares. Or a hundred. Was that the failsafe if things went bad? If players revolted? Bots with guns?

Ash took off his boots, tied them together by the laces, and set them aside. Then he rolled his jacket like a sleeping bag with his gloves, hat, clothes, flashlight and karambit inside. Ash wrapped the lace-connected boots around the jacket to make a tight ball. He rummaged through his rucksack and retrieved black long underwear and socks, which he slipped into.

He collected his bundle and padded silently across the room, barely lifting his feet off the slick wood floor. Ash eased through the half-open door onto the balcony, and dropped his package over the railing. It hit the ground below with a faint smack and puff. He waited, watching to see if lights came on, or if people came out onto the terraces to investigate.

Everything was still.

Static ran down Ash's spine and he jumped, trying to shake the feeling. Was it good or bad it appeared nobody had heard his little drop? Ash was underestimating these people and he needed to stop. Sean was probably watching him even now, from the shadows of his balcony.

No matter. What was done was done.

He slipped back into his room, closed the door, but left it unlocked. Ivy grew on the side of the house, and in a pinch Ash might be able to climb to his balcony. Like the flashlight. When you've got nothing, you must use everything.

Out in the hallway, Ash took extra care, holding the lock open as he slowly eased the door closed. The faint click and beep was unavoidable, so he moved fast, running down the hall in the darkness like a ghost. When he got to the top of the steps he plunged down, stopping five steps down. He lay on the steps with his chin above the second-floor landing, watching the hallway in both directions. Nothing.

He stood and jumped down the remaining steps two at a time, trying to make a little noise. Let them know he wasn't sneaking. The sitting room was dark, as was the kitchen and dining room, but there was salami, tongue, cheese, bread, and water on the sideboard. Ash took a plate, grabbed some cheese, bread, and a bottle of wine, and sat at the table to wait.

Fifteen minutes passed. Ash ate, drank, waited. Nobody came. Not even Otto.

"Rodgers?" Ash called.

The faint chatter of the night chorus and the distant thrum of the house filled the room. Moonlight angled across the valley like spotlights; thin, tattered clouds streaking across the sky.

Rodgers didn't come. He could hide, watch the kitchen. The bot eventually had to return there. So far it had kept to its promise of food being available at all times. That was, if things didn't change.

Ash poured another glass of wine and knocked it back fast.

What if food was somehow withheld? Then what? Would they kill the creatures of the valley for food? Could they? They had the six bullets… maybe five if it had been Sean's shot they'd heard that afternoon. Things had escalated steadily since they'd arrived and there was no reason to believe that wouldn't continue.

After an hour, Ash wandered the first floor of the house, looking in closets, searching the kitchen cabinets. To his amazement, he found batteries, a pack of six new D cells, the size needed for the flashlight.

The euphoria of the jackpot didn't last long, because as he'd feared, the food locker was locked, as was the icebox, a large walk-in type cold box with an area beneath the floor for ice. A pipe came up through the floor and was cold to the touch, the house's geothermal heating and cooling system doing its job. The door leading to the basement was locked, but Ash could pick it easily when the time came. All he needed was a fork with all its prongs bent back except one, and there was plenty of forks.

Ash stopped in the sitting room for a few minutes, then disappeared down the back hallway. He pressed his back to the wall. He could almost feel the camera lenses focusing in on him. When he was comfortable nobody was following, he pulled off his socks, cracked open the backdoor, and slipped into the cold night, leaving the door slightly ajar. His feet stung as he sprinted around the side of the house to where his jacket and boots waited. As it turned out the precaution wasn't necessary, but if he'd been followed, walking around in his long underwear was more defendable than if he'd been bundled up like he was making an attempt to summit Everest.

He collected his bundle and sprinted back to the house. It was cold now, well below freezing, and the ground was slick. Ash's lungs stung, but he picked up his pace, wanting to get back in the house so he could get dressed.

When Ash reached the backdoor, he found it locked. He stood dazed as he searched the house's windows for any signs of life. He slipped on his clothes, pulled on his socks and boots, and encased himself in a warm cocoon. Nothing moved on the thin patch of field that separated the house from the forest. Above, the veranda where they'd all met, shared stories and drinks, stood silent and dark. He felt the karambit through the fabric of his pants and was reassured. He loaded the flashlight with new batteries and dropped the four spares into a back pocket.

Ash worked his way around the house to the north, passing under Sean's balcony and moving around to the front of the atrium. There was a notch where the atrium melded into the foyer of the house, and Ash slipped into it, blending into the darkness like a wraith. He stood still as stone, watching the way he'd come.

Nothing.

Ash was starting to feel the fool. He felt like he was being watched constantly, but maybe nobody gave a shit what he did? Where he went? Problem was, he just couldn't sell himself that. It was possible the backdoor got blown closed in the wind, but the wind couldn't have locked it.

Ten minutes slid by, the cold biting into Ash, and when nobody showed he inched along the outside of the atrium toward the entrance.

He'd only gone a few steps when he tripped. Something lay on the ground in the darkness. Moonlight reflected off the atrium's glass windows, and as Ash bent to see what was on the ground, he jerked back and fell to the hardpan.

A beast that looked half man, half wolf, lay dead, a thin coating of frost covering the corpse's gray hair. It looked to have walked on two, long jointed legs with claws, its arms short and lanky. White film covered dark eyes, a long snout extending off the beast's face and ending in a white nose.

A dark bullet hole marred the center of the creature's chest, a frozen patch of dark blood covering the ice-covered fur. In the moonlight it felt as though the corpse watched him, waiting to come alive and chomp Ash with the razor-sharp teeth glinting within its powerful jaws.

A cough echoed off the house, a faint exhalation that was barely discernable above the push of the wind. Ash rose and pressed himself to the side of the atrium, staring into the forest. Trees swayed and leaves rattled. An owl hooted five times, louder each time, as if saying, "Humans, go to bed. You're drunk." Ash waited still as the seconds ticked by, then minutes.

A tall shadow appeared at the edge of the forest, a slender figure with a long snout and gangly legs. The shadow eased along the edge of the woods, then disappeared.

Ash gathered his courage to follow, but he put his back to the wall again when Otto came around the side of the house, all his attention focused on where the shadow had disappeared into the forest.

Ash pulled his flashlight but didn't follow. He waited, the night symphony serenading him until he felt enough time had gone by. He darted across the open area between the house and the woods, hiding behind a thick tree trunk and scanning the forest. He couldn't see Otto, but the man's fresh footprints were easy to find in the thin coating of frost that covered everything in the valley as the moisture from the storm cooled.

The prints trailed away to the east, following the edge of the woods around the northern side of the garden with the monument at its center. Otto's prints were joined by a second, much thinner and larger set of prints. Otto had found the creature's trail. Or the beast had found his? Ash wanted to turn on the flashlight and scan the ground, look for clues, but that would alert everyone in the valley to his position.

The tracks turned sharply south, cutting across the wide cone of light created by moonlight shining through the giant ring at the top of the monument. The light currently fell on the northern slope, just east of the bear paddock. There was nothing there.

A scream ahead. A pop and a crack.

Ash picked up his pace, looking back over his shoulder every few moments, cognizant of the fact that this could be a trap. There was a roar, then a slap and tear, like meat being torn from bone. A hiss rose above the wind and the chirp and buzz of insects fell away.

He pulled up short when he came around a huge juniper bush, sharp leaves biting his face, small berries squishing against his cheek.

Two lone figures stood in the moonlight, silhouetted before the giant stone monument. One was clearly Otto. He was the smaller figure hanging from the creature's claws.

Ash inched forward until he was thirty feet away, and flicked on the flashlight.

The beast he'd seen the prior day—the Jersey Devil with its wings clipped—bent over Otto, pulling pieces of flesh from his torso and throwing back his head, tossing the chunks of meat down his gullet. The creature froze under the harsh glare of the flashlight, dark blood dripping down its narrow chin, fat and skin stuck in its long teeth. It dropped what was left of Otto, and turned its shining yellow eyes on Ash.

He shuddered, worry, fear, and pain pulsing through him like an electrical shock. His eyes went wide, the scratches on his chest throbbing in rhythm with his heart. Time slowed, the wind died away, and the insect symphony hadn't returned from break.

When the creature spoke, Ash's mouth fell open a crack, and though he wanted to turn and run, his brain just wouldn't issue the order.

"Whatsss it that yousssss wantsssss." The voice was snake-like, and it slithered from the creature's lips like a maggot into rotten meat.

Ash said nothing as he slowly backed away, his brain finally catching up with his flight or fight instinct. Whether this thing was a Jersey Devil or not meant nothing to him, and Deepali's speech ran through his mind as the beast inched forward.

"It understandssss?"

It was calling Ash it. How quaint.

Ash turned off the flashlight, plunging the area around the atrium into semi-darkness. Moonlight knifed across the clearing as he backed away, slipping around a bush, his gaze constantly shifting to Otto's fallen form where it lay crumpled on the hardpan.

The devil's long shadow fell across the tree line as it came at Ash, long arms and legs becoming one as they churned and the creature picked up its pace.

Ash ran, not looking back, arms and legs pumping as his lungs fought for oxygen. He'd try and make the front door. If it was locked, he'd cross that bridge when he came to it. His lungs burned as he struggled for air, pain lancing his knees.

He spared a glance over his shoulder and didn't see the creature, but Ash didn't slow. Sweat dripped down his back, his heart in overdrive, head pounding. He rounded the front corner of the atrium and everything was still and quiet. He skidded to a stop and pulled on the door handle, and to Ash's relief the door opened, and he passed inside.

The atrium was quiet, and Ash stood there, panting, waiting for the door to shutter and shake as the beast tried to get in. But the door didn't move, and only the wind howled. Ash strode quickly through the atrium toward the front door, but he paused when a strange glint from outside caught his eye.

He worked his way through a series of tropical potted plants to the glass wall of the atrium. It had only been an hour since he'd left his room, and he'd already had enough. He stared through the glass at the corpse of the strange beast, heart thumping. The creature's eyes were open, and it looked to Ash as though the dead beast was smiling at him.

25

Nerves crackling and stretching, ears ringing, stomach aching with angst, Ash slipped into the house and left Otto behind. He didn't like the idea of leaving the man's body to be eaten, but without a weapon he didn't think risking his life made sense, given there was no way he could bring Otto back. He was gone beyond this world, and they were down to four. The idea that Otto might be carrying his statue poked its evil head above Ash's barrier of rationality, but was quickly batted down.

He stood in the foyer, blackness leaking from the sitting room. There was no fire, and no lights burned.

Four of nine were left. What was the fifth verse of the damnable poem? Temple, thy dreams with the trees. Nature thy god alone. Worship the sun and the breeze. Altars where none atone. Had Otto atoned? If so, for what?

The house creaked and popped as if speaking, but it wasn't the sound of footsteps or movement. It was a hundred years of cut blue granite pressing on the earth, stretching the wood paneled walls and the thick floor joists.

Ash was paralyzed with indecision. The last hour had taken most of the wind from his sails. Should he go on or go to bed? He was very tired, but he didn't think he'd be able to sleep. So the choice was go back to his room and waste time staring at his dark ceiling, or press forward. There was time to sleep when he was dead. He rolled his shoulders. Bad analogy.

He took one step and the corresponding creak and pop froze Ash in place. There was a bump and rattle from upstairs, perhaps a door closing. He slipped off his boots and tiptoed through the sitting room, past the kitchen and dining room to the hallway beyond.

He paused, a shadow moving at the end of the hall by the door to the basement stairwell. A tinkle, like tiny windchimes twisting in a gentle breeze, floated down the hall. Ash moved quickly, keeping tight to the wall, head low.

The floor popped so loudly it sounded like a gunshot in the stillness and Ash froze.

The shadowy figure spun. "Who's there? I've got Sean's gun."

Ash's abs hurt from containing his laughter. It was Deepali and that was twenty kinds of bullshit, or was it? For all he knew Candice and Sean could be dead. He dropped to the ground like he'd been asked to do pushups, then lowered himself onto his stomach. He lay still on the hallway floor, eyes up and watching Deepali.

She didn't move. Her dark form easy to see from Ash's angle on the floor, moonlight leaking into the passageway from the open kitchen door.

Ash and Deepali stayed that way for a long time, wind pushing at the house, owls hooting and night birds singing. Ash was just starting to cramp when he heard Deepali rummaging around in her bag. If she pulled a light, he'd be seen. So what? What could she do?

A pinprick of light knifed through the darkness at the end of the hall. Metal scraped on metal. The thin cone of light was focused on the basement door lock. Shadows of Deepali's hands furiously working the lock danced on the wall, the woman's bracelets jingling. Picking a lock is hard. Doing it in the dark was harder, but again Ash grudgingly gave the woman respect. If she turned on a flashlight, half the valley would see its glow in the deep of night.

What was Deepali up to? Why did she want to go into the basement? It was nasty, cold, and dark, and Candice had shared much of their adventure in the blackness with most of the group. Deepali knew there was a Yeti-type creature prowling the tunnels, and she knew Ash hadn't found a way out. That told him one of two things. One, she didn't believe what Candice had said and he and Sean had confirmed, or b, she knew something he didn't. Was Deepali, for all her 'we're in a fight for our lives', still playing the game? Or just looking for a way out like he was?

Or was Deepali Treemont?

A creature roared outside. It sounded like a Sasquatch to Ash. He silently chuckled to himself. That was his world now, where he could recognize cryptids by their native calls. That guy sounded angry.

The click of the door lock opening echoed down the hallway. The thin light blinked out, the door creaked open, and Deepali disappeared through it.

Ash pressed himself to his feet like a surfer getting up on a long board, and he was kneeling beside the door before it clicked closed. He grabbed the knob and turned it, so the bolt was drawn back, and held it as the door closed.

Then the tap and click of the lock being turned as Deepali secured the door, the faint sounds of footfalls as she retreated down the steps.

Ash's wrist hurt. He still had the doorknob twisted to the open position, so though Deepali had locked it on her side, the locking mechanism wouldn't engage until he released the door handle and let the bolt insert into the striker plate. He eased the door open a crack and waited, his hand aching from the pressure of holding back the lock bolt.

When his forearm spasmed, he eased open the door and slipped through, releasing the handle and letting the door close with a tap and click.

He stood still in the blackness. He felt the karambit and batteries in his back pocket, the flashlight in his jacket. He listened hard, but all he heard was dripping water, the thrum of the house, and the faint singing wind. The steps were made of wood, and when he got to the bottom, Ash put his boots back on, lacing them up quickly as he sat on the steps in the darkness.

The maze wasn't so much a maze, but a disorganized mess of tunnels that had grown and changed with the house. Old storage rooms, root cellars, and a variety of chambers with bars like prison cells. There were accounts in the sanctuary library about the early days of bringing and acclimating animals to the valley. The cells had been used as a transition tool. The two stumps where the Jersey Devil's wings had been cut off seemed like a pretty severe transition tool to Ash.

He stumbled upon Deepali's flashlight beam as she backtracked to the staircase. She hadn't been with Ash, Sean and Candice when they'd ventured into the basement the first time, so Ash figured she was lost. He hid behind a stack of old crates that had markings on them Ash couldn't understand. The language looked like Arabic.

Deepali cursed, her flashlight beam coming back in Ash's direction. He stayed hidden, keeping an eye on her as she fumbled around in the dark. She was making so much noise he was sure Rodgers or Sean would arrive soon. The woman made no attempt at stealth, but who in their right mind would be down in the tunnels in the middle of the night? Ash suddenly felt the fool for following her.

Ash decided to stay ahead of her and darted into the shadows, running down the dark tunnel. Ash knew the passage well. He'd backtracked down it several times his first time in the basement. The glow of Deepali's light blossomed behind Ash as he worked his way around the large boulder that led to the old mining operation. He entered the chamber silently, dropping into a crouch as he scanned the darkness.

A sword of light cut through the opening to the tunnel, illuminating a section of the old mine. Ash saw his footprints in the dirt covered floor. He saw Sean's, and Candice's, and…

The cave was silent, save for the tapping of footfalls which were getting closer. Deepali's flashlight beam cut across the mine and Ash hid behind the same derailed mining cart he had the first time he'd been forced to hide in the mine.

Deepali coughed and sputtered as she entered the chamber, her harsh flashlight beam spilling over the room. Her bracelets jingled as she came forward.

A shadow, roughly humanoid in shape, slipped into the room behind her.

Ash almost called out, but held his breath. Whoever... whatever the shadow was, it was keeping its distance, watching Deepali as Ash was.

She got to the center of the chamber and stopped, her sigh of frustration rising above the cold breeze. Her flashlight beam jerked around, shadows danced, and it looked like Deepali had turned around and was heading back to the tunnel she'd come from.

A low gurgling growl froze her feet to the cave floor, and she rocked back.

A shadow inched forward and disappeared into darkness. Deepali shined her light around, and Ash heard her panicked breathing, the tinkle of her bracelets.

He pointed his flashlight where the shadow had been and turned it on. A cone of light shot across the chamber, leaking into the tunnel beyond, and behind piles of rubble and under old rusted mining equipment.

The white Yeti stood ten feet tall, its dark red eyes staring defiantly into the light.

Deepali stood between them, eyes wide.

The beast lunged forward, moving past Deepali and charging toward Ash with incredible speed. But even as the beast's long strides took the Yeti past Deepali, it lashed out with its left hand.

Deepali screamed, an earsplitting wail that sent a chill through Ash. She dropped her flashlight and it hit the floor with a pop, its beam arcing into the shadows. Deepali's eyes went wide, and she coughed, her face covered in blood. She dropped to her knees, then onto her stomach as she fell out of Ash's flashlight beam into darkness.

The creature pounded its chest as it came on, screaming and roaring, mouth open, teeth glinting.

Ash clicked the light off and darted right, heading for the far door. He looked back only once, but couldn't see Deepali's body in the blackness. Most likely her bullet was in her jacket, but it wasn't worth the risk to try and get it.

The beast grunted and growled as it pursued him.

The tunnel opened up, and Ash felt warm air mixing with the cold. He slowed. The sound of pursuit had faded.

Ash hid behind a boulder and waited. The beast could be trying to sneak up on him, trick him into thinking everything was OK. Minutes passed, ten... fifteen. After half-an-hour, Ash stood and snapped on his flashlight, scanning the tunnel in both directions.

There was nothing but rocks, spider webs, and stone walls.

The first time around, Ash and his companions retreated back to the house with their tails between their legs. He looked up and down the tunnel again. He was looking for a way out of the valley, and he knew the passage beyond the mine led to the valley.

He pulled his shirt from his pants and put the flashlight beneath his shirt, dulling its beam to a faint orange glow.

Ash continued down the tunnel, easing around a chunk of stone that hid the entrance to a narrow passageway. He worked his way through the new cavern slowly, using his small cloud of light to avoid stones and holes. Most of the tunnel Ash trekked through had been formed naturally when the Andes sprouted from the Earth's crust fifty million years ago, but there were spots that had clearly been blasted or chiseled.

One such spot was braced with black wood supports that sagged under a century of weight. Ash pulled the light from under his shirt and shined its full strength down the narrow shaft. The beam disappeared into blackness. Warmer air pushed from the passageway, and the faint scent of sulfur. He focused the light down the narrow tunnel and went on, staying close to the rock wall. No bugs crawled on the floor, no water dripped. The tunnel was silent save for the whistling of the breeze.

Piles of sand dotted the floor under gaps in the shored-up ceiling. The floor was chiseled stone, and his boots tapped and clicked with each footfall. He'd gone fifty yards when the flashlight beam illuminated a natural cavern beyond. The imaginary mice stopped digging into his shoulders as he passed from the manmade tunnel into the open space.

The space was empty save for several large boulders and an old crate that was nothing but a pile of hinges, a latch, and decayed wood. He went on for what seemed like hours, the cavern expanding and contracting like lungs, the floor tilting, shards of stone spiking from the floor and walls.

He slowed when he saw the blasting cylinder grooves running along the cave walls. The passageway narrowed to a three-foot-wide crack in the mountain, a heavy coating of rubble covering the floor. Ash stuck his light into the passage, and something glinted at its end, stone angling away into darkness above.

As he approached the end of the tunnel, the glint turned into a reflection, and Ash arrived at the end of the passage to find a metal door blocking his path.

The doorframe was set into the stone, big lag bolts and rivets holding the steel in place. Two large hinges were mounted onto the rock, a metal rod running between them and holding the door in position. A circular door handle like a captain's boat wheel sat in the middle of the rectangular door, a key lock with a cover over it at its center. There were no lights, or switches, and as he examined the door, Ash realized it wasn't very old. He traced the outline of the door with his index finger, looking for a gap, but there was none. It had taken someone a great amount of time and effort to put the door in place. But why? The answer to that question was all too clear.

Once in the valley, you weren't meant to leave.

Ash placed the flashlight on the ground, using a stone to angle the beam upward, and gripped the door handle. He strained to turn it, jerking and pulling on the slick metal. It didn't budge. Anger and frustration simmered within him. He'd been bested around every turn and if it weren't for the incompetence of his fellow prisoners, he might already be dead.

He screamed, pounding on the door, the metal booming. He'd had enough. He was done. Ash picked up the flashlight and examined the door again, taking a mental picture. He headed back through the cavern the way he'd come. He went extra slow and quiet when he passed the entrance to the mine, not wanting to alert the Yeti, and his thoughts drifted to Deepali and her crumpled body that lay in the chamber beyond.

That wasn't his problem. Finding a way to get that door open. That was his problem.

26

Ash made his way through the basement in the blackness, slowly easing around corners, being silent. The house creaked and moaned, but he heard no footsteps or other signs of life. In one of the storage rooms he found an old crate still filled with its coconut fiber packing material, and he climbed in and pulled the box's lid into place. His breathing echoed in the confined space, and he leaned his head on the box's side and closed his eyes.

He needed to catch some sleep. His circadian clock was fairly accurate, and he could usually set the alarm in his head, but he was exhausted, and he worried that once he fell asleep, he'd be like Rip Van Winkle.

His head galloped, and he took deep breaths, trying to ease his nerves, which were doing jumping jacks on his spine. Things had gone south so fast he was having trouble keeping it all straight. Otto's death, then Deepali. Weariness overtook him and he fell asleep.

He woke in darkness, bladder screaming, coconut fibers stuck to his face, and he climbed out of the crate and urinated in a corner. There wasn't much—he hadn't had food or drink since his midnight snack and his stomach growled and squeaked.

As he exited the basement into the house, dawn leaked over the horizon, and Ash's third morning in the valley dawned bright and clear. The last of the storm had blown through, and though the air was brisk, the sun beat down on the valley and burned off the morning frost, mist lifting through the trees like smoke. He went to his room and cleaned up, but saw no one.

He ate breakfast alone, sipping his coffee in the stillness on the portico. The selection of food was poor; dry toast, thin butter, and cold scrambled eggs. No juice or drinks, only water. Rodgers didn't appear. As the group of hunters diminished, so did Treemont's hospitality. As far as Ash knew, he, Candice and Sean were the only ones left, and he'd alienated them by siding with Otto. He was on his own. He chuckled to himself. Hadn't he been for a long time?

On his way out of the tunnels the prior night, Ash had been afraid to go back into the mine and retrieve Deepali's bullet and spider figurine. He considered going back down into the basement to retrieve them, but decided against it. He had two bullets, and assuming the shot he'd heard the prior day had been Sean's, he and Candice only had two bullets left.

He also had two statues; the Bigfoot and the bear. Three more and he'd ensure victory. He'd stashed the figurines in the woods, but the bullets were in a back pocket, his folded karambit in the other.

He was walking down the main path, heading for the lake, the sun beating on his neck, when a gunshot echoed off the cliff walls.

Ash darted from the path and slipped behind a tree, searching for the source of the noise.

Ahead, the lake glistened in the early morning sun, shards of light cutting across the path and the woods beyond. Nothing moved at the edge of the forest, and everything beneath the tree canopy was still and full of shadows.

He slipped from cover, but didn't use the path. He stayed in the shadow of the tree line, working his way toward the lake where he expected to find a pedestal with a missing Loch Ness Monster statue.

The echo of the gunshot had died away, and the forest symphony again rang through the valley. The woods gave way to the lake's edge and Ash was forced to leave his cover, but all was quiet. As expected, at the end of the dock a pillar with Nessie carved into it stood empty.

Ash sighed. He assumed Sean or Candice had claimed Loch Ness. A win, win. Now Sean had a knife, his statue, and Candice had her dragon. That left the snake, the Jersey devil, the Bunyip and the mecha creature to be found. If the spider was still with Deepali's corpse, that left the melee wide open.

Another gunshot rang out, and Ash's head jerked toward the woods to the west. Dense forest packed the edge of the shoreline, the thick canopy creating a mix of dancing shadows, the chill breeze pushing around leaves and underbrush.

The mournful cry of an animal in pain echoed off the stone walls.

The dangers that lurked beneath the forest canopy didn't concern Ash in that moment. An anger built in him, desperation. Part of him wanted to seek out the shots. See what was happening, perhaps help. Another part of him wanted to sneak back to the house and get Deepali's figurine. Stay away from whatever trouble was brewing in the forest.

Ash fingered the two bullets in his back pocket. If the gunshots he'd heard were Sean, the Scot was out of ammo.

He darted toward the unbroken fringe of woods that ran along the shore. He saw broken tree branches, trampled undergrowth, and a rough trail zigzagged through the forest as if made by a drunken cow... or something bigger.

Ash hadn't gone far when he reached the first signs of confrontation.

A wounded beast had thrashed around in the underbrush. The forest's tangled mess of weeds were flattened, a nearby tree trunk was scarred, and tree branches were broken. A puddle of dark blood seeped into the ground, the stink of death thick in the air. A small glittering object caught Ash's attention and he knelt and picked it up.

It was an empty cartridge. A .22 caliber.

Ash examined the ground closely and found the footprints of two people. One was clearly Sean's boot, the other, the smaller print, most likely Candice's. The trail of prints, blood, and beaten vegetation ran deeper into the forest, and Ash followed.

Sean must have wounded something with his first shot, but didn't take it down. Maybe he had with his second and final shot? He shook his head. He was making so many assumptions his reasoning meant nothing. He had no idea who he was chasing, or who fired the shot the prior day. For all he knew, Sean could still have all three of his bullets. There were those that could tell the type of gun being fired by the sound of the shot, but Ash wasn't one of those people.

He picked up his pace, ducking under tree branches and traversing thickets of pricker bushes. Stray rays of sunlight pierced the tree canopy and fell on the forest floor like spotlights. Birds sang, leaves rattled.

Ash froze, sniffing. The faint scent of cigarette smoke wafted through the woods, and jarred a memory. What was it? Ash struggled to remember when and where he'd last smelled the scent, but he came up blank.

There were voices ahead, and as Ash passed east of the dragon paddock, he saw Candice and Sean standing over a dead Bunyip. He eased behind a thick bush, peering through the thick foliage.

The giant seal-like beast was covered in blood, and two bullet holes marred its torso. Large, glassy black eyes stared up at the clear blue sky, sunlight glittering off the beast's three-inch claws. Sean and Candice were talking, but Ash couldn't make out what they were saying.

Pain ran down Ash's spine and he shifted his weight. A dead branch snapped beneath his feet, and Sean and Candice's heads jerked in his direction.

***

Rodgers glided through the forest, the sound of his maneuvering jets muffled by the insect chorus and the wind. The bot positioned itself behind a large oak tree, watching.

***

"Show yourself or I'm gonna start firing," Sean yelled. Metal scraped on metal as he slammed the rifle's bolt home.

Ash knew the man was bluffing because he had no bullets—so Ash thought, but why reveal himself?

But why not? Would Sean shoot him for no reason? No. The train might have derailed, but Sean was no killer.

Ash stood and strode from the forest as if he hadn't been hiding.

"Just me," Ash said as he approached. "Whoah," he said, faking surprise when he saw the Bunyip.

Sean eyed him, but said nothing.

Candice came forward and hugged him. "Happy to see you made it through the night."

"You too."

Sean harrumphed.

"See anyone else?" Candice asked.

"Deepali and Otto..." What to say?

Sean and Candice watched him expectantly.

"They're gone," Ash said.

Candice's hand went to her mouth.

"How?" Sean said. The suspicion in his voice was palpable.

Was there any reason not to tell them? Ash's mind raced. He still couldn't get himself out of competition mode into survival mode. What mode were Sean and Candice in? He decided there was no harm in spilling the info. In fact, it might start the process of regaining Sean's trust.

"Otto was taken out by that creature... the Jersey Devil. I saw it with my own eyes," he said.

When he didn't continue, Candice said, "And Deepali?"

"I followed her into the basement last night. Tracked her into the mine," Ash said.

"What was she doing down there?" Candice said.

Ash hiked his shoulders. "That was what I was trying to find out."

"She could've been searching for statues," Sean said.

Ash nodded.

"What happened to her?" Candice asked.

"The Yeti..."

Sean and Candice said nothing.

"You get the Loch Ness sculpture?" Ash said.

Sean looked at Candice, and she nodded. "The Bunyip also. And before you ask, the thing chased us. Sean did what he had to do," Candice said.

Ash nodded. So they were still playing the game, at least on some level. He said, "Those three shots I heard... that all you?"

Sean nodded.

Ash considered giving Sean his bullets as a peace offering, or maybe try and work out some type of share deal.

"Well hello," a deep male voice rumbled over the clearing. The scent of cigarette smoke filled Ash's nostrils as he searched in vain to find the source of the voice.

Sean waved the empty gun around, and Candice cowered behind him, her head peeking over his shoulder.

"So, then there were three," the voice said.

A gunshot rang out and a puff of dirt rose from the ground before Candice.

Ash dropped into a crouch, as did Sean and Candice.

A manic laugh echoed through the valley. "No worries. I'm not going to hurt you.... yet."

Ash sprang for the cover of the forest and another shot pierced the day. He froze, a puff of dirt sprouting ahead of him.

"Now, now. No running away. That isn't nice."

A long shadow fell over the clearing and a man strode from the woods, a cloud of white smoke obscuring his head. Bells rang in Ash's head—the smell of cigarette smoke. It all made sense. Treemont had been with them the entire way, hiding in the valley, watching and waiting. But why had he chosen this moment to reveal himself?

A gust of wind tore away the cigarette smoke revealing the helicopter pilot that had brought the party to the valley. The dour man with a waxy complexion and salt and pepper hair that Ash remembered no longer looked meek and frail. His jeans and blue dress shirt with silver epaulets on the collar was gone, as was the blue cap, replaced by jungle camouflage fatigues. He wore a Glock on his hip and an M4 carbine was pinned to his shoulder and aimed at Sean's head. He came on confidently, never taking his eyes off Sean. Treemont said, "I know there's no bullets in that thing, but put it down anyway."

When Sean didn't comply, Rodgers glided from the forest and took it from him. Sean didn't protest, and the bot silently backed off with the gun pointed at the sky.

"Now with that nastiness handled, we can finish this, yes?"

Ash, Sean, and Candice said nothing.

"Oh, come on. Tell me you're not having fun? You're alive, aren't you? That's more than the rest of the competitors can say."

Sean lost his patience and lunged forward, and for an instant Ash thought he was attacking.

Treemont kept the M4 steady, and Sean skidded to a halt five feet from the man. "What do you want from us? If you want us dead, why not just shoot us? Why all the bullshit?" Sean screamed.

"Want you dead?" Treemont said. "No, I don't want all of you dead. Just eight of you."

"You're fucking crazy if you think I'm still playing your game," Ash said.

"Do you have a choice?" Treemont said.

Ash, Sean, and Candice said nothing.

"Oh, come now? You're not so innocent. None of you are, and it's time to pay the piper, as they say."

Sean balled his fists, his entire head turning bright red, his freckles sticking out like black bugs.

"And who made you judge?" Ash yelled.

In his anger, Treemont jerked the gun barrel in Ash's direction and Sean sprang.

The Scot flew through the air, hands out like eagle talons.

Treemont was faster. He swung the M4 and fired. The gun rattled, fifteen rounds spitting from the barrel in two seconds, empty cartridges bouncing off Treemont's black boots.

Red bullet holes stitched across Sean's chest, but the big man's momentum brought him on, and he barreled into Treemont and took him to the ground.

Candice screamed and fled into the forest, and Treemont didn't even glance in her direction.

Treemont thrashed and rolled, trying to get away from Sean, but the Scot wasn't dead yet.

Blood poured from his mouth and dripped onto Treemont's face as Sean locked his hands on the man's neck. The two men struggled, blood pouring from Sean, his rage and adrenaline giving him one last burst of strength.

Treemont sputtered and coughed as he pulled and tore at Sean's arms, trying to free himself, but Sean held him fast, Sean's head as red as a cherry. Treemont's legs spasmed as his face turned purple and life left him.

Sean choked and splattered blood across Treemont's dead face. With the adrenaline fleeing, the rage drained and fear crept over Sean's face. He looked around, smiled, then fell face forward onto Treemont's corpse and didn't move again.

Rodgers beeped and sighed and floated into the trees.

Ash fell to his knees, fear, joy and anguish fighting for control of his emotions. Treemont was dead. Ash let his head fall into his hands and he rubbed his eyes and twisted his neck. The dust settled and Candice was nowhere to be seen. His heart slowed, his breathing steadied, and his stomach growled.

It was over. Candice and Ash were the only ones left.

27

The trees whispered and sighed, a chill breeze stirring the forest. Nothing moved in the clearing and the sun glared down like an accusing eye as the morning wore away. White clouds filled the horizon at the eastern edge of the valley, and tendrils of mist reached for the ground. No birds sang. It was as if the entire valley knew the leader of the Cryptid Club was dead. Sean's bloody corpse lay atop Treemont's, the two men forever tangled.

Ash got to his feet. His legs were like Jell-O and pain ran to his extremities. He lumbered forward in a daze, Sean's dead eyes staring up at him as if asking a question.

"Sorry, buddy." Ash knelt, looked over his shoulder, and pushed Sean's corpse off Treemont's. Ash took Sean's rifle, which he had two bullets for. To Ash's surprise he found that Sean had three statues. In addition to Loch Ness, he had the Bunyip and the spider.

Ash's mind reeled and he fell back onto his ass. How had Sean gotten the spider? He must have gone down into the basement and found Deepali's body. When had he had the time? Had he followed last night?

Rodgers glided from the forest and came to a stop before Ash, the bot's lens eyes scoping in and out. He squeaked out, "Are you OK, Mr. Cohn?"

Ash said nothing.

"By my count you are in possession of five figurines. Are you not?"

Ash said nothing.

"May I see them?"

Anger surged through Ash. People were dead, and whether they deserved it or not wasn't his job to decide. He wanted to smash Rodgers to dust. Pound the bot until there was nothing left but a pile of smoking electronics. Instead, Ash complied, because in the end he could think of no good reason not to.

He laid the five small figurines on the ground: the Bigfoot, the bear, Nessie, the Bunyip, and Deepali's spider.

Rodgers glided forward and examined the pieces, then rotated away, and before Ash realized what the machine was doing, it snatched up Treemont's M4 and disappeared back into the trees.

Ash sat there, mouth hanging open as he watched the bot go.

A horn blast pierced the day, its sharp bleat echoing over the valley.

The melee was over. Ash had won.

Then another thought wormed its way into his head like a maggot: the game wasn't over. There was no other explanation. If Ash was the last, and Treemont was dead, it was up to Rodgers to make the final decision. That's what the hologram had said. But the hologram was full of shit. He rubbed his eyes again, pain knifing through his head.

If the game wasn't over, who was playing?

Candice. How had he forgotten?

Ash finished searching Sean and found a most unusual item: the pin from Snake's turban. How had Sean gotten it? Ash left it in his room after the search.

A scream floated on the breeze. It came from the north and sounded close.

Candice.

Ash vaulted to his feet and stuffed one of his .22 caliber shells into the rifle and slammed the bolt home. Sweat dripped into his eyes and down his back despite the chill breeze. He plunged into the forest, following Candice's trail. Flattened vegetation led to a thin animal path, and Ash stopped and examined the ground.

Bare human-like footprints marked the hardpan, the thin scratches of two-inch claws at the end of each of the four digits. Small boot prints interspersed with the claw marks, and both sets of prints went east toward the house.

Another wail broke the stillness. There was no doubt. It was Candice.

Ash doubled his pace, surging through the undergrowth, rifle out before him. At twelve thousand feet there weren't many spiders, mosquitoes, and flies, but gnats and small black flies called 'no-see-ums' bit and sucked at Ash's exposed skin as he pushed through the dense vegetation. Birds squawked and yelled as he passed, breaking tree branches and rattling leaves leaving no mystery of his direction. His lungs burned. He'd adjusted to the elevation, but twelve thousand feet was twelve thousand feet, and he didn't think he'd ever get used to it, no matter how long he stayed in the valley.

The main path loomed ahead, and Ash slowed. A massive form stood in the forest ahead, its back to Ash.

The creature Ash had labeled 'Bad Bigfoot' peered through the vegetation, slowly moving forward through the underbrush, watching something on the main path Ash couldn't see.

Ash checked the gun again as he worked his way south, putting space between himself and the massive Sasquatch. The creature's dirty fur was matted with dark blood all along its torso, and dark stains covered the hair around its mouth and claws. Yellow fangs hung over thick lips, and the eyes… even without the creature looking directly at him, Ash felt the weight of those eyes. The terror behind those yellow slits of anger.

Candice stood on the main path, facing a dark figure wrapped in green. She held Sean's knife in her hand, and she slashed at the person, feinting back and forth, lunging with the knife. The stranger wore a deep green jumpsuit with a headscarf wrapped around their head and face. The attacker was screaming and shouting at Candice, but Ash couldn't make out what was being said. He brought up the rifle and sighted the stranger's back.

The Sasquatch roared. A primal scream of rage that made the stranger look over a shoulder.

Ash sucked in a deep breath.

The person in green wore a black sack over their head with a white smiley face drawn on its front. The stranger brought up a handgun and panned it across the forest where the Bigfoot and Ash hid.

Leaves tapped and trees creaked in the wind, gnats divebombed his head, and the scent of shit leaked through the forest

The Sasquatch disappeared into the underbrush and Ash took his eye away from the rifle's sight.

Candice saw her opportunity and took it. She sprang, slashing with her knife, going for the stranger's smiley face.

The person in green wheeled, aimed the gun, and fired.

The shot rang out and echoed through the valley.

Candice came on, the shot missing her and plunking into a tree to her left. She screamed, diving forward in one last surge, knife out before her in a doublehanded grip.

The stranger brought up an arm to block the blow, but the knife tore through fabric and flesh as the blade was deflected. The stranger screamed, blood leaking from the wound.

The gun barked again, a small puff of dirt rising from the ground next to Candice.

The pop of the bullet reminded Ash he had a gun, but before he could get the rifle's stock to his shoulder, a Sasquatch burst from the woods.

Nine feet tall, natty brown hair hanging in thick strands, the beast slammed into the stranger, and the beast, Candice and the stranger went to the ground in a tangle. A cloud of dust filled the air, and Ash took several fast steps forward, positioning himself behind a thorn bush ten feet from the thrashing cryptid and mound of people.

The scene was comical. He'd spent so much time convincing himself he wasn't crazy. That what he'd seen was real. Now, as he watched a Bigfoot wrestle a Brit and a masked assailant, again he felt like reality might be slipping from his grasp.

The gun barked three times and the beast roared.

The creature bucked and heaved as Candice tried to separate herself from the fight. To Ash it looked as though the cryptid had far more interest in the masked attacker than it did with Candice.

Ash sighted the Sasquatch's head and eased off the safety.

The beast turned, yellow glowing eyes searching the forest and finding Ash. Confusion spread over the monkey-like face, the beast's mouth falling open a crack, revealing two rows of sharp teeth.

Candice jerked free of the living knot, vaulted to her feet, and ran for the forest.

A gunshot rang out and Ash jumped. He hadn't fired.

The Sasquatch fell to its knees, blood spurting from its leg.

The person in green kicked the Sasquatch in the chest and knocked it onto its back.

Candice was almost to the woods. Not looking back.

The stranger spun like a ballerina, arm out, pistol at the ready.

A gunshot rang out and Candice spasmed, a red hole appearing on the back of her jacket as she crumpled to the ground.

Ash sighted the rifle and fired. The crack of the hammer striking home, the pop of the gunpowder expanding, and the whoosh as the bullet left the barrel filling his head.

The shot missed and thumped into the ground, a puff of dirt rising into the air.

Ash pulled back the rifle's bolt, dropped his last bullet into the firing chamber, and slammed the bolt home.

The pop of gunfire filled the clearing as the stranger fired in Ash's direction, and leaves were cut from branches, bullets ricocheted off rocks, and wood splinters flew as the shots peppered trees.

The stranger dropped into a crouch and Ash fired.

He didn't wait to see if he'd hit the masked person and used his shot as a diversion. Ash bolted into the forest, branches slapping his face, gnats invading his nose, mouth and eyes. He headed away from the house. There were no sounds of pursuit, and when he believed he'd gone far enough, he paused to catch his breath behind a thicket of thorn bushes with small yellow leaves.

Ash pulled for air as he gathered his courage, and when his heart had slowed, and his nerves had calmed, he followed his own trail back to Candice. He couldn't abandon her. She'd always been kind to him, and Ash had always thought she had a thing for him, but like many things in his life since the incident, he hadn't taken it seriously.

When he arrived back at the scene of the attack, Ash found the Sasquatch and the person in green gone, drips of blood leading away into the forest. Candice still lay where she'd fallen, her long blonde hair splayed across her face. A pool of dark blood spread beneath the corpse, her eyes staring into the next world. Ash knelt and looked for a pulse.

Candice was gone.

Ash cried then. All the emotions of the last four days spilling from him in a deluge. He didn't know any of these people, didn't really care if they lived or died. But Candice, Sean, Otto... and the others. They didn't deserve to go out like this, at the whim of a madman... or madwoman.

Neither did he.

Suddenly, Ash felt eyes on him again. That feeling he'd had since he'd stepped off the helicopter. Those fears brought all the questions forward like a crowd of kids trying to get to the ice cream truck's window. Who was the person in green? Was it one of the other eight? Someone else? Clearly the pilot wasn't Treemont, if there'd ever been a Treemont. Ash was starting to doubt even that. Everything they'd been told was a lie, but he'd figured that out a little too late.

Ash took the knife Candice had gotten from Sean and covered her body with stones as the midday sun arced overhead. When he was done, he worked his way up to the house. He was careful, staying in the shadows, keeping undercover. Whoever the person dressed in green was, they'd had no trouble shooting an unarmed woman in the back, and Ash realized though he was the last, he hadn't won anything. To the contrary.

He was being hunted.

Ash encountered no living creatures on his way to the house, and when he reached the blue stone structure he paused, looking back the way he'd come. The stranger didn't make an appearance, and neither did Rogers. Ash thought he'd heard the bot's maneuvering thrusters several times as he snuck through the woods, but he'd been unable to catch a glimpse of the tin can.

The backdoor was unlocked, and Ash entered the long hallway, memories of his first night in the valley rushing back. Dark blood still stained the wood floor, and splattered the walls. Snake had been the first to go, or had he?

Ash searched his memory, looking for any clue that might tell him who the stranger was. Frustration sent a tingle of angst down his spine and his stomach grumbled, so he made his way up to the dining room. He found a stale loaf of bread and a hard chunk of white cheese with green fungus gnawing its fringe.

Thankfully nobody had messed with the wine supply, and Ash opened a bottle of red and wandered out onto the portico with some bread. He pulled a seat over and leaned it against the side of the house, protecting his back. He sat, his view of the northern and eastern sections of the valley unobstructed.

Ash drank from the bottle. He felt drained, numb, and he didn't know what to do. Sit around and wait for the mystery stranger to pick him off like a duck at a carnival? He didn't think that was the plan, however. Everything so far had been orchestrated, and Ash had to believe the mastermind of this shit show had come up with a better ending than picking him off at long range with a gun. But perhaps things hadn't gone according to plan?

Ash sat on the porch for a long time, staring at the forest, the empty rifle resting on his lap. When the bottle of wine was gone, dusk had seeped through the forest, the eastern end of the valley filled with a pink and purple cotton candy sky.

He thought of Ophelia, all his mistakes, all the bad decisions that had led him to this end. He should've blinked and walked out of the damn forest and buried what he'd seen deep, gone on with his life. Then he never would've become a hunter, never would've met Candice, or Sean, or any of them.

The sun set, darkness spreading over the valley like a blanket. Stars blinked above, the line of dark clouds in the east growing as they approached. He leaned back, and his eyes slipped closed and he jerked them open. This was no place to fall asleep.

A beast cackled in the forest and the call was answered by a screech and a roar. All the creatures of the valley were trapped here, just like him. They'd been captured, tricked and manipulated.

Ash recalled the last verse of the Atavism Special Animal Sanctuary poem:

Callous to pain as the rose,
Breathe with instinct's delight
Live the existence that goes
Soulless into the night.

He didn't know how it had been done to him, or who had done it, but Ash sure felt soulless and alone.

28

For the second night in a row Ash slept like a squirrel. With a killer on the loose, he loathed the thought of going up to his room, so he went back into the basement and found his crate. Sleep never fully came. It teased and cajoled as it often does. Ash gave up, climbed out of his coffin-like bed and headed upstairs.

Stars still blinked in the darkness, the thick clouds tearing apart as they reached the Andes. It had gotten much colder, and Ash shivered. The old, blue granite house was silent, and when he arrived in the dining room, he found Rodgers waiting for him.

"You did not go to your room this evening," the bot stated.

Ash said nothing as he examined the same bread and cheese that had been laid out the prior night.

"Have you slept? You'll need to be rested to face the coming day."

Anger swelled in Ash, the matter-of-fact way the bot talked to him, like he had no choice except to play the game. The garbage pail had been MIA for the last twelve hours. Ash surged toward Rodgers, intent on pounding the bot to scrap, but he pulled up short. "What the hell do you know about it? All you do is skulk around. Where the hell were you when Sean needed help? Candice? Who the hell is pulling your strings?"

The bot chirped, its eyes zoomed in and out, but Rodgers said nothing.

Ash spun on the ball of his right foot and swung his left leg in a wide arc, his foot connecting with the bot's pseudo head.

Rodgers was knocked back a few feet, regained its balance, and jetted forward until it hovered where it had been, eyes scoping. "Do you feel better now, sir?"

"Why the hell are you here?" Ash looked at the pitiful food. "You said you'd take care of us. What is this shit?" He pointed at the hard bread and green cheese.

"Things are coming to an end, Mr. Cohn. How do you not see?"

"Then why shouldn't I smash to you pieces just for fun?" Ash knew it was a stupid thing to say.

The bot seemed to know also. It squeaked, then pushed air through its grill-like mouth.

"Did you just sigh at me?"

"Sir, I do have a purpose here, but first I think I can put your mind at ease," Rodgers said. "The illusion of control is a dangerous thing, Mr.

Cohn. The more of it you think you have, the less you actually have. Do you understand?"

Ash was coming to detest the bot's squeaky mechanical voice. "You're saying I have no choice?"

"Precisely. If you were to destroy me, I would be replaced."

Ash said nothing.

"What is the human saying?" Rodgers chirped and beeped. "The devil you know?"

"You said you had a purpose. Care to share it?"

Rodgers spun and glided from the room.

Ash downed a glass of water, grabbed a couple of slices of stale bread, and followed. He caught up with the bot as it exited the backdoor.

"Care to tell me where we're going?"

"Haven't you wondered what the monument light falls on? What it marks and when?" Rodgers said.

Ash rubbed his chin as he fell in alongside the bot, but he said nothing. At first Ash didn't know what Rodgers was talking about. Monument light? Then he recalled how the moonlight shined through the hole at the top of the sculpture and marked a spot in the valley.

Stars blinked down at them as they skirted the edge of the house and followed the path to the monument. They passed the red stain that had been Otto. The Jersey Devil was long gone, and Rodgers powered north into the forest, heading for a thin path that would take them toward the bear and snake paddocks. A chunk of moon was visible at the very southern edge of the valley, rays of fading moonlight arcing into the valley.

"Is that where we're going? Where the light marks?" This all made no sense. Ash was no astronomer, but he knew the phases of the moon changed continuously, and thus the spotlight created by the monument would shift and move as each day passed into the next.

"Yes."

Ash harrumphed. "That's it? Why now?"

"It's time for you to see what the valley lacks."

"Lacks?"

The odd pair cut deeper into the forest, the thick tree canopy stifling most of the starlight and moonlight.

"You will see."

Ash's frustration boiled over. Perspiration bloomed on his forehead, stomach burning, a chill clammy tremor running through him. "Why do you have to show me? Isn't that what all this crap is about? The game? The challenge? Why not let me figure it out on my own?"

The bot chirped, beeped, and went silent for a time, its maneuvering jets hissing in the stillness. After several minutes, Rodgers said, "As you've seen, the cone of light created by the monument is quite large. Therefore, there are several days throughout the year where the Dreamer Garden's location is marked with the light. Now is not such a time, however, and Mr. Treemont wanted you to see this. Hoped you'd find it on your own, actually. The valley isn't large and it's just another of the sanctuary's attractions."

Ash didn't like that the bot was making the valley sound like Disneyland, and as he trudged through the forest, dawn still two hours off, he wondered if he wasn't being led into a trap, or at least some type of confrontation? But like many things he'd encountered in the valley, did it matter? As Rodgers had pointed out, he had no real control, so he might as well go with the flow.

But Ash didn't roll like that.

He stopped walking and Rodgers disappeared into the darkness. He stood still, tuning his hearing—eliminating the push of the wind, the whine of the night symphony, and the occasional whelp, gurgle or bark that echoed through the woods. He didn't hear Rodgers' thrusters, and the steady strum of the valley he'd gotten used to had gone still.

Ash had to get the tunnel door open. The seed of an idea sprouted, and Ash mentally counted the dead batteries he'd used in the flashlight. Ash had hidden the useless light and spent fuel cells the prior day. Never knew what they could be used for, and as a plan formed in his head, Ash smiled.

That was for later, however.

He waited. Ten minutes turned into twenty... thirty. "Shit!" Ash screamed when Rodgers didn't return. He could head back to the house, but what purpose would that serve? No, he needed to walk willingly into the net, see what his host wanted him so desperately to see. Ash followed Rodgers and found the bot waiting a hundred yards down the path.

Without a sound, Rodgers glided through the woods.

A hissing ran through the forest, but it wasn't near. Ash and Rodgers slipped behind a large boulder as dawn filled the eastern end of the valley, gray light leaking through the forest. The hissing died away, and the duo continued on until they reached an overgrown garden with an odd assortment of sculptures made from a variety of materials at its edges.

"Please excuse the weeds and lack of trimming. Ms. S... The valley's caretaker doesn't care much for tradition."

"Who is Ms. S?"

Rodgers said nothing.

"Fine. What tradition?" Ash knew that was the exact question the bot wanted him to ask, but he wanted to get on with whatever show was planned. Now that he had an idea how he might escape the valley, that's all his food and sleep deprived mind could think about.

"Look closer," Rodgers said.

The closest sculpture was a Kraken, its giant bulbous head made of stone, its many twisting legs metal rebar, its eyes emerald stones. To its right a rendering of a man with wings. At first Ash thought it was a Jersey Devil, but there was no menace in the creature's expression, no fangs or claws. Chiseled into the white and black speckled granite statue at its base was the word Mothman.

Ash rolled his shoulders and cracked his neck, an odd sense of unease spreading through him. He looked at Rodgers, who hadn't moved. The bot hovered, camera lens eyes focused on Ash.

A large bird wheeled overhead, and a long bellow came from the direction of the lake. Ash wandered through the overgrown cemetery-like park. There was a gray statue of an alien with a large round head labeled Gray, a giant ape, and a huge bird with wide spreading wings unfurled labeled Phoenix, and several other odd creatures with names Ash had never heard of and couldn't even pronounce.

"These creatures… these are the beasts nobody has been able to capture?" Ash said.

"When the sanctuary began, Sir Heuvelmans wanted those who visited to never be complacent. To never get lost in all the mystical things here in the valley. The Dreamer Garden was meant to inspire, remind every hunter who came here that there were still many mysteries to uncover."

"Why bring me here? Why would you think I'd care? This little game of bullshit is getting old. I need—"

A gunshot pierced the day and a bullet plunked into the torso of a beast made of wood and stone.

"You still don't understand, do you?" The voice was clearly disguised, the brash haughtiness unachievable without effort.

"What do you want from me? You want the valley, it's yours. What the hell is this all about?" Ash yelled.

Another shot rang out and Ash ran. He'd had enough. He'd retrieve his batteries and get to work on his escape. He was done.

The faint sound of hissing grew as he ran on, and he thought he saw Tallboy watching him from behind a tree, but when he looked closer the Sasquatch was gone, or it had never been there. Ash was starting to see threats around every bend and in every shadow.

Shrill laughter followed him through the jungle, the sound of snapping branches and footfalls marking his pursuit.

Ash darted past the snake paddock, his mind running backward, remembering the creature had escaped. The hissing got louder, and the sounds of pursuit grew.

"Where are you running to, Mr. Cohn?" Rodgers' speaker enhanced voice rang through the woods.

Ash burst from the trees into a clearing.

The massive snake lifted its head and turned its obsidian eyes on Ash, its tongue lashing through two-foot fangs. The beast's body undulated and expanded as it uncoiled, the hissing getting so loud it blocked out all other sound except the galloping of Ash's heart. He stood frozen, the snake blocking his way, and Rogers and the stranger stopping his retreat.

The massive snake moved with amazing speed for a creature of its size, and it was halfway to Ash when his brain issued orders and the flight or fight decision was made. He bolted into the forest, a thick tree branch grazing the side of his head as the snake lunged, its jaws snapping on air. The beast cried in frustration, a mix of an angry scream and a cry of pain.

"You can't hide anymore, Mr. Cohn." It was Rodgers. Logic be damned. If he got the opportunity again, he'd take pleasure in smashing the life from the bot. Ash didn't care about its replacement.

Snapping branches and the sounds of vegetation being crushed filled the woods as the snake pursued Ash. He couldn't outrun it, couldn't fight it, so his only hope was to find a place to hide. Could snakes climb trees? Even in his frantic state he knew they did, so that old staple of security wasn't an option. Plus, the thing could lift its head twenty feet off the ground!

He zigzagged through the forest, cutting as close to trees as possible, slipping through thickets of pricker bushes and between stacked lines of trees. None of these measures slowed the beast, and when Ash glanced over his shoulder, the snake's flat, angular head was only feet behind him. The creature's huge head lowered to the ground, its body twisting and surging through the underbrush, a forked tongue the size of a firehose shooting through fangs that dripped with the saliva of anticipation.

Ash threw himself into a cluster of bushes to his right, branches spearing him like knives, leaves raking his face. A loud crunch reverberated through the forest and gunshots tore through the woods, plunking into the ground, tree trunks, and underbrush.

The hissing ceased.

Ash jumped, grabbed a branch, and swung in a wide arc, changing his direction yet again. He stopped running when he saw the snake wasn't moving, blood leaking from a hole between its eyes.

Why kill the beast? It was after Ash. Almost had him. A sick feeling settled in Ash's stomach, a warning that told him something wasn't right and that things were about to go sideways.

As if reading his mind, the false voice of the stranger echoed through the valley. "I want to kill you myself." The malevolence in the voice surprised Ash. What had he done to make this person hate him so? He recalled something Sean had said about injuries undeserved, but there was no accounting for insanity, and whoever had trapped him here was surely insane.

With the snake dead, Ash felt exposed and he looked around for cover, but anger and defiance fought with the rational side of his brain. The side that said survival was the goal. But the human race had been hurting itself since the first bipedal creature inched from the sea, and Ash was no different. He sat on a stone, indignant. "I won't play your game any longer. I'm done. So go fu—"

A gunshot rang out.

Pain pierced Ash's right leg and he rolled off the stone onto the hardpan, covering his head.

"You will, or I'll put a bullet in your head."

"Piss off asshole," was the best Ash could come up with.

The manic laughter returned, but it wasn't close.

Ash lay prone and examined the gunshot wound. It was only a graze and the bullet had buried itself in the ground. The gash was deep, however, and a thick stream of blood ran from the wound. The scratches on his chest screamed as Ash squeezed the cut, forcing more blood out, trying to clean the new wound as best he could without water or alcohol. He pulled the knife he'd taken off Candice's corpse and cut a patch of fabric from his shirttail. He made a bandage, and cut two thin strips to hold it in place. Blood turned the bandage red in seconds, but it was stopping most of the blood flow and helping the wound close.

He peered over the edge of the stone he hid behind, scanning the forest, but he didn't see Rodgers or the stranger. Ash got to his feet, testing his leg, applying more weight until he stood steady. The gash ached, but he could walk, even run if he had to. He'd been lucky, but he had the ominous feeling his luck had run out.

29

The new day brought the rain, thin sheets of drizzle that soaked Ash through as he trekked through the forest. He was chilled to the bone, and his leg ached, but the bleeding had stopped. His stomach screamed, his mouth dry as paper, but he didn't feel that bad considering what he'd been through.

The creatures of the night had gone silent, and the beasts of the day had yet to pick up the cadence, and the early morning stillness made Ash uneasy. He was normally comfortable in the woods, but he doubted he'd ever be able to take a stroll through nature again. Silence covered the forest like a blanket, and a dingy gray light spilled through the dense tree canopy. The cry of a startled bird floated through the woods and Ash froze, slipping behind a tree trunk. Something was working its way through the underbrush behind him, pacing itself, going slow, trying to be silent as it followed his path of crushed vegetation, but in the early morning quiet the sounds rang through the forest like an alarm.

Panic knifed through Ash. He should've been more careful, paid more attention and left no signs, but even as those thoughts flitted through his head, he knew it wouldn't have mattered. Treemont, or whoever the hell he or she was, had been watching everything since the beginning, and he had no reason to believe that wasn't the case now. He glanced around at the trees and weeds, expecting to see Rodgers watching from the shadows.

Suddenly a sense of urgency gripped him, and he snapped from his reverie. There was a thick evergreen to his right, its long branches drooping under the weight of its many small green leaves. He could hide under the tree's bows, but if the stranger had dogs, or could track him, or Tallboy was along... He had to run.

A branch snapped very close and Ash slipped around the evergreen, but he saw the glint of Rodgers' metal body picking through the woods. Nowhere to run. Ash mounted a thin oak. He shimmied up the foot-round trunk, using branches as steps, his feet slipping, leaves falling. He realized how much noise he was making and decided to hide. He lay prone on a thick branch, arms wrapped around the limb. There was a branch directly below him packed with leaves the size of a hand, and he could barely see the ground directly below him.

Maybe it would be enough.

He inched further out onto the branch so his legs wouldn't be seen if someone stood next to the tree's trunk and looked directly up. The limb bent and twisted, and Ash froze. He peered through a tangle of branches and green leaves, and watched the stranger thread through the forest, Mira trailing after.

Ash hadn't seen Mira since the challenge behind the house in the snow, but he figured she'd seen him. The odd creature was half machine, half flesh, and its six steel, multi-jointed legs picked through the underbrush.

The path his pursuers followed was leading the stranger right to his tree. He looked for nearby branches. Maybe he could move through the treetops. Me not Tarzan, he thought, and the tree he was in swayed slightly from his weight and couldn't take his movement. If he started moving around, they'd see him for sure. He took a deep breath, the forest chorus picking up speed and strength, as if the creatures of the wood were trying to help him.

The stranger still wore the black sack with a smiley face.

Rodgers joined the group, looking as he always did, but Ash couldn't stop staring at the mecha beast. Its torso of metal, circuits, wires, blood vessels and flesh was bloodied and torn, and the creature shuffled forward in a spider-like sideways gait, legs churning. Blood vessels and muscle encased in wires and intertwined with circuits and metal supports gave way to a short torso, from which hung four arms, three long talons protruding from the ends of each. The beast's pumpkin-like white head turned side-to-side, its four dark, glassy, softball-sized eyes scanning the underbrush.

Ash gasped, and put his hand over his mouth like a southern bell.

Skewered on one of Mira's talons was Emica Sasai's head.

The stranger put up a hand and the trio paused, the masked pursuer lifting his head as if sniffing the air.

Tears leaked from Ash as he watched his pursuers continue along the path.

Emica's head was crushed, the mecha's leg piercing the top of her skull. Dark lines of dried blood ran down her forehead, and her eyes had been gouged out. The creature didn't seem to know the head was there.

He hadn't known her well, but Ash felt his insides melt, his skin trying to crawl off his body. He'd seen enough death in the last four days to last a lifetime, and sorrow washed over him.

The faint sound of metal tinkling on metal froze Ash to his tree limb, arms tightening, chest scratches wailing, leg wound burning.

The trio was close now, so close Ash saw the dark eyes of the stranger through the holes in the sack. He knew those eyes, and as the party got closer a knot so tight, and so dense gripped his chest, that for a moment he couldn't breathe.

The stranger paused ten feet from the tree, and bent, examining the ground next to the evergreen where Ash had stood. The stranger sniffed, and the person looked up, dark eyes searching the evergreen canopy.

If the stranger had been alone, perhaps Ash might have pulled his karambit and dove from the tree, making a desperate attack. But with Mira and Rodgers there, and the M4 in the stranger's hand, Ash's options were nil. He hated that feeling. It was worse than fear or loss; that rumble in your stomach and tightness in your chest that told you there was no control. It was all an illusion.

The hunter stood, stretching as if sore, then put hands on hips, and the tingle of metal on metal again rang through the forest.

Rodgers circled the area, and Mira stood still behind the stranger in green, dark eyes scanning the ground.

The stranger pulled off the hood, revealing the beautiful light brown face of Deepali.

Ash couldn't breathe. When he first heard her bracelets he'd known on some level, but he hadn't accepted it. How had this happened? He'd spent so much time with the woman. Had the fight in the mines been fake? Was the Yeti fake?

His mind spun, and a thick drop of sweat slipped off his forehead and fell to the ground. Rain leaked through the canopy, so when the drip of sweat landed on a dead leaf with a splat, only Mira's eyes shifted in the direction of the sound.

Deepali's dark brown eyes scanned the tree canopy, as if somehow she knew Ash hid within. His path had led the insane woman right to him, but the crushed vegetation also hid the evidence of his climb. Her eyes found Ash's tree, and followed the tree's trunk as it rose into the dense canopy.

Ash went rigid, back spasming, his leg and wounds thumping in rhythm with his galloping heart. She would see him. There was no doubt. He closed his eyes and gathered his courage to jump. If he could land on Deepali and get away before…

Then Ash remembered the empty rifle slung over his back.

Deepali's eyes stopped scanning the tree when the branches thickened.

Ash eased the rifle ever so carefully from his shoulder, but before he could toss it as a diversion, something caught his eye.

Tallboy stood within a thicket of brambles, watching the scene unfold. Feeling Ash's stare, the beast looked up at him, dark monkey-like face twisted with worry, eyes shining through the tapestry of branches, its fangs buried under thick gums.

Deepali smiled and looked over her shoulder, and Tallboy disappeared into the thick underbrush.

Ash threw the rifle, and immediately regretted it.

Lying flat, balancing on the branch, he had little leverage, and the rifle only went a couple of feet before it started its fall to the ground, bouncing off branches on its way down. It landed with a crash several feet from the base of the tree, and Deepali looked up, her smile gone.

She shook her head. "I thought you'd provide more sport than this. Have you no pride?"

The woman's voice was no longer honey, but vinegar.

Ash didn't speak. She knew he was in the tree somewhere, and she could open fire with the M4 at any moment and there was nothing he could do.

Rodgers collected the rifle and brought it to Deepali.

Mira didn't move.

Deepali accepted the gun, turned from the tree, and started back the way she'd come. Mira fell in behind her, the sound of servos whining and the tap of the mecha beast's metal claws tapping rocks as it retreated.

Rodgers stood at the base of the tree, still, its lens eyes focused up into the tree canopy.

When Deepali and Mira disappeared into the trees, Ash let out a deep breath. He felt like he hadn't breathed in an hour, and his chest ached with stress and fear. What the hell was going on? Deepali had followed his trail, knew he was here, but didn't finish him. How could she be alive? He'd seen her die, or had he? The memory of Deepali falling into the blackness stung him like a wasp, and he'd avoided her corpse because of the Yeti.

Those thoughts sent pain coursing through him. Why hadn't Deepali ended it? Ash knew the woman was insane, that was pre-established, and insanity had no bounds.

The drizzle ended, but everything still dripped with moisture, a cold wind pushing through the valley and chilling Ash. Terror washed over him. She had the M4, Mira.

He needed to get through that door.

Rodgers still stood beneath the tree, as if waiting, and Ash gathered his courage. He could take the bot. It didn't have any weapons.

Ash climbed to the ground and stood before Rodgers, holding his knife before him, as if it could do anything against metal.

"I suggest you move along, Mr. Cohn. This short respite is almost at an end," Rodgers said.

Ash plunged into the forest and left Rodgers behind. He didn't know where to go, so he changed his direction every few minutes, trying to shake off pursuit, though he knew that wasn't possible. He'd have to face Deepali at some point. The valley wasn't that large.

He needed a few things to make his plan work, and he thought he'd be able to find what he needed up at the house, but Deepali would definitely be watching the house. He remembered the mine exit into the valley. He could sneak into the house that way, but that would mean traversing the Yeti, but did it? Clearly what he'd seen the night Deepali died was a trick, and the thought of going down into the dark with only his karambit didn't fill him with hope.

No. He'd wait until he was ready to deal with the door.

Ash inched through the woods, hiding as he went. He thought of traps he might set, but every idea he had required time, tools, and effort. He had no time or tools, and if he didn't get some food soon, he was going to collapse.

The dark clouds were breaking up as they pushed over the Andes, and rays of golden sunlight leaked through the gloom. The air smelled of moisture, earth, and flowers. His tension eased, but then Emica's crushed head filled his mind. The way the dead eyes had watched him with blame.

The memory hit him like a shot of anisette. He'd met Emica before arriving in the valley, the memory so clear he couldn't figure out why he hadn't remembered before.

He'd been doing research at the small Bigfoot library in Stony Creek, and she'd entered like she owned the place. The library, which was no more than a room behind the closed post office, had binders of newspaper articles relating to Stony Creek's history with Bigfoot. There were some texts, interviews, but it was nothing compared to the sanctuary's collection.

She'd looked much different then—jet black hair, pink nails and all black clothes. That much at least hadn't changed. He picked his way through a dense patch of brambles and paused, staring back over his shoulder, searching the forest for pursuit.

There was nothing there except trees and weeds.

Emica had given her name, asked him a few questions, then stormed out without a thank you. He hadn't seen her again until he arrived at the helicopter, and now she was dead. He felt responsible—that was the bane of his life—but he knew none of this was his fault. If he hadn't come, Deepali, or Treemont, who the hell ever, would have replaced him, and everyone who was dead would still be dead.

Thoughts of home brought memories of Sean, and Candice, and Ash felt Candice's wet lips on his cheek, the kiss from the prior day the memory he'd chosen to cling to. Her bloodied body, long blonde hair covering her dead eyes, was an image he knew he'd fight to chase from his memories for the rest of his days.

He hugged himself as he exited the forest onto the main path. Nothing moved, and there was no sign of Rodgers, Mira, or Deepali.

"Ash... Ash.... Where are you going?"

Deepali stood on the portico above, training a rifle at his head.

Ash dropped and rolled.

The gun barked, a puff of dust lifting from the ground next to Ash. He kept rolling, like a child going down the side of a sledding hill, arms at his sides, legs tight together.

Deepali fired again, but the shot didn't come close, and plunked into a tree to his left.

Ash slowed his roll.

Gunfire erupted, but all the shots were pelting the ground to his left. She wanted him to go right, so he complied. He pressed to his feet and cut between two tall conifers and skidded to a stop, a nine-foot Sasquatch, blood dripping down his leg from a wound, blocked his way.

Bad Bigfoot's fur was matted with dark blood, and red and black specks of flesh clung to the creature's fangs and bared teeth. Yellow eyes glowed in the dim light beneath the tree cover. The beast grunted, flexing its claws as it came forward.

Ash pulled his karambit and opened it with a flick of his wrist. He spun the blade on his finger, making a show of it, trying to scare the creature. The black knife's fiberglass blade whizzed through the air, and the beast slowed, but didn't stop.

With a roar of fury, the creature attacked.

Ash braced himself, rolling his shoulders as he brought up his fists, curved blade out.

30

The Sasquatch roared as it swiped at Ash, its sharp claws coming up just short of his face. Ash feinted left, punching with his right hand, the karambit's blade slicing across the beast's hairy chest. The blade slashed hair, thick dreadlock-like strands falling to the ground, but didn't break the skin. The beast looked down at his missing hair and growled, and when it looked up, its eyes radiated hate.

The creature lashed out again, claws out.

Ash's leg stung as he pivoted, but he managed to avoid the strike. He kicked as he spun, connecting with the back of the beast's legs.

The blow didn't even pause the creature.

It did, however, piss it off. A low groan that rose to a bark, then a roar, escaped the beast like a rising thunderclap.

Ash backed away, never taking his eyes off the sasquatch, cycling the karambit back and forth as he flipped it on his index finger. An urgent communication reached Ash from his brain, and he turned and ran, arms out before him as underbrush slashed and tore at his face.

The Bigfoot gave chase, Ash heard its harsh breathing and the sound of breaking branches.

Deepali's maniacal laughter floated through the forest, an ill sound that sent a chill through Ash. He'd been attracted to her, but hadn't seen through the veil she was wearing. It takes a truly deranged individual to lie and deceive with such credibility and ease. She'd fooled him, and that wound was deeper and hurt more than the others. Old Ash would have never been taken in. Ash the scientist would have immediately questioned the woman's story, her motives, but Old Ash was gone, and if he didn't get past that, his life was over whether he survived the valley or not.

He doubled his pace, anger burning through him, memories of Ophelia driving him on. He couldn't let her win, let them all win. He wasn't crazy, and if the last four days had taught him anything, it was he wasn't nuts, but many of the truths he'd held dear had been shattered. There were magical things. Things that shouldn't exist, and he'd seen them. The idea of bringing Ophelia to the valley stirred the pleasure zone of his brain, but that pesky reality craving bastard always reminded Ash that there was no way Ophelia would come here no matter what he said or did.

And that was OK. Time to move on, build a new life.

He reached the edge of the forest and paused. He couldn't see the veranda, so he dashed for the backdoor. The tent pavilion was gone, and nothing moved on the thin strip of turf that separated the forest's edge from the house. He paused at the back door, looking over his shoulder.

The ten-foot Sasquatch watched him from the tree break, its head outstretched, mouth open, teeth shining in the sunlight.

Ash waited, watching, but the beast didn't come on. It was almost as if there was a forcefield separating the house from the rest of the valley. Ash knew that was crazy, but was it? People trained dogs with shock collars and invisible fences, and the memory of the Jersey Devil with clipped wings reminded him that past leaders of the Cryptid Club hadn't been above surgeries and other modifications to control the creatures of the valley, Mira being a prime example.

A gunshot rang out in the stillness. A plunk to Ash's right, splinters flying from the doorframe.

Ash dropped into a crouch, searching the side of the house and the forest.

"Where might we be going?" Deepali yelled. Then her unhinged laughter filled the valley.

Ash crawled through the back door and locked it behind him. He considered running around the house and locking all the doors and windows, but he quickly discarded the idea. Deepali was probably still up on the portico, and she and Rodgers surely had keys, plus there were many first-floor windows that could be broken.

He still couldn't wrap his noodle around the idea that Deepali was coming for him. With the M4.

He limped into the kitchen. He was able to run and walk fine, but now that he was able to slow down, he tried to keep some weight off the leg. He fetched a bottle of wine and opened it, taking a long pull that eased his fighting nerves. He wet a towel, stripped his makeshift bandage off the gunshot wound, pouring some wine on it before taking another long pull. He searched beneath the kitchen sink, in the cabinets, but he found nothing of use. He needed hydrogen peroxide, even a diluted sample would work. There were four unopened water bottles on the counter, their plastic caps still sealed. Ash took one and slipped it in a back pocket.

The house creaked and moaned in the stillness, the wind gusting through tiny gaps in the windowpanes creating an eerie melody. Ash took a pull of wine and went in search of the cleaning supplies. The house was cleaned regularly, that was easy to see. The bathroom, while of the most basic variety, was always spotless, as was the rest of the house. Ash had smelled bleach, wood polish, so he was certain there was a stash of cleaning supplies somewhere, and diluted hydrogen peroxide was a common ingredient in surface cleaners because of its disinfectant properties. Ash remembered his mom pouring the stuff on his cuts. How he would cry when he saw the brown bottle emerge from the medicine cabinet. The times do change, however, and Ash knew mothers didn't do that anymore because research had shown that hydrogen peroxide damages newly forming cells.

These useless thoughts clogged his head as he shuffled down hallways, anticipating encountering Deepali around every turn.

But he didn't see her, or Rodgers.

The doors to the dining room were locked.

A clock ticked, a floorboard popped, and windows rattled in their panes.

Ash searched the hallway broom closet, but found nothing. He wandered to the front of the house, searched another small closet off the sitting room, but found no cleaning supplies. He went upstairs. Nothing. He was beginning to despair when he thought of the basement, or perhaps the downstairs bathroom itself. He'd seen no cabinets in the washroom, but he remembered where his mom used to keep the toilet brush and cleaner and hope surged through him.

The washroom was plain, and though Ash had used the toilet and sink, he'd never taken advantage of the stall shower. He lifted his shirtfront and sniffed. "Damn, you sme—"

The click of a door lock engaging echoed through the silent house and froze Ash in place.

There was a lock on the bathroom door and Ash reached out to turn it, then paused. The room had no windows, and he had no idea where the air vent on the ceiling went, and he didn't want to get trapped.

He dropped to a knee, craning his neck so he could see behind the toilet.

"Jackpot," Ash said.

A toilet brush rested in a white plastic cup, and next to it a yellow bottle with a narrow spout sat beneath the toilet's tank. The yellow bottle was labeled Krypto-killer, a cleaner even a superhero can't beat. Ash lifted the bottle and examined the white label on its back. The writing was microscopic, and he couldn't read it in the half-light.

He stood and opened the bathroom door a crack.

Nothing moved in the hallway.

He slipped out, closed the door behind him, and headed for his stash of batteries.

Ash needed a couple more things—a nail, or similar item and something to hammer it with. That, along with a sealable container, which should be easy to find, would complete his supply list. If the cleaner he'd found was at least 3% hydrogen peroxide, which was common.

Sunlight angled through the windows and dust motes floated in the air as Ash slunk through the house. It was odd to be putting his back to the walls, searching the shadows. Just forty-eight hours prior he and the others had walked these halls, drinking, discussing their situation. Now everyone was dead, and a crazy bitch was trying to kill him, and having fun while doing it. You couldn't make this shit up.

He found a corner at the end of the hallway where a picture window displayed the eastern side of the valley. Dark clouds dotted the sky, beams of sunlight angling into the valley. He held the cleaner up to the window and traced his finger along the list of ingredients, and there it was, hydrogen peroxide (3%).

Back in the kitchen he recovered a teapot with a sealable lid, and one of the dull knives he'd left behind when he'd rummaged through the kitchen at the start of his little adventure in the Andes. A small wood mallet used to tenderize meat completed his search, and Ash put everything in a paper garbage bag and headed for the basement stairs.

Ash would recover the batteries where he'd hid them in a basement storage room. Then he'd find a good hiding place within the maze, make his bomb, and get the hell out of the valley.

The stairs creaked and popped as he climbed down into darkness. The batteries were stashed under a pile of old rags that looked drenched in dark blood with green fungus growing around their edges. There were no functioning batteries left, which wasn't really an issue because he wouldn't have used a flashlight anyway. With Deepali searching for him the last thing he wanted to do was help them find him.

Darkness pressed in on him as he slunk through the maze, the deepening cold penetrating him as the perspiration on his back and forehead chilled. The twelve C batteries were exactly where he'd left them, and he piled them into the sack with the rest of his supplies. Then he realized with a sickening horror that without light there was no way he could build his bomb. What he needed to do required precision and attention to detail.

He had to head back to the house, or... Ash shifted on his feet, his mind trying to convince him that going through the tunnels to the exit into the valley would be less dangerous than heading back up into the house, if that was even possible. If Deepali had done her homework, and at this point Ash had to assume she had, she might follow him down into the basement and send Rodgers or Mira to track him into the tunnel from the other entrance.

There were places in the maze where he could hide, but he had to consider the Yeti. Had it been real? It sure had looked real, but Ash couldn't figure out how Deepali pulled off her trickery. If the Yeti was real, there was no way she would've been able to control the beast, but if the creature was fake, a guy in a suit? Ash shook his head. That was nuts. There had to be another explanation. He decided to head back the way he'd come, and sneak up to his room.

He pulled his karambit and took his time heading back to the stairs, going slow, listening for every creak, every moan of the house. If Deepali or Mira were moving around up there, he couldn't hear them. Rodgers, however, could be anywhere.

He saw nobody as he went through the house and up the steps. If Deepali meant to track him into the maze, he'd somehow missed her.

Not one to look a gift horse in the mouth, Ash entered his room, locked the door, and propped his desk chair under the nob.

The process of making a pressure bomb from batteries is simple, but extremely dangerous. Most people who try end up burned and in the ICU.

Ash opened the door to his balcony a crack, but didn't go outside. He sat Indian style on the threshold, his bag of junk on the floor between his legs. He took the twelve batteries out of the bag and stood them on end in a row. He selected one randomly and put the tip of the knife on top of the negative contact. Ash turned his head and looked away as he gently tapped the knife handle with the meat mallet.

After several taps a hiss of air escaped the battery as the pressure within was released. Ash released the breath he was holding. With the battery no longer under pressure, the fuel cell was basically harmless with the exception of sulfuric acid, which was part of the battery. Using the knife, he carefully broke open the top of the battery.

Within, there was a rolled-up piece of white paper with metal shards sticking from it, and all around that core was black powder, magnesium oxide.

"Jackpot." Ash pumped the air with his fist. Something had finally gone as expected.

Using the knife, Ash scraped all the magnesium oxide into the teapot and ground up the large chunks. Thankfully the black stuff was already dry, or he would have needed to set it out on the windowsill for a few hours.

He repeated this process eleven more times, and when he was done there was a nice mound of magnesium oxide in the bottom of the kettle. Sweat rolled down his forehead, and he wiped it away with the back of his hand. He was done. All he needed to do once the bomb was placed was add the hydrogen peroxide, seal the teapot, and run.

Perspiration dripped into his eyes again and he used his shirt to dry his face. Ash pulled the bottle of water from his pocket and took a long pull, emptying it and letting the bottle fall to the floor. His stomach ached for a second as the sudden infusion of liquid induced nausea, then faded.

He gathered the teapot bomb, his bag of supplies, and got to his feet.

A wave of dizziness washed over Ash, and he put out a hand to steady himself on the washstand.

The sound of footsteps echoed in the hallway outside his room.

Ash looked around, frantic. He felt drunk, slow, and all his joints shrieked with pain. He looked down at the empty water bottle. But it had been sealed. With the sickening realization that he'd made a huge mistake, Ash knew plastic caps could be removed without the safety seal being broken if one was careful. Ash's mother echoed in his head, like whenever he did something stupid. "Didn't I tell you not to take food from strangers."

He fell onto his side. Where the hell was mom's voice when he was debating coming to the valley?

The room grew dim, the footsteps louder.

Lights out.

31

Ash came awake with a start, memories of Ophelia, Sasquatch, and the valley washing over him as he opened his eyes. Bright light, pain. He squinted, and rubbed his temples, his forehead aching. His leg wound screamed, the scratches on his chest pulling and stretching, and his head pounded in rhythm with his hammering heart. Metal tinkled on metal and he jerked his head toward the sound and found that he was restrained. Birds tittered and insects sang as Ash pulled against his bonds, but they held him tight.

The whiteness faded, and he saw Deepali's dark eyes staring into his, a slight smile sliding over her face. He looked away.

Ash was strapped to a pole at the center of a clearing, and the small path of hardpan was surrounded by thick walls of evergreen trees so tightly packed it was hard to make out one tree from another. Two paths trailed away from the clearing, one north and one south. There were no weeds or grass, and the brown patch of rock-strewn hardpan was stained with dark patches of dried blood.

Deepali took Ash's chin in her hand and turned his head so they once again looked into each other's eyes. She shook her head and let Ash's chin fall to his chest.

He heard the click of his karambit opening and he looked up.

Deepali spun the knife on her index finger, smiling. When she saw him looking at her, she said, "Nice little weapon. Love the fiberglass blade so airport security can't pick it up. Did you make it?"

Ash said nothing, and did his best to look belligerent, which wasn't hard.

Deepali spun and lashed out with the blade, slicing Ash's forearm. He flinched, blood dripping from the scratch. "Sharp," she said, and laughed.

"What do you want with me?" Ash's voice cracked, and he flinched. He already sounded dead, beaten.

Deepali made a show of spinning the knife, sliding side-to-side in a fighting stance. Ash could tell the woman had been trained in martial arts by the smooth way she moved from one stance to the next.

"Why not just kill me? Then you win."

She froze mid form, her eyes sliding to his. "Would I? Really?"

Ash said nothing.

"No," she said. She shook her head as she continued moving around with the blade. "I'll let one of the beasts finish you. Then I will have truly won."

"You're insane."

Anger flashed in her eyes and she struck out with the karambit again, putting a thin scratch across Ash's cheek.

Ash did his best not to react, but as the hot blood dripped down his face, anger welled in him and his cheeks burned. "I'm gonna kill you," he said, and blinked. He couldn't believe what he'd said. He'd never threatened a person's life, despite having had the thought many times.

Deepali's eyes widened, then narrowed as her lips thinned to a red line. "I'm showing you respect. Don't you get that?"

Ash said nothing, pain reminding him he was tied to a pole. Respect? But he had to stay quiet. She was getting ready to spill it. He could feel it coming like a twenty-foot wave.

"I just figured you, the real winner, at least deserved an explanation before I take it all away from you."

Ash let that revelation sit there like a fart in a movie theatre. The real winner?

She sighed. "Look, I understand you're pissed and confused. I played you like a violin. Nobody likes being used."

Ash said nothing.

"And you're probably wondering the hows and whys?" she said.

Ash let his eyes stray around the clearing as he tried to act disinterested. He wondered where Rodgers was.

"I guess the best place to start is at the beginning," Deepali said. She sat on a stone, bracelets tinkling.

"Any way you can let me down from here?" Ash said. His hands and feet were turning a light shade of purple as the circulation to his extremities was restricted.

She laughed. Not a normal, jovial laugh, but the manic, deranged cackle of someone who was gone. Someone who had left reality behind.

"I got the invitation at the perfect time," she said, ignoring Ash's faint squeals of pain. "I was on the balls of my ass, as you Americans say, and I was headed for the street again." She paused and looked hard at Ash. "The streets are like prison, and I'm never going back there."

Ash nodded slightly. He needed to buy time, figure a way to get free, but he had little hope and even less strength. Even if he managed to get free, the M4 hung over Deepali's shoulder and she could gun him down at any moment.

"I got here early. Seduced one of the locals pretending to be a rich countess." She looked up at the clearing sky and chuckled. "The dumbass didn't have a chance. So Treemont and his little bot weren't prepared when I arrived early, and..." A strange crooked smile inched over her face. The look of an insane woman. "I started the competition a little early. You might say I took control of things."

"There really is a Treemont?" he blurted. "What did you do with him?"

She smiled. "So we are paying attention? Yeah, there was a Treemont. The invitation, the whole thing, it was all legit. He had some rare form of cancer, only had a few months to live, so no guilt there."

How had Ash not seen this woman for who she was? He'd seen none of the signs. She was beautiful and engaging, and she'd taken advantage of him.

"Anyway, he meant for us to compete, as the invitation said. No doubt he expected casualties, but from what I could tell, he didn't mean any of us harm. He seemed like a nice man, actually."

"And you just murdered him?" Ash said. His anger and frustration grew, eating at him, his worries of survival ebbing, taking a backseat to his rage.

She punched with the blade, pulling up just short of his face. "Make no mistake. I have killed a few good men, and many more bad ones. Do you know how I decide which is which?"

The blade danced before Ash's face and he said nothing, but the bottom of his stomach dropped out.

"I was raped when I was eight. Eight, Ash."

Ash sighed. Deepali had been broken long before she'd come to the valley. He suspected, and he was sure this revelation, and self-justification, was just the tip of the tuna.

"So don't tell me about murder. I'm sure he deserved it. You haven't seen the lab," she said.

But he'd seen some of the work performed there. Ash's stomach turned, pain leaking through his chest.

"Yes..." she laughed again. "I see you know what I mean."

He said nothing.

"It wasn't hard getting the access codes to Treemont's research computer. Treemont was a frail old man. He gave me the code for Rodgers also, with a little... coaxing. Oh yes, the tin can helped, all along the way, watching, reporting. The bot knew most of the plan. So once Treemont was out of the way I was able to see what Treemont had planned."

She stopped flipping the karambit and slipped it in a pocket.

Curiosity was now racing with his anger, taking front position. "What was the deal with the poem? The statues?"

She cackled loud and hard. "Yes, quite the little mystery. I'm no UN Owen, however, but I tried to keep up appearances, make you all believe you were still playing Treemont's little game," Deepali said. "I stood back and let Treemont's plans unfold until they became... detrimental to my overall goals." When she saw the recognition in his eyes, she continued, "The deaths of Snake and Auggie went off without a hitch, but then things went off the rails a little."

Ash stared forward, mind spinning, but he said nothing. Something caught his eye in the periphery of his vision, but he didn't dare shift his head and look.

"Old longings nomadic leap. Chafing at custom's chain. Again from its brumal sleep. Wakens the ferrine strain," Deepali recited. "Obvious now that we're at the end, no?"

"How did you do it? Make Tallboy kill? I've seen him several times, and whatever you did was temporary. Drugs?" Ash asked.

She nodded. "I may have given Tallboy a larger dose than Treemont had planned." She smiled a wicked grin. "I figured Auggie wouldn't be able to control himself. Just like you. Given the opportunity to prove he wasn't crazy. That Bunyips truly existed, was more important to him than anything, and he let his guard down."

Ash looked at the ground, then to the forest.

Two yellow eyes shined from the shade beneath the tree canopy, the ape-like face of Tallboy easing from the shadows.

"But why? How?" He had to keep her talking.

"Snake was first because he knew who I was. He told you all on the helicopter ride in, if you recall. He deserved what he got. After I administered the drug to Tallboy, I had Rogers create a diversion that led Snake right to Tallboy. The Sasquatch was in an ultra-aggressive state, and add Snake's rashness and ego, and things fell right into place," Deepali said.

The ease with which she spoke, the total lack of remorse, worried Ash more than the M4 on her shoulder. "You were with me when we found him. You... that was a neat trick. Fooled me. Well played. Well played."

"Don't beat yourself up, Ash. It's just business. Not personal."

"Everything about this is personal now."

She ignored him, and said, "Auggie went exactly as planned. I knew he wouldn't be able to stop himself... but Edo's death was the first curve ball."

Ash recalled the sound when the spider had landed on Edo.

"After the torpor of will. Morbid the inner strife. Welcome the animal thrill. Lending a zest to life." Deepali laughed again. "This one was supposed to be my challenge. The spider, and Rodgers was to watch the scene and drive off the beast if needed, but I changed things up a little."

"So, like I said, you're a murderer." As soon as the words left Ash's lips, he wished he could have them back.

A dark cloud of anger spread over Deepali's face, then dissipated. "No, I'm not totally innocent, and in Snake's case maybe guilty, but the competition was designed to test your limits, and I'm sure, as I've already said, Treemont didn't expect you all to survive, despite whatever personal feelings he may have had."

"But was he going to kill those who lived?"

It was Deepali's turn to say nothing.

A beast shrieked in the jungle, a wail of anger and hunger.

"We're running out of time, Mr. Cohn," she said.

"So you and the bot just killed everyone else? Played this stupid game with the statues?" Ash sensed their talk was coming to an end, and when that happened...

"No. Rodgers wouldn't allow it. He's got some kind of core programming that won't let him harm another human. Very iRobot."

"What about the rest of them?" Ash didn't know much about homicidal killers, but he'd seen enough James Bond movies to know that the mastermind always wanted to reveal their brilliance. Show the losers how they were beaten.

"I tried to stay with the poem, and the melee was preplanned, so I just let that happen."

"And Emica, Otto, the others?"

"Voices of Solitude call. Whisper of sedge and stream. Loosen the fetters that gall. Back to the primal scheme." She guffawed. "Back to the primal scheme. Rodgers told me Treemont meant to have us living off the land by day three." She harrumphed. "Back to the primal scheme my shapely Indian ass."

Deepali shot Ash what he thought she believed to be a seductive look, but instead looked more like a demented clown.

Ash flinched.

She frowned, and stuck her chin out in defiance. "Mira helped with Emica. She takes basic instruction as you've seen, and is somewhat brainwashed to follow the commands of whoever feeds her. And Otto?" She waved a hand before her face and the rifle slipped from her shoulder. She inched the gun's strap back into position, and said, "Otto was simple. I left some bait for the devil, left a trail of breadcrumbs for Otto, who followed them without question."

"The pilot?"

"Ah, yes. I have to give Treemont credit for that one. That was all set up long before any of us arrived, so I just stood back and watched."

"And if he'd lived?"

Deepali shrugged. "After that... well, you saw most of it."

Ash remembered how Sean had attacked the pilot, died from the gunshot wounds. "You were with me? Consoled me?" Ash was doing his best to sound hurt, but even he could tell his fury was seeping through.

Deepali said nothing.

"Candice? You killed her in cold blood."

Deepali rubbed her arm and Ash recalled Candice getting a piece of her with Sean's knife. "That one I regret, a little. I wanted to see which one of you would betray the other."

"And if we didn't?"

Deepali padded the M4.

"So what about you? I saw you die. How did you pull that off?" Ash was out of questions and out of time.

Tallboy's face faded back into the forest as another primal roar echoed through the valley and pushed over the clearing. The breeze made Ash shiver, and he pulled on his bonds.

"What did you see?" She was smiling. So very proud of herself. "It was a bit of deception. See, Rodgers told me the Yeti can't see very well in the dark."

"But I saw it strike you down?"

"You did?" She smiled so broadly Ash thought she might hurt her face. "I admit that was the most difficult part of the entire affair. The drugs helped, though, but it was still scary." She cackled.

With nothing left to say, and no plan, Ash said, "So, you'll let the beasts get me and you're the new king of the hill?"

She nodded. "That's the plan. Any last words? Anyone back home you need me to contact?"

Ash felt like he'd drunk a shot of molten lava.

"Oh, that's right. You've got nobody. But, hey, at least you saw Bigfoot, right?" She stepped forward, smiled, and pecked Ash on the cheek. "Sorry about this. Really, I am. You know how I tricked you?"

Ash said nothing. Didn't even look at her. His eyes were focused on the forest, where he hoped to see Tallboy's face, but there was nothing there except the thick evergreens.

She pushed the hair from his face with her index finger. "I like you, Ash. That was real."

"Why kill me then? I'll leave. You can have the valley. I don't want it."

Her eyes went wide as quarters.

"Or we can stay here in the valley together."

Ash threw up in his mouth a little.

Her face grew tight, then slackened. "I'm not going to kill you. I'm just going to win the game."

"What does it matter? You've cheated."

She cackled. "I changed the rules. Big difference." She lowered her head and stared at the hardpan. "Goodbye, Ash. Good luck in the next life."

Then she scampered off into the forest, bracelets tinkling.

Late morning turned into afternoon, and the sun had arced past noon when something pushed through the forest. Ash's bet was on Mira. He pulled on his bonds, but his hands and feet were numb, and both his legs had fallen asleep. The scratches on his chest ached, the wound on his leg pulsed, and the new slash on his forearm yelled for attention. Ash doubted he'd be able to stand, let alone fight.

If it wasn't Mira, the devil, a Bunyip, Sasquatch… Ash found that he just didn't care anymore.

Branches cracked, leaves fell, and the woods went still as the massive beast emerged from the undergrowth. It looked like a Sasquatch, but walked on all four limbs. Its hair was short and gray, not a tangled mess of brown and black fur.

When the beast saw Ash strapped to the pole, it paused, looking him up and down. Then with a scream of rage that made Ash's ears ring, the creature charged.

***

From the shadows of the forest, Rodgers watched.

The game wasn't over.

Two remained.

32

Tallboy stepped from the trees, threw his massive head back, and roared. Slime dripped from his thick fangs, and his face was twisted with rage.

The charging bear-like creature glanced in Tallboy's direction, but didn't slow.

Ash cringed and waited to be mauled.

Tallboy roared again, and this time when the advancing creature turned in his direction, the Sasquatch was on the move. Hope stirred Ash's emotions, and he silently urged Tallboy on. The Sasquatch was a blur, and before the strange beast could react, Tallboy slammed into the creature.

Grunts and snarls filled the glade as the cryptids rolled and pulled at each other. Tallboy's right arm jackhammered up and down as he relentlessly pounded the beast's head as the creature fought to sink its two-inch claws into the Bigfoot. Clouds of dust and dirt lifted from the hardpan, filling the small clearing. Nothing moved in the forest beyond, at least nothing Ash could see. Were the unseen eyes watching him still? Was Rodgers hiding in the underbrush?

Tallboy raked his claws across his adversary's chest and blood geysered through the gashes, spraying the gray fur, turning it black.

The wounded beast bellowed and rolled away, whimpering as it pressed its hands to its chest, trying to stop the bleeding.

Tallboy gathered himself to his full height, looking down on the wounded beast.

The creature growled, but backed away until it was at the edge of the forest, then it turned and disappeared into the undergrowth, snapping branches and shifting vegetation marking its departure.

Tallboy stared after the creature for several minutes, standing still as stone as the sun vanished beyond the lip of the valley.

Ash hung limp from his pole, watching Tallboy, hoping beyond hope that the beast wouldn't notice him, or would leave him alone. But that was crazy. He'd seen what the creature had done to Snake, but then Ash remembered what Deepali had said, and the poem. Again from its brumal sleep. Wakens the ferrine strain. But Tallboy had been drugged. Was he again wrapped in brumal sleep?

He couldn't feel his legs or hands, and his arms tingled to his shoulders, wounds thrumming.

Tallboy turned his angry glare on Ash, and he felt a zap of energy cramp his neck and run down his spine. He shuddered, the cold breeze bringing the scent of blood.

The Bigfoot lumbered forward, matted hair swaying, muscles rippling. His footfalls were like the coming of an elephant, and clouds of dust rose from the hardpan as he approached. His ape-like face wasn't angry, nor was it serene. The beast's yellow eyes had lost their murderous glare, and the creature's claws had been retracted beneath the mounds of fur that covered its hands, but anger lines still crisscrossed its black leather-like face.

The Sasquatch came forward until he was standing so close to Ash, he could smell the beast's rancid breath. The Bigfoot leaned in, putting his face an inch from Ash's.

Ash trembled like a tiger was prancing around him. Sweat dripped from every pore, and his vision went red as he held his breath.

Tallboy lifted a hand, but no claws were extended. The Sasquatch brushed Ash's face with the back of his monkey-like hand, and it took a monumental effort not to flinch. The beast's eyes shifted, and Tallboy inched past Ash.

Seconds dripped away. A minute.

Ash felt the tension in his bonds slacken and he wiggled his wrists.

The slashed rope bonds fell away.

He shuffled his feet and almost fell.

Ash didn't leave the safety of the pole. He kept his back pressed to the wood, waiting for Tallboy to appear before him. When the Sasquatch didn't appear, he mustered the courage to look over his shoulder and found that Tallboy was gone.

He dropped to his knees, legs numb, arms stinging. He rolled onto his side, head pounding. Slowly, he flexed his arms and legs, twisting and cracking his joints. His chest wound stung and the cut on his leg pulsed with pain, but the slash on his arm had stopped bleeding and no longer hurt. When he got feeling back in his arms, he shook his hands wildly in the air, whipping them back and forth, circulating blood. He made fists over and over and the redness faded from the tips of his fingers. He flexed his legs, repeating the procedure until his entire body hurt.

Scattered clouds fleeted by, patches of faint blue sky fading to dusk as the sun dropped below the western edge of the Andes Mountains. He felt cold, hungry, his head pounded, and angst gnawed at the edges of his nerves. He'd been so confident when he'd arrived in the valley. So certain he could handle whatever was thrown his way, but as he stared up at the sky, his eyes leaking tears, he just didn't give a shit anymore.

He sat up, still flexing his arms and legs. Deepali had taken Sean's knife. He got to his feet and searched the forest where she'd thrown the blade and Ash found it easily. He cracked his neck and rolled his shoulders as he walked, pain stretching through him like lightning.

Ash's options were few. He could see if Deepali had messed with his makeshift bomb. Most likely she'd taken it, but if she hadn't, perhaps he could continue with his plan to blow the door in the mines. There had to be a way out of the valley that way.

Or...

He could find Deepali, finish the dangerous game she'd started, and take the valley and everything in it for his own. Turn things for the good. He felt no great guilt for those who'd been killed, he'd hardly known Sean and Candice, and the rest he hadn't known at all, but he wasn't a murderer. There was something in Ash, that most basic of human beliefs that told him killing another human is a crime against nature. Something one never forgets, unless they've slipped into darkness.

Had he slipped into darkness?

He didn't know, but what he did know was he couldn't stay in the clearing, which judging by the blood stains was some type of feeding area. He flipped the twelve-inch knife, the clipped blade made of black carbon steel. Ash admired the notched blade, and the dark wood handle with gold and brass mosaic pins. He remembered how Sean had chosen the weapon and left his statue behind. It had all been a crock of shit.

He threaded through the forest, staying silent, slipping in and out of the shadows. Regardless of what he decided to do, he didn't want Deepali to know he was alive. With his legs and arms back in working order, pain knifed through him from his leg wound and the multiple bruises and knife slashes on his arms and face. His joints ached, and his stomach screamed for food, his mouth dry, and a new worry wedged its way into the conversation. He could no longer trust the food and water provided to him, and that was a big problem. Even if he managed to survive and get out of the valley, he was days away from supplies, and he had no money.

The grayness of dusk leaked over the valley as Ash exited the forest onto the main path. The blue granite house sat to the east, its dark angular roof sticking above the trees.

He found Deepali sitting at the edge of the lake, her back to him. Kressel's long gray neck stuck from the lake, a mound of whitewater surrounding the massive beast. The creature squeaked and whined as Deepali tossed fish into the water.

The M4 rested against one of the dock's supports several feet away from her.

Any thoughts of attack, or of stealing the weapon fled when Mira appeared out of the vegetation. The mecha beast patrolled up and down the beach, its dark eyes scanning the lake and the forest's edge.

Ash looked over his shoulder at the house. With Deepali outside, he could slip into the house, find some food, and head down into the mines, but something held him in place.

"You going to just let her get away with it? After everything she's done?" It was mom's voice again. He rolled his shoulders and cracked his knuckles. She had a point.

He bent, picked up a stone the size of a golf ball, and hurled it into the forest. It slapped through some leaves and thumped into a tree. Mira didn't even notice, and Deepali tossed fish to Kressel. He tried again. And again. Nothing.

Ash grabbed a smaller stone, weighing it in his hand as he bounced it in his palm. He drew back his arm and threw a dart right at Deepali's head. The rock plunked off her skull and she screamed, jerking her head around, searching the forest.

She bounced to her feet, snatched up the M4, and leveled the weapon at the woods. Deepali opened up, sweeping the gun back and forth, her arms shaking, the gun rattling as thirty shells spit from the weapon in ten seconds. She screamed with rage as bullets peppered the forest, but the shots were wild and came nowhere near Ash where he hid twenty feet away behind a stone.

"Find what threw that rock. Now!" Deepali yelled, and Mira scurried into the forest. "If that's you Tallboy, I'll have Mira beat your ass red!"

Deepali snapped the empty clip from the M4 and searched in her pocket for the spare.

Ash bolted from the forest, throwing himself forward in an uneven gait that sent shards of pain running through his legs. Sweat dripped into his eyes, pressure spreading through his chest, his leg wound screaming.

Deepali pulled the clip free of her pocket, and she braced the rifle on her leg as she focused on inserting the fresh magazine. As the clip clicked home, she sensed Ash and spun, bringing up the gun and firing blindly. A ribbon of bullets stitched across the hardpan to Ash's left.

He dove forward, bowling into Deepali like a linebacker filling a hole. His shoulder drove into the woman's chest, and he wrapped his arms around her, driving her to the ground.

Deepali's ribs cracked and popped, and a gust of air escaped her lips as Ash pressed her to the ground. He gripped her wrist, pressing the rifle to the ground. With his other hand he slapped her hard across the face.

She went for Ash's eyes and he punched her in the jaw.

Deepali fell back and screamed. A sickening dread fell over Ash. He'd never hit a woman. Never even put a hand on a woman in an aggressive way.

This was survival, but still a lifetime of moral brainwashing made him pause for an instant in his fury.

Deepali rolled away, gasping and crying, jerking the gun free, aiming it at Ash.

He pushed the gun away, and pressed her and the rifle back to the ground. He reached inside her back pocket, the one he'd seen her drop the karambit into, and when he felt the knife's smooth plastic, he pulled the blade free.

Deepali pulled the trigger and the M4 barked, the wild shots randomly peppering the woods, the pop and crack of the gunpowder expanding echoing off the stone walls of the valley.

Ash opened the karambit with a flick of his wrist and slashed Deepali across the neck.

Deepali froze, her eyes widening, then she choked up blood as the gash on her neck opened and her head fell to the side. Her skull hit the ground with a thump and puff of dirt, and she lay still, a pool of dark blood leaking into the dirt around her.

Ash wept, all the emotions of the last five days spilling from him. He dropped to the ground, chin falling to his chest. He sat staring at Deepali's corpse for a long time, the bloody karambit hanging from his index finger.

It wasn't until he heard the *womp womp* of an approaching helicopter, and the whir of Rodgers' maneuvering jets, that he allowed himself a brief sigh of relief.

Darkness stretched its shadowy fingers across the valley as Ash strolled around the house. The thumping of the helicopter rotors grew louder, and it wouldn't be long before the whirlybird arrived. How could that be? Ash wasn't sure. He could only speculate that the craft had been waiting nearby for Rodgers' signal.

Ash avoided the house, though he saw no real reason he had to. He was the last, and if he wasn't, so be it. He'd had enough. He followed the yellow stone path to the clearing where the helicopter had dropped them off, and in the distance, Rodgers hovered next to the monument, watching him.

Ash threaded through the tall grass, working his way toward the bot. He looked over his shoulder, and though the helicopter's rotor wash thundered through the valley, he still couldn't see the craft.

"So, Treemont was a man of his word?" Ash said when he reached the bot.

"All goals are achieved, each parameter met, and only one remains," Rodgers said. "Per Dr. Treemont's instructions, I am declaring you the winner. Ash Cohn, you are the new leader of the Cryptid Club, and the master of this valley."

The darkness deepened and stars blinked overhead as a chill breeze pushed through the Andes, stirring leaves and twisting tree branches.

A beast howled, and the cry was met with a series of yelps, roars, growls, and grunts.

Ash didn't know what to say. He felt dirty. He literally still had blood on his hands.

"What is it you command?" Rodgers said.

A spotlight arced over the mountain peaks as the copter banked hard to the south, the pilot bringing the craft in slow as it dropped to the ground. The pounding of the rotors tore at the vegetation and dirt lifted into the air as the copter landed with a thud, its tinted windows dark.

"Sir, what is it you command?"

Ash said nothing. He considered grabbing a stick and smashing the robot to hell, but then who would take care of the valley? Make sure the beasts that needed help got it?

Rodgers beeped and buzzed.

"Keep the place running," Ash said.

"But, the valley is yours, Mr. Cohn." The bot's lens eyes scoped out.

"Call me Ash." He stared out at the Andes, looked back over his shoulder at the house, then over at the copter.

Ash strode toward the helicopter and didn't look back.

"Mr. Cohn? Mr. Cohn? Where are you going?" the bot's voice whined.

Darkness pressed in around Ash as he vanished into the night.

The End

Other Severed Press books by Edward J. McFadden III: Dinosaur Red, Drop Off, Jurassic Ark, Keepers of the Flame, Throwback, Sea Tremors, Primeval Valley, Shadow of the Abyss (#1 Amazon Bestseller), Awake, and The Breach (#1 Amazon Bestseller, Amazon #1 Hot New Audio Release). His other novels include Quick Sands – A Theo Ramage Thriller, Dogs Get Ten Lives, The Black Death of Babylon and HOAXERS. Ed is also the author/editor of: Anywhere But Here, Lucky 13, Jigsaw Nation, Deconstructing Tolkien: A Fundamental Analysis of The Lord of the Rings (re-released in eBook format Fall 2012 – Amazon Bestseller), Time Capsule, Epitaphs (W/ Tom Piccirilli), The Second Coming, Thoughts of Christmas, and The Best of Pirate Writings. His short stories have appeared in over 75 magazines and anthologies. He lives on Long Island with his wife Dawn, and their daughter Samantha.

CHECK OUT OTHER GREAT BIGFOOT NOVELS

THE BEASTS OF STONECLAD MOUNTAIN
by **Gerry Griffiths**

Clay Morgan is overjoyed when he is offered a place to live in a remote wilderness at the base of a notorious mountain. Locals say there are Bigfoot living high up in the dense mountainous forest. Clay is skeptic at first and thinks it's nothing more than tall tales.

But soon Clay becomes a believer when giant creatures invade his new home and snatch his baby boy, Casey.

Now, Clay and his wife, Mia, must rescue their son with the help of Clay's uncle and his dog, a journey up the foreboding mountain that will take them into an unimaginable world...straight into hell!

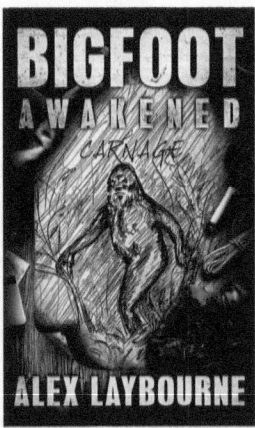

BIGFOOT AWAKENED
by Alex Laybourne

A weekend away with friends was supposed to be fun. One last chance for Jamie to blow off some steam before she leaves for college, but when the group make a wrong turn, fun is the last thing they find.

From the moment they pass through a small rural town they are being hunted by whatever abominations live in the woods.

Yet, as the beasts attack and the truth is revealed, they learn that despite everything, man still remains the most terrifying evil of them all.

CHECK OUT OTHER GREAT CRYPTID NOVELS

SWAMP MONSTER MASSACRE
by **Hunter Shea**

The swamp belongs to them. Humans are only prey. Deep in the overgrown swamps of Florida, where humans rarely dare to enter, lives a race of creatures long thought to be only the stuff of legend. They walk upright but are stronger, taller and more brutal than any man. And when a small boat of tourists, held captive by a fleeing criminal, accidentally kills one of the swamp dwellers' young, the creatures are filled with a terrifyingly human emotion—a merciless lust for vengeance that will paint the trees red with blood.

TERROR MOUNTAIN
by **Gerry Griffiths**

When Marcus Pike inherits his grandfather's farm and moves his family out to the country, he has no idea there's an unholy terror running rampant about the mountainous farming community. Sheriff Avery Anderson has seen the heinous carnage and the mutilated bodies. He's also seen the giant footprints left in the snow—Bigfoot tracks. Meanwhile, Cole Wagner, and his wife, Kate, are prospecting their gold claim farther up the valley, unaware of the impending dangers lurking in the woods as an early winter storm sets in. Soon the snowy countryside will run red with blood on TERROR MOUNTAIN.

 SEVERED**PRESS**

CHECK OUT OTHER GREAT CRYPTID NOVELS

BIGFOOT WAR
by **Eric S. Brown**

Now a feature film from Origin Releasing. For the first time ever, all three core books of the Bigfoot War series have been collected into a single tome of Sasquatch Apocalypse horror. Remastered and reedited this book chronicles the original war between man and beast from the initial battles in Babblecreek through the apocalypse to the wastelands of a dark future world where Sasquatch reigns supreme and mankind struggles to survive. If you think you've experienced Bigfoot Horror before, think again. Bigfoot War sets the bar for the genre and will leave you praying that you never have to go into the woods again.

CRYPTID ZOO
by **Gerry Griffiths**

As a child, rare and unusual animals, especially cryptid creatures, always fascinated Carter Wilde.

Now that he's an eccentric billionaire and runs the largest conglomerate of high-tech companies all over the world, he can finally achieve his wildest dream of building the most incredible theme park ever conceived on the planet...CRYPTID ZOO.

Even though there have been apparent problems with the project, Wilde still decides to send some of his marketing employees and their families on a forced vacation to assess the theme park in preparation for Opening Day.

Nick Wells and his family are some of those chosen and are about to embark on what will become the most terror-filled weekend of their lives—praying they survive.

STEP RIGHT UP AND GET YOUR FREE PASS...

TO CRYPTID ZOO

www.ingramcontent.com/pod-product-compliance
Lightning Source LLC
Chambersburg PA
CBHW031955170626
46807CB00006B/2503